I0634671

TRUST IN LOVE

A MCCORD FAMILY NOVEL
BOOK 2

AMANDA SIEGRIST

Copyright © 2015 Amanda Siegrist
All Rights Reserved.

This material may not be re-produced, re-formatted, or copied in any
format for sale or personal use unless given permission by the publisher.

NO AI TRAINING: No part of this material may be used in any AI training
of any kind. Without in any way limiting the Author's exclusive rights
under copyright, any use of this publication to "train" generative artificial
intelligence (AI) technologies to generate text is expressly prohibited. The
Author reserves all rights to license any and all use of this work for
generative AI training and development of machine learning language
models.

Every part of this material was human created, including all written words
and the cover.

All characters in this book are a product of the author's imagination. Places,
events, and locations mentioned either are created to help inspire the story
or are real and used in a fictitious manner.

Cover Designer: Amanda Siegrist
Photos Provided by: CURAphotography/Krivosheev
Vitaly/Shutterstock.com
Edited by: Editing Done Write

ALSO BY AMANDA SIEGRIST

A happy ending is all I need.

Consequences Novel

Dark Consequences

Cruel Consequences

Fatal Consequences

Haunting Love Novel

Third Time's the Charm

Thirteen Days Gone

One Mistake Too Late

Holiday Romance Novel

Merry Me

Mistletoe Magic

Christmas Wish

Snowed in Love

Snowflakes and Shots

Holiday Hope

Sleigh All the Way

Lucky Town Novel

Escaping Memories

Dangerous Memories

Stolen Memories

Deadly Memories

Forgotten Memories

HE WASN'T LOOKING FOR LOVE.

SHE WAS AFRAID TO TRUST AGAIN.

WHEN FATE BRINGS THEM TOGETHER, WILL THEY TAKE A CHANCE ON FOREVER?

1

THE DRIVEWAY STOOD as solid as a rock, yet felt like liquid fire under her shaky legs. Her nerves flowed in all directions, draining her as she stood staring at the dilapidated house. The horror of its despairing look slammed into her with brute force, knocking in the sense that her life wasn't going to get any better.

Sophie wasn't sure what was worse, the fact she moved here for a fresh start to such a revolting place, or that her father even left this appalling place called a house to her.

The shutters on the front windows hung crookedly. One little touch of breath and they would probably shatter to the ground.

A porch swing swayed in the afternoon breeze, the hinges creaking. The poor thing probably couldn't even hold her meager weight of a hundred and fifteen pounds soaking wet.

The porch steps looked fragile. On the top step, to the left, a small hole wallowed in pity. With the swing appearing beaten and bruised, she was starting to wonder if the steps would support her.

This had to be a sign.

She shouldn't step inside the house at all.

The house looked like it used to be a deep red, beautiful at one time. Now, peeling paint, cracks scouring everywhere, reminding her of bloody knuckles after a beatdown of great proportions.

Her vision slowly trailed from the house to her hands.

Cracked skin from numerous punches, the blood slowly seeping out.

Shivers consumed her. The memories...

She didn't want to remember. She just wanted all those memories to fade away.

The longer she stood there, the faster her anger simmered to the surface.

She hated red. Hated this house. Hated her father who ran out on her mom and her at the age of five. Now he decided to leave this miserable house to her in his will. He left without a backward glance, and twenty years later decided when he croaked he wanted to leave this disgusting house to her.

He knew exactly where she was to give the notification when he finally slipped into death from liver cancer. She couldn't remember much about her father, but she remembered the excessive drinking. With the way he drank, perhaps it was fitting he died in the manner he did.

Should she feel remorseful? Maybe, but all she felt was rage. Hot, burning rage that he thought he needed to put this dreadful house into her name.

Just as suddenly, burning terror bombarded her.

This house had become her haven. She had needed to run away from her life, and for once in his life, her father had given her the perfect escape. One small thanks could be given for that.

"Hel—"

Sophie screamed. A strange looking man stood way too close to her liking. Where had he come from?

"Are you crazy? Just walking up to someone without a thought or care." Sophie took a wobbly step back.

The man looked speechless—and somewhat filthy. Dirt and sweat hung off his face, with a shirt just as dirty, tattered in the front with little holes littered about. His jeans had a rip in the knee, dirt stains trailing down the length, right to his mud-caked boots.

"I—"

"I don't appreciate being walked up to like that. Is it common practice for you to frighten people?" She slowly moved farther away from him.

He still stood too close for her comfort.

Oh, no.

Was this a horrible neighborhood?

Her house didn't give the appearance that it was a nice neighborhood. This man didn't help convince her either as he continued to stare at her strangely.

"Who are you? What kind of neighborhood is this? You need to leave or I will—" Sophie started to say she would call the police, but stopped. She didn't trust the police. They weren't there to help people. They never helped her when she needed them the most. "I'll throw you off this property myself," she finished with as much firmness as she could muster.

Like, whoa. Where was this bravery coming from anyway?

He glanced down at his clothes, then looked back at her. "I—"

"You need to leave now."

"Stop. Just listen to me for once. Quit interrupting me.

This is a great neighborhood. The only bad house here...is this one," he exclaimed, throwing a hand toward her house. Sophie reacted instantly by taking two large steps back.

"I saw you standing here and assumed it was yours now. The yard needs a good mow, and I was just going to offer to mow it for you. Welcome you to the neighborhood and all. That's it. Calm down," he said, pointing to the yard this time.

Sophie glanced at his hand and then at the yard. Her focus had been on the house for so long she never took notice of the lawn. The sad state of despair dug deeper inside.

At least a foot tall, if not more, the dire need to mow the lawn slapped her in the face. She had never mowed a yard in her life. She didn't even know how to work a lawn mower.

The longer she stared, the deeper the despair slipped in. But she didn't know this man and didn't trust any man.

Not anymore. They were all bad.

She looked back at him and gathered the little strength she had left from the long, trying day.

"I don't need nor want your help. Please do not step foot on my property again." She abruptly turned around, ignored the look of shock on his face, and walked quickly toward the porch steps.

Hesitating to enter the house earlier, now she burned with the need to get inside safely.

Staying carefully to the right of the steps, having no desire to fall through the hole already formed on the left, she quickly took her key that she had been twisting in her hands and shoved it into the lock. Thankfully, it unlocked without issue.

Shoving open the door, she stepped inside as fast as her feet would carry her and slammed the door shut. Twisting the lock immediately, a deep breath escaped. She put her back to the door and slid down with a slow pain, the tears finally falling.

Why was she crying? Did that strange man cause her tears? Was she that frightened of him?

She honestly didn't believe so. But they felt good releasing from her body, a sort of cleansing that she needed.

She wanted this to work. Desperately needed her life to move in a good direction for once. She could only hope it would as she sat on the dirty floor, crying her eyes out.

AUSTIN STOOD IN THE DRIVEWAY. What just happened?

Absolutely crazy woman. She interrupted him, threatened him, and denied him of a good, decent offer to mow her lawn.

He had gotten home from the farm and noticed the woman standing in the driveway to the house next to his. The previous owner had passed away two months ago. He never knew the man, considering he just moved in a month ago, but he knew by the other neighbors that he had no care in the world, especially about the upkeep of the house.

What was wrong with trying to be neighborly?

He hadn't meant to scare her. He honestly thought she heard him walk up, or at least saw him approach. The way she stomped up those steps and slammed her door, he couldn't tell if it was fright to get away from him or anger burning inside because of him.

Trying to figure it out would just cause him a headache. The best course of action would be to ignore her, not even attempt a hello. He couldn't even get his first attempt out.

What did he do to get such a reaction?

A quick glance at his clothes, he knew how the dirt and

grime that clung to him from helping Ava plant her garden she'd been dying to have made him look a little unpresentable. But a criminal?

No more dating crazy women. Once was enough.

Not that he intended to date his neighbor to begin with. Crazy or not.

Never in his life had a woman reacted to him like that. All women usually swooned over him. They swayed with vigor, flashed a pretty smile, and bowed at his feet. Well, not necessarily bowed, but women did crazy things sometimes to get his attention.

Hell, he'd be the first to admit sometimes it didn't take much to get his attention. Beautiful face, gorgeous body, and his interest piqued instantly.

Either she was a little crazy in the head or he was seriously losing his touch. He didn't even try to flirt with her in any way.

Oh, man. The reaction he'd get from her if he did.

Life needed to be simple, carefree. Testing that clearly unstable woman wouldn't bring him any good at all.

He finally walked to his own home and headed for the shower. Within thirty minutes, he was showered, dressed, and had his keys ready to head back to the farm, about a ten-minute drive, if that.

It would've been nice just to chill out in his new house, but Ava insisted he come back for supper and cake. He had insisted on a shower first because he hated trampling dirt into the house for Eleanor to clean. She did enough around the house. She didn't need to clean up after his dirtiness, too.

He could've showered and changed there, but he liked the new house he bought. Nothing but pleasure hit him each time he came home. He had lived on the farm with his brother, Zane, never once leaving to live on his own. Zane had recently married Ava, and Austin decided it was time for him to branch out on his own, give them their duly deserved space.

Not to mention, Ava always disapproved of the women he brought home. He hated seeing that critical look in her eyes. The women usually didn't accept a second date from him with one nasty look directed their way by Ava.

If she didn't approve of his women, it never amounted to much. Now he knew how his brother, Jimmy, must've felt when Ava went all mother hen on him when he lived in New York City.

He loved her, though. He had to admit she had a keen eye for things of that nature.

But love? He didn't want that. Just a good time.

Which meant, he'd probably never have to worry that Ava would scare a good woman away. He didn't date the *good woman* type.

He shot a wary eye at his neighbor's house, the crazy woman not in sight, and got into his truck. Despite his own warning about dating his neighbor, he had to admit she was rather cute.

A short pixie haircut, dirty blonde, as some people liked to call it, with a cute pert nose. He decided if she ever smiled, it would light up her face with a beauty that could blind a man. Small, yet radiant. Maybe two sweet dimples to add to the beauty. Her lips curved in a delicious invitation, begging him to try a taste. And taste he would.

He could almost feel her smile on his lips.

Why was he thinking about her smile? He shouldn't think about her at all. The best thing she ever did was freak out on him. Dating his neighbor would be bad. If it didn't work out, which he knew it wouldn't, then he'd be in serious trouble having to live next door to her.

He wasn't in the market for a wife or a long-term relationship. He liked his short, fleeting relationships and had no intention of wavering from that lifestyle.

Ever.

Definitely no dating his neighbor.

Sighing with contentment, he pulled into the driveway of the farm. No matter how far he moved away, this would always be his true home. Entering the house quickly, he took a seat at the dinner table just as Eleanor set down the last plate.

"You smell better, Austin," Zane said with a grin.

"A shower does that to you, bro. This looks delicious, Eleanor, as usual," Austin said smoothly to Eleanor, who sat right next to him.

"Thank you, Austin. Wait until we have cake. Ava did an excellent job. And she says she's not a baker," Eleanor said sweetly.

"Well, you did help a little. Not sure I'll ever get the hang of baking," Ava replied.

Zane leaned over and kissed her cheek. "Your apple pies are delicious. If they weren't my favorite already, they would be after you made them."

Austin made gagging sounds as he winked at Ava. "You two are ridiculous sometimes. It's because of me that you're together. That idiot would've never figured anything out without me."

"I would've eventually come to my senses. I could never live without this woman by my side," Zane said sincerely, gazing lovingly at Ava.

"You could have a wonderful relationship, you know, if

you would just quit dating trash. That last woman was disgusting." Ava raised a brow.

"You think all the women I date are disgusting. Just because I like beautiful, available women, who like sex just as much as me doesn't make them disgusting," Austin pointed out as he cut a piece of his pork chop and popped it into his mouth.

"Yes, they are. Don't think for one minute just because you moved out I don't see who you're bringing home. What's her name—Dakota something. You brought her home a few nights ago. Now, my dear little brother, she's all wrong for you. I mean, her name is Dakota. Need I say more?" Ava said.

"How in the hell do you know I brought a woman home and what her name is?" Austin dropped his fork.

"I know all, Austin. Do not mess with me," Ava said with a smirk. "I also happen to work for the police department, in the crime lab, if you forgot. My officers are very good at their jobs."

"Since when are they *your* officers? Why are they checking up on me?"

"Everyone obeys Ava. Haven't you figured that out, Austin? I even learned that right away," Zane said as he broke open his bread roll and slathered a glob of butter on it.

"You're in love. You obey her for that reason," Austin pointed out. He glanced back at Ava, who still grinned deviously at him. "What? She was a nice woman."

"I worry about you, Austin. Are you ever going to settle down? And yes, I will keep tabs on you if I have to. I protect my family, and you are my family. I can't help but worry," Ava said seriously.

Austin picked his fork up, sighing heavily. "Look. Not everyone gets a happily ever after like you two. I don't want it, actually. I date around like I do because that's what I enjoy. I don't plan on changing, so please don't send every woman I bring home away. I do like to enjoy them for a little while at least. They know up front what kind of guy I am, so it's not like they have dreamers in their eyes when it comes to dating me."

"Austin, you're delusional if you think when you tell a woman there's no future they actually believe that. They all have those dreamers in their eyes. Why? Because you *are* that kind of man. Women want you and hope to be the one to finally settle you down. To make you a marrying kind of a man," Ava said honestly.

"Not every woman," Austin muttered under his breath.

"What does that mean? Who shot down the big bad Austin?" Zane joked.

"Huh?" Austin asked.

Zane and Ava stared at him expectantly. Even Eleanor sitting next to him gave him a grin with anticipation on her face. "It's nothing. I didn't even try to be honest with you. Because if I actually tried to ask her out, she wouldn't have talked to me the way she did."

"Ooh, I like this woman already," Ava said with a gleam in her eye.

"You don't even know what I was going to say," Austin said.

"Doesn't matter. If she talked back to you with force and attitude, I like her. She could be the one. End of story. Every woman you date bends over backwards for you. You need someone to challenge you," Ava said, pointing her fork at him.

"I don't want a challenge. I like nice simple things in my relationships. Sex...sex is simple. She's my new neighbor.

I'm not dating my neighbor. She bought the decrepit house that's next to mine. I saw her standing in the driveway and walked up to her and offered to mow her lawn—being neighborly, I thought. She freaked out on me saying I tried to scare her. She barely let me say hello when she started hollering at me. No, in fact, I didn't get the whole word hello out. All I got out was hel. That's it, hel. Can you believe that?" Austin said, as Ava still grinned at him like crazy. "Stop looking at me like that."

"Like what? Like the way you looked at me when you thought Zane and I were crazy for not telling each other how we felt last year. I like this woman. I want to meet her. She sounds perfect for you," Ava said.

"Forget it. You're not allowed to visit me if you're going to meddle in my life with my neighbor. I'm not dating my neighbor. She's crazy. I'm telling ya. How did we get on this conversation? Where's my cake? I'm done eating. What's the cake for? Are you leaving again? Because the last time you made a cake was to tell us you were leaving," Austin said.

"Let me go get that delicious cake." Eleanor stood up, quickly walking out of the dining room to the kitchen.

"Correction. Last time she made a cake was to tell us the good news that the person who started the fire on the farm last year was finally caught. She just added in she was leaving at the same time." Zane grabbed Ava's hand.

"Here we go. What a great looking cake, Ava!" Eleanor beamed with pride as she set the cake on the table.

Austin smiled at the cake, imagining the huge mess Ava probably created to make it. She decorated it with a fine layer of white icing and sprinkles scattered on top. Eleanor was spot on. A great looking cake. Delicious looking, too.

He looked at Zane. "You make a good point. What's the cake for this time? Last time I tried getting your guys' goat by saying she was pregnant and you—" Austin paused as his mouth dropped open with shock. "Are you pregnant?"

Ava smiled wide as Zane pulled her hand to his mouth, lightly kissing it.

"We are," Ava said as she smiled with love at Zane.

"Oh, man! Congratulations, you guys. That's the best news ever. I can't believe you made me wait all day to hear this. I'm going to be an uncle. This is crazy." Austin stood up and circled the table to embrace Zane in a huge hug. "Congratulations, man. I'm so happy for you. Jimmy would be so excited, too."

"Thanks, Austin. We're excited," Zane said.

Austin grabbed Ava in a big hug as well.

"Do you know what you're having?" Austin asked Ava as he went back to his seat.

"I'm only eight weeks along. We won't know for a while yet. As long as the little one is healthy, that's all that matters," Ava said, rubbing her stomach.

"Jimmy would be so happy to hear this. Congratulations to both of you," Eleanor said as she got her hugs from the two of them after Austin did.

"He would. I was thinking of making a trip to New York to visit him. Tell him the news. I'm still trying to talk Zane into it. Will you come with, Austin?" Ava asked as she grabbed Zane's hand.

"Hell, yeah. Come on, Zane. You have to go," Austin urged.

"I've been to New York three times now, and each time was quite an ordeal, thank you. I can't imagine what the fourth trip would be like," Zane said with quiet sadness.

"Well, we didn't bury him in Minnesota, so you have to come with to visit him. I thought you would do anything to make your wife happy. She's pregnant now. You have to make sure the baby's okay as well," Austin said.

"Thanks for making me worry ten times worse now," Zane muttered as he glared at Austin.

"Just pointing out the obvious. You're protective of Ava. Now she's pregnant, so that protection increases. New York is awesome if you just give it a chance," Austin said.

"That's what I keep trying to tell him and he never listens to me," Ava said.

"Do I need to repeat myself? Not one trip I made turned out well. And the last one, it should've, but it didn't." Zane looked at Ava, who had sorrow in her eyes. "Fine. I said I probably would. I don't think I could have you out of my sight for very long anyway. I'd miss you too much."

"That's what I like to hear," Ava said with a smile.

"Oh, man. Here we go again with the lovey-dovey crap. Might be time for me to go home," Austin said with a teasing tone.

"Eat your cake, young man. You can't leave until you help me clear the table first," Eleanor said with a smile.

"Of course, I'll help. It's great cake, Ava. You did a good job." Austin glanced at Zane. "You did a good job picking out a beautiful, amazing woman. I can't wait for my niece or nephew to get here."

"I did do good," Zane replied, squeezing his wife into a side embrace.

"Now if only you'd find a beautiful, amazing woman and settle down," Ava said with a pointed glare at him.

Austin groaned and shoved another bite of cake into his mouth.

That was never going to happen. Love wasn't for him.

2

SOPHIE TOURED the house after she cried all the tears left inside. She honestly didn't think any more could pour out. A good half hour had passed before she calmed down even a tiny bit.

Dreadful. The only word to spring to her mind after she finished walking around the house.

The inside was almost as bad as the outside, except she found no holes in the floors or walls. That was a plus.

Yet everything was dirty. The entire house stunk to high heaven. She went around opening all the windows, trying to air it out, briefly glancing around to see if that man was still lingering nearby.

Thankfully, she didn't see him.

She hoped she wouldn't run into him again. He obviously didn't understand personal space. Something she direly needed.

After completing that task, she ran outside to her car to grab her meager belongings and threw them in the house before anyone else tried to come up to her and scare her.

Three suitcases and one box. The existence of her life.

Four things stuffed with her belongings, most of them clothes. Her life boiled down to that. Nothing else. No family. No friends. No big moving van. And sadly, no hope this move would help her.

The burning anger she held for her father outside lowered every time she walked around the house.

Her house may not look the greatest in the neighborhood, it may not smell like roses, but this house was her home. Her new safe haven.

She thanked him every time she saw something that would make this new life easier. She had a couch. She had a bed. Stains littered all over them with a funny smell rising, but it meant more money to spend on other essentials, like groceries.

She had no job yet. Although, she was going to try her hand at selling crafts she made. She dabbled with it on the side, but now she had the chance to make her talent as a full-fledged job.

First, she needed to buy supplies with money she didn't have. Who needed to eat a lot of food anyway? Not her.

Once she started making and selling her works of art online, everything would be fine.

She made great things. Creative things.

Everything would work out. She needed it to work.

Next, she looked at the three bedrooms. Two of the rooms had beds. The last one was completely empty.

The master bedroom, she figured, had been her father's. The thought of sleeping in there disturbed her.

Without hesitating, she put her suitcases in the other room with the smaller bed, grabbed the sheets from it and tossed them into the washer for fresh linens tonight.

A true smile touched her face as she pressed the start

button to the washer. A nice clean bed for tonight. In her new home. Her safe home.

Gladness also swept through that the washer and dryer worked.

Her smile wouldn't leave. Her father wasn't letting her down. All the appliances worked. The house may look like crap, but all the appliances were well maintained, as far as she could see.

The night flew by as she cleaned her room, washed every speck of dirt in sight, remade the bed, and put her clothes away.

She grabbed her last piece of luggage—the lone box— and carefully opened it.

Sadness drifted to her eyes. It wasn't even packed to the top.

She pulled out a few picture frames, dusting off the imaginary dirt as she gazed at them. They were all of her mother, young and carefree. Such a beautiful woman. Nobody was more beautiful. Each picture had been taken before life became what it was. A woman saddled with a baby, heartache, terror, and a deep loneliness that Sophie now understood.

Shifting a few things, tears threatened to fall once again.

Her beloved angel peeked out from under a frame.

Sophie grabbed it with delicate hands, tracing the edges. A simple design with wings of glory and praying hands to her chest. A brilliant-white porcelain angel that was her most prized possession. Her finger stopped its movement as it reached the angel's left wing. A jagged edge stared back, the wing broken from a horror she hated remembering.

But she did remember.

The most pivotal moment in her life. So crystal clear.

How her hand had hovered over the trashcan, the angel dangling from her fingers. Yet, she made no move to drop it.

Not only did the beautiful angel remind her of her mother, it now reminded her of her strength.

It had been the day she finally left. The day her weakness had come front and center, smacking her in the face. The tip of desolation had cracked when her guardian broke. Speaking in whispers, it had told her to get up and get out. Run for your life. That's exactly what she did.

She walked over to her dresser and gently placed the angel on top. Standing back, she smiled again.

A disgusting stench drifted throughout the house. Dirt layered in every corner. Cracked and peeling paint. The grass too tall for neighborly manners.

None of it mattered.

This was her home. It would work because she would make it work. When it became too much, she would come here to this exact spot, look upon her guardian angel, and never forget why she left— why she ran.

"YOU WERE FLIRTING with that man. I saw you, Sophie. How could you embarrass me like that in front of my colleagues?" Kevin shouted, the rage filling his face.

Sophie shrunk back into herself, knowing how he transformed into another human being when he was angry. "I wasn't flirting. I was just being friendly. I swear, Kevin."

"Friendly? He put his hand on you," Kevin roared as he advanced at her.

"Please, Kevin. I shook his hand to be polite. You don't want me to look rude for not shaking the man's hand, do you?" Sophie pleaded, retreating from the rage.

"*No man will ever touch you but me. I'm the only one for you,*" Kevin whispered menacingly. He raised his hand and swung down, hitting her face. The force of the impact sent her flying into the dresser, knocking several things to the floor. Her shoulder jammed into the corner, the pain shooting throughout her body. She fell to the floor, her body too weak to do anything else.

Sophie felt his presence move closer as she struggled to sit up. Suddenly, without notice, a foot wedged into her stomach, knocking her breath out. He delivered several more blows. Sophie writhed in pain, unable to do anything but lie there taking the abuse.

Her eyes centered on her angel that had fallen to the floor, its wing shattered into pieces, just as her heart had. She tried to block the pain, the blows, and the blood spilling from her body by staring at the figure that followed her through life.

A rough scream escaped when he slammed down on top of her, grabbed her by the neck, and slowly started to squeeze. "*You will never disobey me again, Sophie. You will never look at another man again like that. Allow a man to touch you in such a manner. Never again, Sophie, never again.*"

Sophie struggled to draw in air as his eyes glossed over in madness, the power in his hands deepening. Her mind started to waver, her eyes closing as a deep blackness hovered. Just before it completely swept her away into the heavenly gates, a knock sounded from below.

Kevin snapped out of it, cursed loudly, and abruptly let go of her neck. "*Don't you ever disobey me again. I won't tolerate that kind of behavior. You're mine. Only mine.*"

Sophie stared at his back as she lay bruised and damaged on the floor as another knock echoed throughout the house.

A PERSISTENT KNOCK SHOUTED for her to answer it. She glided a shaky hand over the broken figurine and made her way to the front door.

Frowning, she noticed for the first time she had no peep-hole to see who was on the other side.

Another forceful knock.

She stood frozen in her spot.

Should she answer it? Who could possibly be banging on her door so late at night?

He found her.

She wasn't good at this cloak-and-dagger stuff. She wouldn't be surprised if he found her right away, considering she didn't try very hard attempting to hide.

The moment she had been notified of her father's death, she fled. Kevin hadn't been home at the time.

Her meager attempt at living in peace was failing before she could even begin. Before she could even try.

Life wasn't fair. A mantra she heard often enough through life from her stepfather. The miserable excuse for a man was right for once.

Life wasn't fair.

She jumped in place, her hands shaking even more when another round of banging occurred. She inhaled a deep bout of strength, unlocked the door, and swung it open.

Tremors ran through her body as she stared at the angry face.

It overwhelmed her sanity, making her fall into the blackness she had unwittingly been spared from last time.

3

Austin barely caught the woman before she slammed into the hard floor. He gently scooped her up, ignoring the strange feeling coursing through his body as he held her close.

Looking down, he laughed at the mangy mutt he had seen scratching at her door tugging lightly on his jeans.

"Down, boy. Down. I don't want to drop her." He closed the door behind him with a shove of his boot, then walked to his left, noticing the suspect couch lingering in the dark. Tenderly laying her down, he hesitated to walk away. Except he needed some light.

He found the light switch with ease and flicked it up. Bright light illuminated the room.

There was no hiding the cringe. The place was filthy.

He crouched back down by his peculiar neighbor. Why would a woman of her beauty be in a place like this?

A hand reached to caress her cheek when the dog jumped into his lap, sending sloppy kisses onto his face. "Stop it. Stop! I don't do dog kisses, boy. I don't like those kinds of kisses," Austin said, laughing, as he ruffled the dog's hair.

All the anger that simmered to the surface when he saw the dog pawing to get into her home evaporated when she fainted. He couldn't help but laugh when the adorable beast was so happy in his arms.

He wanted to know why she locked him outside, though. He couldn't stand people who abused their animals. It was uncalled for. Growing up on a farm wasn't the only reason he had great respect for animals, but it helped. Hell, most of the animals on the farm were considered their pets, which in turn made them family. Courtesy of Ava to Zane's undying irritation. Austin laughed again.

"Do you find breaking and entering into my home funny?"

Austin's head snapped to the woman's terrified face.

"I wouldn't call it breaking and entering. You fainted. I caught you before you fell to the floor. I carried you inside, not sure what else to do. I'm positive you wouldn't have appreciated being on my living room couch," Austin replied smoothly, trying to add a touch of his charm women normally swooned over.

This was where they would get the little butterflies in their stomach, shyly smile back, do a little hair flip, and bat their lashes at him. One simple smile and some smooth words usually did the trick.

"I'm positive I don't appreciate you in my home. Please leave."

He had to be losing his touch. Austin stood up, ignoring that awful thought. "Okay. You're welcome, by the way, for saving your head a headache. I'll just add in I don't appreciate you treating your dog so cruelly. I watched for several minutes while he begged to be let in. Whining, pawing at the door, while all you did was ignore him. You can be mean to me all you want, but you won't be mean to this animal." The anger wove its way back into his words, his stance tightening as he felt the dog sit by his feet.

She glanced down at the floor where the dog sat nicely at his feet, wagging his tail with happy vigor. She quickly glanced back at him. "That's why you knocked on my door so late at night?"

"Yes. Trust me. I have no desire to bother you. You're not someone I want to tangle with. But I won't hesitate when it comes to the treatment of animals." Austin ruffled the dog's head with care. "This little guy is sweet. He doesn't deserve to be kicked outside when the temperature is dipping down as it is."

"That's not my dog. I would never treat an animal like that, I assure you," she said, glancing at the dog again.

A shabby looking dog. All white with long, curly hair. Some spots were ratty, knotted, dirt lingering almost on his entire body.

"That's funny. Why was he begging to be let in your door? I'm telling you, I stood there for a while watching him. I even called to him and he refused to move from his spot. It's your dog," Austin insisted.

"That is not my dog. I've never owned a dog in my life. The treatment would've surely been—" She cut her words short as her frightened expression morphed into surprise. "I've never owned a dog before."

Austin stared at her, puzzled. "This isn't your dog? You promise?"

"I wouldn't lie about that. I would never treat an animal with such cruelty. I can tell it's dirty. I can even smell a bad stench from him. Unless, of course, that's coming from you," she blurted, then suddenly backed farther into the cushion.

Austin laughed to dispel her unexpected jolt of fear, aware of the way she flinched away from him. "Good one. I'm sure I did smell the first time we met. It's not me this time, darling," he said with a wink for added reassurance that he wasn't offended. "Now I just feel dumb. Well, I apologize for banging on your door and scaring you to pieces to the point of fainting. I never meant to do that. I just hated seeing him in such torture."

"You're apologizing to me?" she asked with the shock clear in her voice.

"Yeah. That's what you do when you're in the wrong. I'm sorry. If he's not your dog, I'll just take him home tonight and try to find his horrible owner tomorrow."

"Okay."

"Okay," Austin repeated, suddenly unsure what to say next.

Such a strange, confusing woman, who he was sure had many facets to her personality. He decided in a split second that he wasn't the man to find out what they were. He wouldn't pursue his neighbor, no matter how much the desire rushed through his body.

"I won't bother you anymore, I swear. I know you don't like me." He patted his leg, looking at the dog. "Come on, boy. Let's go home. Clean you up. The lovely lady is right. You stink!"

Austin winked again to lighten her mood. The waves of tension still rose from her body. Smiling, he walked out of the living room to the front door. The dog jumped on her lap, licked her face once, and ran after him.

He quietly shut her door.

Sophie stared at the door. What just happened?

She went from terrified of that man to uncomfortable to almost secure.

His attire spoke much more highly of him this time. He had combed his brown hair to the side in a graceful manner, not one piece out of place. A clean black T-shirt had clung to his body in a raw, sensual manner and blue jeans that hugged his thighs just right for a man. His boots were clean, free of dirt, shining with a power she couldn't describe.

When she had opened her eyes to see him laughing with the dog, something had touched a place in her heart that she thought to have been destroyed. His angry glare a minute later should've frightened her, yet she had only seen that tender smile when her eyes first landed on him.

Strange.

Even stranger had been his lack of reaction to her loose lips, insulting him the way she had. She hadn't been able to stop the words from leaving her mouth. She never spoke to people—men specifically—in such a way. The hurt they would dish out for such insolence wasn't worth contemplating because she knew what happened when she spoke that way.

Yet he laughed instead. Smiling. Winking. Not one hurtful hand came her way.

She couldn't blame him for being angry at the appearance of that adorable dog. Filthy, yes. But oh so adorable. She had no clue when it came to dogs what kind he was. It had been obvious no one was taking care of it as they should.

He clearly didn't mind how dirty the dog was because he planned to take him home. Another thoughtful, caring gesture.

Just who was that man?

When would she see him again? Never would be good.

Then his sweet smile penetrated her thoughts and she hoped soon. What happened to avoiding men?

She took a solemn breath and urged herself to look at her angel to remind her why men were bad. How well they could fake sweetness, kindness, and the next minute rip you to shreds.

"WHAT THE HELL IS THAT THING?" Zane demanded as the mangy dog ran around Austin's feet.

"What do you mean? It's a dog. My dog," Austin said with pride.

He had given him a bath last night. A huge water mess had splattered everywhere on the bathroom floor mingling with the dirt that had flown off the many times the dog felt the urge to shake his body. Austin decided the dog did need a haircut, but he would wait until he found his owners. He had no intention of giving him back with the state of despair he found the sweet, lovable dog in.

Dirty, smelly, knotted hair in many places, and even a few spots of dried blood where he had itched to the point of madness. But he planned to give them an earful on their treatment of animals and report them to the authorities. He'd also get Ava in his corner, knowing he would get the dog into his hands with ease.

One look and he had fallen in love. He wasn't giving him up without a fight now.

"When did you get a dog? You left last night dog free and now you have a dog," Zane said dryly.

"Is it that big of a deal? He's cute. A little messy last night, but we've become fast friends."

"I don't get it."

"I saw him sitting on my neighbor's porch last night and he was dying to get in. I banged on her door, ready to yell at her for treating him like that. Turns out, it's not her dog. He was dirty as can be and I cleaned him up, deciding he was my dog now. I'll try to find his owner, but he's mine now," Austin said with certainty.

"The same neighbor that you had issues with yesterday afternoon?" Zane asked with a grin.

"Yes," Austin groaned hesitantly.

"Yes? That's all you're going to say. You're not planning on elaborating how that conversation went?"

"No. It went. That's it," Austin muttered, walking toward the hog barn. "We have work to do. Come on, Axel."

"Who in the hell is Axel?"

"The dog," Austin exclaimed, turning around to glare at Zane.

"You named him Axel? Axel's a name for a big booming German shepherd or a Rottweiler, not...whatever the hell that thing is."

"He's a West Highland terrier. I know it's hard to tell with his hair as long as it is, but he's definitely an Axel. That's the first name that came to my mind and I'm sticking with it."

"What did your neighbor have to say about his name? What's her name, by the way?" Zane asked with a grin.

"What is it with you and Ava and this obsession with my new neighbor? I didn't tell her what I named him, and I'm not talking about her anymore. I have no idea what her name is and no desire to know either. Let's get to work already," Austin said, swinging the barn door open and stomping his way inside.

ZANE SMILED, itching to tell Ava the new development with Austin's neighbor. She was right. Maybe this woman would be good for him. He wasn't usually surly when it came to talking about women. He enjoyed all kinds of women.

Very interesting indeed.

He saw Ava coming from the red barn and his smile grew wider.

"Just the beautiful woman I had been hoping to see," Zane said, pulling her into his arms for a demanding kiss. He came up for air, a twinkle in his eyes as he pulled her tighter against him.

"What was that for?" Ava asked as her eyes betrayed that she wanted more.

"I missed you," Zane said simply.

"You saw me like ten minutes ago," she said dryly. "Spill it, mister."

"Austin got a dog. Named him Axel, and he doesn't look like an Axel. Trust me. He talked to his neighbor again last night, and I don't think it went well. He had a grumpy attitude when I tried to pry the conversation out of him. I got nowhere. He's keeping the dog, too." Zane watched as Ava's eyes lit up with amusement.

"I have to meet this woman. She's getting under his skin. You were just dying to tell me, weren't you?" Ava grinned deviously.

"Of course I was. Nobody better to whip some sense into him than you. He needs to stop dating the women he is and settle down. I know he doesn't want to, but he's going to spiral out sooner or later. I just know it. Any woman who can bother him like that is worth taking a chance on. We should meet her." If he didn't like the woman, he would back off.

"Leave it to me. I want to see this doggy now," Ava said happily.

"He's in the barn. He's no doggy. He doesn't even look like a dog. He looks like a sloppy mop."

Ava lightly tapped Zane on the butt. "Be nice."

Zane grabbed her hand and pulled her closer as they walked to the barn. "Watch where you put your hands, sweetheart. I'm liable to toss you over my shoulder and have my wicked way with you back in the bedroom."

She smiled as she pulled her hand from his, running it down his back in a slow caress, landing on his bottom again, pinching in delight. "I like the sound of that."

Zane grabbed her into his arms, cradling her to his body as he pushed her against the barn wall. "I love you. I can never say that enough." He brought his mouth down, crushing any words that may have escaped from her sweet lips. He treasured the heat that flowed around them, the magic that swirled in their mouths.

He pulled back slightly, resting his forehead against hers. "We need to get to work. Quit distracting me."

"You distracted me first," Ava pointed out as she grabbed another kiss. "Let's go find Austin. I can't wait to meet Axel."

Zane groaned at the ridiculous name and followed Ava into the barn.

4

—————

SOPHIE STARED in pleasure at the website she had created. Her shop was all set up. Thankfully, she already had a small customer following or it would've been harder to start a new life. She had managed, somehow, surprisingly, to create her artwork without Kevin becoming too mad about it. He eventually would have made her stop.

It had been her only source of income when she was with him. So pathetic. Reliant on him and his money. But no more. From now on, she would make her way in this world with her own hard work. She would never allow herself to become reliant on anyone else. Never again.

It'd be her way, or she would die trying.

She was behind on a few orders, sending apology emails with discounts for their next purchase, almost making it free for them. She couldn't afford to lose her faithful followers.

She enjoyed toying with projects, creating interesting and unique designs made out of anything really. She made a coat rack once out of a pitchfork. She had curved the prongs into hooks, adding a touch of whimsy to it. Then, she painted the handle with a delicate pattern, drawing out the beauty of the wood. For the bottom, she found a metal funnel with the hole just large enough to fit her handle through and hold the weight of it.

With the right tools and frame of mind, anything was possible. She had both.

The past week had flown by with hard work she had never doled out in her life. She had cleaned the house from top to bottom, every speck of dirt swept away with a painful brush of her hand. She forgot how many times she filled her bucket up with new water, it turned brown so easily, so fast. Now cleanliness filled the air.

Smelled fresh, new, and a little like freedom.

She had gone grocery shopping, buying a few more essentials for the house, supplies for her work, and gas for the lawn mower that sat in the shed waiting to be used. Except when she filled it up, changed the oil, and pulled the string to start it, nothing happened. No roaring sound pierced her ears.

She tinkered with it for a while, but she had no clue whatsoever what she was doing.

Her mystery man.

Why couldn't he magically appear again?

She hadn't seen him once all week, almost as if he never existed. She didn't even know where he lived, but she assumed somewhere in the neighborhood.

Why hadn't she taken his offer to mow her yard? Her lawn mower was broken, she had no clue how to fix it, no money to buy a new one, and the grass was growing way beyond the appropriate height.

He was right. Her house was the only run-down, neglected house on the block.

No worries, though.

She would just fire up another search engine on the

computer and find how-to instructions on fixing a lawn mower. She created obscure and odd things all the time; she could figure out how to fix a lawn mower.

She wasn't dumb. No matter how many times someone had told her that as she'd grown up.

"WHAT THE HELL YOU DOING?" *he bellowed in a disgusting tone, the stench of alcohol perforating her senses.*

"Setting the table," Sophie replied timidly.

"You're doing it all wrong. You're the dumbest kid I know. Get the hell outta here and get your damn mother. I want it done right," he yelled, spit flying as the words flew out.

Sophie nodded, turning abruptly, the tears in the corners of her eyes as she ran upstairs to where her mother was folding the laundry.

"Mama, I can't set the table right. He wants you to do it," Sophie whispered behind her mother, who had just finished folding a towel.

She turned toward Sophie. "Did he shout at you?"

Sophie nodded. "I'm too dumb, Mama."

Her mother crouched down to Sophie's level and grabbed her shoulders in a comforting embrace. "You're not dumb, Sophie. Don't let anyone tell you otherwise. He didn't mean to yell at you. He's a good man. He takes care of us."

"He's been drinking, Mama. You know how he gets when he drinks. How is that taking care of us?" Sophie asked, hating that her mother put up with him, defended him constantly. She wished he would run out on them like her real father had. He wasn't a good man in her eyes.

"He provides a roof over our heads and food in our bellies. He gets a little angry when he drinks, but he doesn't drink that much.

We have no choice right now, Sophie. He's a good man deep down. We just have to see that part of him. You're not dumb. I'll help you set the table."

Sophie nodded as she followed her mother to the dining room. She knew it was inevitable, the ensuing rage that would end the night.

"OH, YOU FANUZELING PIECE OF CRAP." Sophie whacked her wrench over the lawn mower with brute strength, not making one tiny dent.

She had been working for hours, or at least it had felt like hours, trying to fix the lawn mower with no luck whatsoever. She had no clue what she was doing and neither did the internet.

Another whack might help. Well, it'd help the frustration, that's for sure.

She raised the wrench when a slobbering kiss melted her senses.

Turning her head to the side, she received another slobbering dog kiss and giggled at the intrusion. "Well, hello there. Thank you for the kiss and the much-needed distraction from demolishing this horrid device." Sophie ruffled the dog's hair.

"He's an expert kisser. Learned none of it from me, but he has good skills," said the voice of the man she had wished for earlier.

Sophie turned toward him with a look of surprise. Yet she couldn't explain why. He had been with the dog the last time she saw him. Suddenly, without thought, she said, "And you know how to kiss well, is that what you're saying?"

His lips curled with delight. "I would like to think so. Would you care to find out?"

Sophie grimaced in horror at his words—and her loose lips. Why couldn't she control what came out of her mouth with him?

"Or Axel and I can leave you to finish demolishing your lawn mower. Sorry about interrupting you," he quickly said with an apologetic smile. "Come on, Axel. Let's go, boy."

He patted his leg for Axel to follow, turning to leave.

"How did you know his name was Axel? Did you find his owners?"

He glanced back at her. "No, I didn't. I called around to the local Humane Society and a few other animal shelters, but no one put out a missing report for him. I'm not really surprised with the state he was in. We bonded that first night and I couldn't bear to part with him, so I named him."

"Axel? That's different," Sophie said hesitantly, petting Axel, who hadn't moved from her side.

"It was the first name to pop into my head. I like it," he said with a shrug.

"I like it, too."

"Thanks. You'd be the first to like it. I'm sorry about what I said to you. I didn't mean to make you uncomfortable. I tend to joke around and just have fun sometimes. I didn't mean to offend you."

Sophie stood up, wiping her hands on her pants. "It did surprise me. I don't mean to be rude either. I'm sorry."

He took a step toward her. She instinctively stepped back. Either he noticed her retreat, or hadn't planned to come that close to her, but he stopped moving.

"Well, now that we got that awkwardness over. I'm Austin. I live next door," he said with a friendly smile, gesturing his head toward his house. "Offer still stands to mow your lawn, just as a neighborly gesture. I can see you're struggling with yours. But if not, that's okay, too."

Sophie shuffled her feet slightly, hating that she wanted to accept his offer. He seemed so nice, so genuine. They always acted like that at first. She had a horrible intuition when it came to men. The longer she looked him in the eyes, the harder it was to resist.

"Well, the fanuzeling machine just won't work, no matter how hard I try to fix it," Sophie said, irritated, kicking the lawn mower, hoping to jumpstart it that way.

Austin laughed. "Fanuzeling? I'm not sure what that means."

"You know—fanuzeling," Sophie said with a shrug, slightly embarrassed.

"No, I don't know. It sounds cute coming from your lips, though."

Sophie blushed. "Another version of swearing. I hate foul language. It sounds better to me to say fanuzeling."

Austin grinned. "It's a pretty word when it leaves your lips. I like it."

Sophie's blush crept farther around her face, traveling down her neck. "Well, like I said before, it just won't work."

"Would you like me to mow your lawn? I don't mind. I can even look at the lawn mower and see if I can fix it."

"I'm not dumb. I can handle it."

He stumbled back a step. "I never thought so. It was just a friendly offer, nothing else. Or we can do it together. I don't know much about lawn mowers. Actually, nothing about them, but sometimes a second pair of eyes helps."

"I appreciate the offer, but I can handle it. Excuse me." Sophie gave Axel one last pat on the head and walked quickly back to her house.

She wouldn't fall under his spell. He had experience and

player written all over him, especially when he smiled. As she shut the door to the house, she also tried shutting the door on his glorious smile.

To her extreme annoyance, she was unable to do so.

———

AUSTIN WATCHED as she walked away without a backward glance.

How did it go wrong so fast, again?

She was a puzzle. He had been unable to help himself with a little light flirting. The longer he stood there, the more her beauty had wrapped around his senses.

Even covered in sweat and grime, she looked beautiful. The sun had shined brightly on her, haloing her loveliness, making it difficult for him to remember why he needed to stay away from her.

Oh, yeah. She was his neighbor. He could not dabble with her.

He hated the fact he missed seeing her, and the fact her face penetrated his thoughts more than he wanted. She still hadn't been nice to him once since they met. But she liked Axel's name. That made him happy. Zane didn't like the name, and Ava didn't mind the name but offered better choices, which he refused.

He liked Axel and wasn't going to change it.

Always mucking things up with her. No matter how hard he tried, he couldn't manage to get on better ground with her.

A very touchy woman, the littlest thing set her off. There was something about her behavior that struck him as odd, but he couldn't quite put his finger on it.

Not his problem. He had to stay far away from her.

Unfortunately, he had to keep repeating that to his thick brain. He wanted to unravel the mystery surrounding her and he hated that.

He pulled his phone out, scrolling through the contacts until he found the one he wanted.

"Hey, Bethany, just the beautiful woman I was thinking about. How about hitting up a movie later tonight? I've been missing your gorgeous face," Austin said, but even as he did, Sophie's face intruded on his thoughts.

"Great. Can't wait to see you, darling." He hung up the phone, feeling more miserable. He blew out a frustrated breath, glanced one more time at her house, then slapped his leg. "Come on, Axel. Let's get ready for our date. We have better things to do than worry about our crazy neighbor. She's not that beautiful."

As he walked inside the house, Axel trailing his steps, he knew he was lying to himself. She was beautiful and he wanted to see a real smile light up her face.

AUSTIN WALKED QUIETLY into the house, his footsteps barely making a sound.

"Did you have fun?" Zane asked quietly as he sat on the couch in the living room, barely visible in the dark.

Austin jumped from the intrusion, a hand jamming to his chest from the scare. "Geez, Zane. What the hell you sitting in the dark for?"

"Where have you been? It's past curfew," Zane asked as he stood up, walking toward Austin.

"What are you, my dad? Nope, you're not," Austin shot back sarcastically.

"I can go wake up Dad for you if you like. Although, I think it's better I'm sitting here waiting for you than him."

Austin sighed. "What's the big deal? Maybe you should try breaking curfew for once. If Dad were so concerned, he'd be up waiting with you."

"I worry about you, Austin. You'll be graduating soon, and look at what you're doing."

"What am I doing? Having fun. What's so wrong with that?"

"Jimmy said there's a rumor going on around school that you got a girl pregnant. A Chrissy or something. Is that true? Dad will skin your head if it is."

"Jimmy needs to keep his damn mouth shut! I didn't get any girl pregnant. I didn't even sleep with her. She wanted to and I chose to decline because she's been with too many guys already. If she's pregnant, it's not mine. She started that because she saw me with another girl. Don't worry about it."

Austin started to walk away when Zane grabbed his shoulder. "I will worry about it. You're my brother, and I don't want you to screw your life up. If you didn't sleep with her...fine. Just make sure you use some damn protection when you're with a girl. Better yet, wait for the right one to come along instead of sleeping with every damn girl you find attractive. You're only seventeen."

"I don't sleep with every girl I find attractive. So I have a reputation with the ladies. Big deal. I haven't actually slept with that many. I do have some morals. I enjoy making out thoroughly, though," Austin said, grinning deviously. "I use protection, Zane. I'm not dumb. Quit worrying about me. And no, I didn't have sex with any girl tonight either. Good night."

Austin walked away without another word.

5

Sophie stood with her fist in the air, ready, waiting, poised for action. Yet the longer she stood there, the worse it became. Completely frozen.

Why was she standing on Austin's porch to ask to borrow his lawn mower? What was she thinking?

She needed to stay away from this man. He would be nothing but trouble with that gorgeous smile and smooth words he constantly doled out. She didn't need that in her life. She had purposely escaped that sort of thing to lead a normal, quiet life.

Not that she should compare Austin to Kevin because they were nothing alike. Kevin was polished, mannered, and came from where money talked frequently. Austin was more loose, fun, and smooth with his words. She had no idea what he did for a living, but she imagined it wasn't a nine-to-five job dressed in a tailored suit. She had yet to see him dressed in anything close to that.

A small smile lit up her face. He'd be handsome dressed like that.

Ugh! Get your head out of the gutter.

To her unforgiving irritation, she worked tirelessly all day on the lawn mower with no luck. She regretted dismissing his offer of help, hoping he would come back but knowing he wouldn't.

Why would he?

They had a brief moment when they were very polite, perhaps even friendly to each other. But then she ruined the moment by abruptly declining his offer—again—for help and walked away without another word.

It was for the best. She didn't need him.

But then she glanced at her checkbook.

She needed him.

After many hours of irritating tinkering, she figured out the motor was busted. The estimated cost to have it fixed would roughly cost the same amount as it would to buy a new lawn mower, if not more.

Plain and simple, her lawn mower was kaput. She had to mow her lawn and figured the best solution was to borrow Austin's until she sold a few more items to cover the cost of a new lawn mower.

She could always open a credit card and charge it, but she didn't want to be in debt so soon. She wanted to make it on her own without more worry pressing into her mind.

She sincerely hoped he didn't harbor any hard feelings and would kindly let her borrow his lawn mower. She had at least ten orders she was working on right now, and they would generate a nice allowance, but she wouldn't be finished until the end of the week. She couldn't delay cutting the lawn anymore.

The sweet older woman, Carletta, who lived on the other side of her house, had stopped her just the other day, making a brief comment on the lawn. She had been nice about it in her own friendly way, but basically told Sophie she was making the neighborhood look like trash with the way the lawn appeared. She was right, of course. She wished she could ask Carletta to borrow her lawn mower but noticed the other day that she hired a lawn service. She barely interacted with any of her other neighbors, her hesitation to let others in so ingrained from her past.

That left only Austin.

Sophie took a deep breath, tried to wipe the fear from her body, and finally completed the motion of knocking.

Her knuckles barely grazed the door.

No way he would've heard that, even if he was standing on the other side.

"Don't be a ninny, Sophie."

She raised her hand again to knock harder.

The doorbell.

She would never get a loud enough knock out of her. Her nerves were wired too high.

Lowering her hand, she gently reached for the doorbell and pressed lightly. The ring echoed throughout the house.

She almost fainted with apprehension as she waited in dread for him to answer the door.

———

AUSTIN GROANED as an irritating sound perforated his mind. He threw an arm over his eyes to block it out.

It didn't work. He could still hear the annoying sound. What the hell was it? It made the headache he had worse.

"Austin, someone's at the door," Bethany whispered in a sleepy voice.

Austin lifted his arm and glanced at Bethany. How in the hell did she get in his bed?

He drank way too much last night, all because he was trying to get one woman's face out of his mind. She didn't even like him that much and she was messing with him. His way of life.

He couldn't even remember having sex with Bethany.

Another groan almost escaped, irritated that she was in his bed.

He could only blame one person—himself. He was the idiot who called her. He just wanted something to take his mind away, and he definitely got that. It was the first time in his life he regretted sleeping with a woman. What was wrong with him?

Bethany nudged him. "The door, Austin. Are you going to get it?"

Austin muttered under his breath and grabbed his head in pain as he sat up. "I'm getting it. I have to head to the farm. I had a nice time, Bethany."

Austin grabbed a pair of sweats lying on the floor, put them on with an aching pain, and walked out of the room without another word. That was his nice way of saying *get the hell out* because he was done with her company.

Austin groaned the whole way. Who was at his door this early in the morning?

He glimpsed the clock.

Ten o'clock already. Okay, it wasn't that early.

Damn. Zane hadn't even called yet wondering where he was. Although, Zane knew he liked to enjoy his Friday nights.

What a nice brother letting him sleep in.

Of course, Zane probably left the nasty, annoying grunt work for him to finish. Maybe it wasn't so nice.

Austin opened the door and nearly fell over in surprise. "Sophie? Good morning."

"You don't have a shirt on," Sophie blurted as her eyes slid up and down his chest.

Austin grinned, his headache suddenly gone from her roaming eyes, enjoying the way her delicate stare brought him to an instant ache. "It didn't really occur to me to grab one."

"Well, I mean, anyone could be on the other side of this door. Do you always answer the door in such a manner?"

"No. This is the first time. I had a headache. I wasn't really thinking about it when the doorbell went off."

"You have no headache now?"

"Nope. Seems to have suddenly disappeared," Austin said smoothly.

"Oh, well, you should get a shirt. You know, never mind. I'll just leave," Sophie said, clearly embarrassed, as she turned around.

Austin reached out and grabbed her arm gently.

She jerked away. "Don't touch me."

"I'm sorry. Please don't leave." Austin held his hands up in an innocent gesture. "You knocked on my door for a reason. I apologize for making you uncomfortable. I obviously do a good job of that."

"No, I'm sorry. You're right. It's not your fault I freak out over the littlest thing...oh dear," Sophie said as Bethany came up behind Austin dressed in the slinky black dress that she wore last night.

Austin turned to Bethany, for the first time in his life horrified to have brought a woman home.

"Call me, Austin. I had a great time." Bethany kissed him on the lips quickly before he could turn away. "Who's your friend?"

Austin looked Sophie in the eyes, noticing her uncomfortable posture. "My neighbor Sophie. I'll see you around, Bethany."

Bethany grabbed another quick kiss, winked at him, and turned around. "Good morning, Sophie," she said as she sauntered past her.

Sophie didn't respond and watched the woman walk to a car that pulled to the curb and wave good-bye to Austin as it drove away.

"Your girlfriend seems nice."

Austin rolled his eyes, her missing the action. "She's not my girlfriend."

"Oh. Who is she?" she asked curiously, turning her eyes back to him.

"A woman I date occasionally."

"So, you mean sex?"

Austin laughed. "Way to get to the point there, Sophie. Yes, I guess if you want to call it that. I don't do relationships. I just date casually and enjoy myself."

"Why? You don't want to get married?"

"I don't ever plan on getting married. I'm not the marrying kind of guy, if you get my drift. I like women. They like me. That's all I want. That's all I really need."

"Wow."

"You seem surprised."

"You're very honest. Men generally aren't truthful."

"You haven't met the right man. I would never lie to you." How did this situation escalate into what it did? Although, he did enjoy the fact she knocked on his door. But why?

"Why are you here, Sophie? Besides dissecting my love life. Or lack thereof."

"Oh, right. My lawn mower decided it doesn't ever want to start again in its miserable life. I was hoping I could borrow yours until I find the money to purchase a new one. If it's not too much of an imposition." She shifted on her feet as if she were about to bolt.

"Sure. I can—"

"Nope. If you're offering to do it yourself, I can handle it. It's my lawn, and I will do it. I just need a machine that will actually work."

Why was he surprised? She would never give in to his help. He couldn't believe she was asking to borrow his, but then again, if she had no money, it made sense. He imagined it took a lot of effort for her to knock on his door. "Let me grab a shirt and get the keys to the shed. Come on in."

"I'll wait out here, if you don't mind." Sophie backed up a step.

Austin noticed the retreat and the slight fear in her eyes. He scared her. Why? He had never been rude to her.

"Okay. I'll be right back," he said, trying to act casual.

Austin ran upstairs, grabbed a clean shirt from his closet, and ran back downstairs to the kitchen where the shed keys hung on the wall by the fridge. He snatched them from the hook and made his way back to Sophie where she stood fidgeting in place waiting for him.

"Okay. Here we go. Let's head to the shed." He started to walk out when the phone rang. "Or not. That's probably my brother calling. Here. I'll just give you the key."

"Thanks. I'll go grab it and return your key promptly." She took the key from him. Her fingers lightly brushed his.

"No worries or rush. It'll probably take a while to mow the monstrosity out there. But I guess I don't have to offer my help because you know it's there if you need it." He glanced behind him as he heard his phone go off again. "Just return it when you're done. I better get the phone. Enjoy your day, Sophie."

"Thank you so much, Austin. You, too." She quickly turned around and hopped down the steps as if she were eager to get away from him.

Austin sighed as he watched her walk away. What he wouldn't have done to pull her into his arms when their fingers briefly touched. She was slowly becoming hard to resist. Everything inside him ached to find out more about her. He sensed there was a tremendous amount of secrets lying deep within her.

He cursed softly when the phone started to ring again. He slammed his door shut in frustration and raced to the kitchen, picking up the phone in a rush.

"Hello." He paused to listen to his brother give him a brief speech on wasting the morning and that he needed his help on a section of fence that went down in the north pasture.

"Settle down, Zane. I'm on my way now. I was heading out the door just as you called." Austin hung up, grabbed a bottle of water from the fridge, a granola bar from the cupboard, and left the house, trying not to catch a glimpse of Sophie before he left.

He made it to the farm ten minutes later. He stepped out of his truck at the same time Zane walked out of the house.

"So, was your evening enjoyable?" Zane asked, amused.

"Yeah. Beer, a beautiful woman, what more can a man ask for?" Austin grinned.

"Companionship, love, a deep relationship with a magical woman," Zane replied seriously.

"Drop the love speech, Zane, please. I'm not in the mood."

"Oh, hungover, are we? Sorry, let me get my 'I feel sorry for you' mood going. Wait, I can't, because your damn dog hogged the bed last night. No more sleepovers with Axel. I enjoy snuggling with my wife, and I can't when I have to share the bed with that mongrel."

"Oh, someone didn't get any last night, did they? Well, I got enough for the both of us. You're welcome," Austin said, thinking it was true, but honestly still couldn't remember how the sex was last night. He'd never drink to that extreme again. Not to mention, now that Sophie wasn't with him, his headache had come back full force.

"Not funny, Austin. I'm serious. He goes home with you tonight." Zane motioned for Austin to follow him to the barn.

"Fine. I was going to anyway. I missed him. Where is he?" Austin asked as he looked around.

"Ava went for a walk and took him with. She's falling in love with the damn thing, and the next thing you know, we're going to be buying a dog. It's all your fault. I don't want a dog. It'll probably be bad for the baby."

"No, it won't. Not if you get a good dog. You should get one. If Ava asks, you know you'll give in. You always give in to her."

Zane abruptly stopped and glared at him. "Don't you dare say anything to her or encourage her to get a dog. You'll regret it."

"What are you gonna do? Throw more pig shit at me?" Austin asked with a grin.

"Worse. And I won't tell you what it is because the element of suspense will kill you."

"Not scared, Zane. Never have been and never will be," Austin replied. "Hey, does that old push mower we have still work? I think it's in the red barn. We never use it since we bought the rider."

"I imagine it does. It has been collecting dust, so I have no idea if it'll start. Why?"

"I officially met my neighbor yesterday. We talked nicely for once, and her name is Sophie. She knocked on my door this morning asking to borrow my lawn mower because her lawn mower is broken. I thought if it still worked, we could just give her that one. Mowers aren't cheap."

"Really? You want to give your neighbor, who you haven't gotten along with until yesterday, our lawn mower. Just like that. In return for what? A romp in the sheets?" Zane asked with a suspicious gleam in his eyes.

"Geez, Zane. Is that how you really think of me? I'm just trying to be polite. It's sitting collecting dust and would finally get some use. She mentioned she doesn't have the money at the moment to buy a new one and—forget it," Austin said irritably, walking around Zane, ignoring his questioning look.

"I don't think of you like that. It was an honest question. I've never known you to give a woman a gift before."

Austin turned around. "What do you mean? It's not a gift. It's just being neighborly or nice or whatever. I've given flowers and whatnot to a woman before. I don't see her that way anyway."

"Are you sure you don't? Flowers are one thing. A lawn mower, a whole other ball game."

"What does that even mean? A diamond ring might raise questions, but a lawn mower, I don't think so."

"It means you say you don't like her, and yet, I think you do. You don't just give anyone a lawn mower," Zane said with a teasing smirk.

"You're impossible. Let's fix the fence already. I'm done talking."

"Sounds like what I always said when you pestered me about Ava," Zane hollered at his back.

"I barely know the woman to like her like that. Knock it off," Austin shouted, closing the barn door on his face.

6

———

AUSTIN BLEW OUT A SMALL BREATH, ruffled Axel's hair for a measure of confidence—something he never lacked before —and knocked soundly on the door.

He smiled wide when Sophie opened the door, cute and delectable in a white sundress that accented her beauty way more than he wanted it to. It hugged her breasts in a teasing manner, making him wish he had the right to cup them softly and appreciate them to the fullest extent. The dress ran just above her knees, telling a man there was something delicious waiting for him just a little farther up. It wrapped delicately around her waist with a soft bow just where her belly button would be, waiting for him to unwrap what lay beneath.

Three days had gone by.

Three long, agonizing days of torture from not seeing her beautiful face.

"Austin...hi. I suppose you're here for your key to the shed. I've been meaning to return it, but I've been so busy with my orders that I lost track of time. I'm so sorry." Sophie started to bite her bottom lip.

"No problem. That's not why I'm here. You look beautiful, by the way," he said, unable to hold it in. Biting her lip in that manner wasn't helping him to tame down his attraction. Temptation tingled throughout his body to step forward and have a little nibble on her lips himself.

"Umm...thank you. Why are you here?" she asked uncomfortably.

"I have something for you. We don't use it, sits collecting dust really, and it works great. I figured you'd get better use out of it than it sitting in the barn doing nothing."

Sophie looked confused as she raised a brow. "What is it?"

"Oh, right. A lawn mower." Austin smiled, pointing to her driveway where he had set it down after unloading it from his truck.

It refused to start when he first tried it, but after a few replacement parts, he got it running without an issue. He had to spend a few dollars—nothing extreme—to fix it. He would leave that little part out from Sophie or she probably wouldn't accept it. Ava probed him the entire time he worked, but he refused to talk about it.

Zane and Ava were enjoying his discomfort in the matter. He assured them it was nothing more than him being nice. A new friend. That was it. He refused to allow anything to happen with her. He wouldn't go any further than a simple friendship.

Sophie glanced over his shoulder and gasped. "Oh, I can't accept that, Austin. That just isn't right."

He frowned. "Why not? Like I said, we aren't using it. We recently bought a rider for the farm. I totally forgot about this lawn mower when I bought the one for my house. Stupid of me, but works out great for you. I want you to have it."

"But I can't. It would—"

"Sophie, please. I don't want anything in return. Since the first day I met you, I've only been trying to be nice. I get the impression you aren't used to that, and I'm sorry. I can't imagine anyone being horrible to you because, even when you're getting stern with me, you're sweet and eloquent about it. I'm sure there are reasons for it, but you don't have to tell me. Don't argue with me for once and just accept the damn mower." He felt horrible when he saw her cringe at his swearing. "Danuzeling mower, sorry."

"What?"

"You don't like swearing and I said damn. What do you say instead? Danuzeling?" Austin asked with a goofy grin.

Sophie chuckled softly. "No, I've never said that before. It has a nice ring to it. I try really hard not to use any replacement words either. I appreciate the effort, Austin. Most people laugh at me."

"I would never laugh at you unless you're purposely trying to be funny. Please take the mower. If it kills you that much to accept it without giving me something, then just make me a pie," he said without thought.

"A pie? What kind of pie?"

"A grape nut pie. A family favorite of mine and never missing in action around Thanksgiving."

"I've never heard of it. I don't know how to make it."

"Oh, man, really? It's delicious. You have no idea what you're missing. It's like pecan pie, but way better. Do you bake? I know Ava isn't a huge baker, but she sure tries." Austin laughed, thinking of the chaos she created when she baked.

"Ava? Another girlfriend or woman of yours?"

"Oh, no. My brother Zane's wife. You'd like her if you met her. She's great, but a sister to me. Nothing more."

"Oh, okay. Yes, I can bake. I suppose I can accept the mower in exchange for a grape nut pie. I would need the recipe, though."

"Of course. I'll call Eleanor and get it to you right away. I think I'm getting the better deal. My mouth is watering just thinking about it."

"Eleanor? Another—"

"Geez, no. Not another woman of mine. She's our long-time housekeeper and all around second mother. I don't have that many women." As those last words left his mouth, he realized he did have a lot of women. What did that say about him?

"Oh. Well, you said you enjoy women and they enjoy you, so...never mind."

"I did say that. Neither of them are one of my women. How do we always get on this topic?"

"I don't know." She laughed as Axel jumped up on her. "Hey, you. I missed you the other day. Where were you hiding?"

Austin enjoyed her laugh. She didn't do it enough. "He was at the farm with Zane and Ava. Sleepover, to my brother's extreme annoyance. Now he's afraid Ava will talk him into getting a dog."

"He doesn't want one?"

"Ava's pregnant. He worries about when the baby gets here. Worries about a lot of things now since she found out she's pregnant. He's just overly protective of her and rightly so. I can't imagine losing her or her getting hurt, but I told him a dog wasn't such a bad thing."

"Why so protective? Why would she get hurt?" Sophie asked with a slight shudder in her tone.

Austin noticed her slight retreat into the house. "She was hurt last year. Almost lost her from it and we—well, it's hard to talk about it. She means the world to me and Zane. More so Zane, I imagine. He would do anything in his power to protect her, make her happy. That's what makes him happy. All she has to do is ask for a dog and he'll go get her one. He'll moan and groan about it, but that's how much he loves her."

"And yet you don't want love?"

"I tried it once. It wasn't for me. How about you? Ever been in love?" How did they always get off track? Yet he was desperate to hear her answer.

"No, it doesn't exist. For me, anyway. The way you talk about your brother, it sounds like for him it does. Let's see that lawn mower," Sophie said, walking wide around Austin, abruptly changing the subject.

He stepped back to give her space that he knew she wanted, almost losing his footing from the hole in the porch.

"Oh, my! Be careful, Austin." Sophie grabbed his arm.

He clutched her back, relishing in her soft touch and the concern on her face. "We should fix that. I'm sure there's some wood lying around the farm that would patch that up real quick." He glanced down at the hole.

She let go of his arm. "The farm? You keep saying that."

He started down the steps to the mower, Sophie right behind him. "Yeah, my brother and I own a farm not too far from here. This is the first time I ever ventured out on my own. About a month before you moved in, I bought the house next to you. Zane and Ava are married and starting a family. It just seemed appropriate." Austin rolled his eyes. "And Ava didn't really approve of the women I brought home. It's difficult to maintain a second date when she's clawing down their throats with death glares. She's still making it difficult, and I'm not even there."

"Well, I see what she means." She almost bumped into him when he stopped and turned around.

"What do you mean?"

"Well, you admitted to me that you only date for sex, if that's what you want to call it, and you're not really bringing home the nice girl types, are you? When the baby comes she won't want those kinds of women around."

"You don't hold back, do you?" Austin asked with a grin.

"I don't mean to have a loose tongue. I didn't mean to offend you. I'm so sorry. I won't say anything again." She shifted farther away from him, the fear etched clearly in her features.

"No. I appreciate honesty. I know where I stand with you. It's nice, Sophie. Most women say what they think I probably want to hear. I guess I don't really bring home the nice girl types because they look for relationships and I'm only looking for fun."

"You'll never want more than fun?" she asked as the terror slowly left her eyes.

"Do you want more than fun?"

Sophie looked away toward her house. "I just want peace in my life. I don't want a man, or love, or anything but me." She glanced back at him. "I don't trust men. Maybe you can tell or maybe you wrote that off as me being...a very naughty word. You say you're being nice, but in my experience, there's always an ulterior motive."

"With me, you get what you see. I'm not hiding anything. I'm just looking to be a friend. I won't say you're not beautiful because you are, Sophie. You're my neighbor and that's bad business right there. I have no ulterior motives other than being a nice guy. You don't want me to bother you, I won't. But if you need me, all you gotta do is knock on my door. Not all men are bad. I'm sorry one had to make you think that."

"Not just one, Austin, but every single man to enter my life." Sophie's eyes got huge after she said that, almost as if she hadn't meant to say such a thing.

"Well, you moved to the right place. I'll change your mind about men, or at least about me. I'm hard to resist because I'm just that irresistible," he said, as Axel jumped up on his leg looking for a scratch under the ears. Austin chuckled, thinking that Axel agreed with his words.

"I hate admitting, against my better judgment, you have been slightly changing my mind. Or maybe I just want this free lawn mower," she said with a tentative smile.

He laughed, glad to have removed that moment of fright from her eyes. "It's not free. You owe me a pie. I'm really dying to have it now."

"Well, while I put this away, go grab the recipe and I shall make you a pie."

"Don't have to tell me twice." He winked at her and walked toward his house, Axel right by his side.

SOPHIE SIGHED IN DEFEAT. She was letting him weasel his way into her life. The harder she tried to resist, the easier it was for him to enter.

She could still remember how he looked that morning, half-naked, holding the door open, his bronzed chest displayed in all its glory right before her eyes. She had never seen such beauty and, strangely, had the intense urge to rub her hands over his sculpted chest. Defined muscles flawlessly covered every corner of his body, begging to be touched. She had difficulty looking away.

Or when her fingers had brushed his when she took the shed key from him. An immediate heat had flashed, her eyes darting to his to see if he had felt the same thing. He still had the same friendly look on his face, so she assumed he hadn't.

Figured. She couldn't compete with the woman who had walked out of his house. She wasn't that kind of woman. Not that she wanted Austin that way, because she didn't. That tingling sensation meant absolutely nothing.

Fleeing from his porch, mowing her lawn as her excuse, she had decided she needed to limit contact with him as much as possible. She would not fall under another man's charm.

And then he knocked on her door.

Another opportunity presented itself to touch him. A horrible one. Because the last thing she wanted was for him to fall through the hole in her porch. His warm touch as he grabbed her back had ignited tiny flames of desire. She could almost feel his heat lingering, missing his touch.

At least she knew where she stood with him—off his radar. They were neighbors, and he wouldn't add her to his list of women.

Somehow, as she pushed the mower to the backyard, that made her oddly sad.

She increased her footsteps, trying to shake that sadness out. She didn't want to be added to what she assumed was a long list. But she did appreciate his honesty.

She had pictured him as a playboy but never expected him to admit it. She couldn't explain or understand the refreshing feeling that zipped through her to experience such honesty from a man.

His delicious body flashed before her again. The pure perfection of his chest. His soft hands.

It'd be nice to experience it just once.

No.

Not going to happen.

The best thing she could do was make him the pie and avoid him.

With that thought firmly planted in her mind, she walked back to the house, waiting eagerly to get the recipe and get him out of her life.

7

SOPHIE CAREFULLY WALKED down the basement steps to the washer and dryer with a basket of dirty clothes under one arm and her free hand holding the handrail. The steps felt rickety and loose in a few spots.

Perhaps she should mention to Austin about grabbing more wood from the farm to replace a few of these. Tumbling down the stairs wasn't on the top of her to-do list.

Against her better judgment, she had somehow let the man weasel his way into her life, even after she explicitly told herself not to. She made him a pie that first time for the lawn mower, which he thoroughly devoured in two days, to her shock.

He knocked on her door with the clean pie pan and some wood to fix the hole in her porch. He grinned that silly grin of his, saying the wood was hers for another pie. When he looked at her that way, it was hard to say no.

Of course, he offered to fix the hole.

Self-sufficient, her new middle name. She could handle it on her own. He didn't argue once when she declined his help.

She managed to fix the hole, and a week later, after making a few great sales, she bought stain and re-stained the front porch. Such an amazing feeling to look at a completed project. She couldn't believe what a fresh coat of stain or even paint could do to bring new life to something. Even a bit of new life inside of her.

Since that fateful day, he hadn't stopped bringing her things. She received more wood, some odd-shaped pieces of metal, and whatever else, according to him, that was lying around the farm. He said he'd never lie, so she decided to take his word as the truth. Every time she would make him a pie. After the third time, she switched it up and made a cherry pie. Then came a blueberry pie, an apple pie, and when she really wanted to see the light shine in his eyes, she made another grape nut pie. It really wasn't that difficult to make the man happy.

He managed to help her fix the porch, the swing, the back door that wouldn't close properly, a window in an upstairs bedroom, the shutters outside on the porch, and supplied great material for her works of art. She had shown him what she made and he had been deliriously impressed by it. He couldn't believe she created such things and even bought a chair she made out of pallets that he wanted to give to Ava. She almost gave it to him for free, but he had insisted. She put hard work into making it and he would support that by purchasing it.

Four weeks.

That's all it had taken for him to worm his way through her defenses and slowly crumble them down. Sometimes, after he left, she would run upstairs and stare at her angel, reminding herself why it was bad to trust him. She swore each time she did, the angel smiled back at her as if to say that he wasn't that bad.

Could she trust him? So far, he gave no impression that she couldn't. But she still had her worries.

She never invited him in and he never pressed the issue. He always dropped the supplies at the door, knocked to let her know he was there with gifts galore, and offered any assistance to which she politely refused. After she made the pie, she would knock on his door to deliver it. He would invite her in for a slice, but she always politely refused to enter.

He never, not once, pressured her either way. He would grin in his sexy way and say, "Okay, Sophie. Until next time. Axel and I will miss your delightful face, darling."

She just adored Axel. He was never far away from Austin. She liked that about him. That he loved that animal so much.

The only non-enjoyable thing to occur was seeing Austin's occasional women roll in and out of his house. It wasn't as regular as she assumed it would be, but enough to make her sick. She didn't want Austin that way because she was done with men.

Every time she saw him leave or come home with some-one, she changed her mind and wanted to be his woman.

They all looked the same.

Beautiful, well-endowed, sexy women who knew what he wanted and didn't mind giving it to him. She hadn't met Ava yet, but decided she agreed with her. She didn't like any of them. If she happened to be outside when she saw one of them, she gave a death glare that she hoped would make Ava proud. Of course, she made sure that Austin didn't see. That would create questions she didn't want to answer. Even to herself.

Sophie jumped with enthusiasm off the last step,

grateful she made it down in one piece. Austin's adorable face punctured her mind. When would he stop by again?

Normally, she didn't ask for anything. She just used what he gave her to fix whatever needed fixing. Perhaps, just this one time, she would go to him and ask for wood to replace some of the steps.

She froze midway between the stairs and the washer.

The biggest spider to ever step in her pathway stood a foot away.

The spider's body was grotesquely big, about the size of a grape. She couldn't remember a time she ever saw one that big.

Long black legs that sat waiting for action, and its beady eyes—not that she could see them, but she imagined—were staring her down just as she stared right back. Like a show-down, two gunslingers waiting for the walk of death. Who would pull the trigger first? Her or the spider?

She hated spiders.

She refused to be beaten down by a man anymore. She surely wasn't going to let a spider beat her down either.

Slowly, the laundry basket descended, her eyes never leaving the sight of the spider. She let go of the sides of the basket, the spider making no move. Gently, she lifted her foot and removed her sandal. There was no way she could stomp on it, but she could reach really far and whack it with her sandal.

With one careful step, she waited for the spider to scamper away, yet it made no move. Perhaps it thought it would win this war. She was about to prove it wrong.

Reaching out with the longest stretch she could muster, she slammed down on the spider's body.

Instant relief swamped her.

Until dozens—no, thousands—of tiny little baby spiders scurried around the basement floor.

She lost the war.

A loud scream belted from her lips as the sandal slipped from her fingers. She dashed back up the stairs.

Disgusting!

Her skin crawled with unease as the impression of tiny spiders inhabiting her body consumed her, even though none had touched her. She didn't stop, but raced for the front door and yanked it open.

She fell right into Austin's arms.

"Are you okay? What's wrong?" he asked, concerned, as he held her gently.

"Oh my, Austin. It's...it's a spider. In the basement," Sophie muttered as she breathed in his wonderful scent. He smelled of fresh outdoor air with a hint of farmness—a mingling taste of manure, hay, and whatever else she assumed belonged on a farm. It should make him stink unpleasantly, but it only made him smell divine.

As soon as the realization that she was in his arms pricked her senses, she stepped back.

HE HID the disappointment when she stepped away. He had never gotten that close to her, and it had instantly played hell on his body. She had felt so good pressed against him, he almost kissed her.

"In the basement, you say. I'll kill it for you." He winked and stepped inside the house.

She didn't stop him, so he took that as acceptance that he could enter and walked downstairs to the basement.

Some of the boards felt loose under his feet. He'd have to remember to grab more wood and bring it over.

He had stopped by today with an old metal toolbox he found hidden away in the barn. He didn't know if she could do anything with it, but he saw some of the great things she created and knew she would think of something awesome.

He liked that about her—a lot. He needed to quit thinking about her day and night.

A laundry basket sat in the middle of the floor. Must've been where she saw the spider.

Her sandal lay by its lonesome and the guts of what looked like was once a spider not far from the basket. Confused, he picked the sandal up and headed back upstairs.

She already killed the spider. Why was she freaking out about it? He laughed. She was probably one of those types who felt bad after they killed a bug.

The front door was open. Sophie stood in the yard instead of on the porch.

"I have your sandal. It looks like you already killed the spider. Why didn't you tell me that?" he asked with a laugh.

"I did kill it. You should put that down, Austin," Sophie said with alarm, eyeing her sandal.

He looked confused. "Why? It's a sandal."

"Yeah, but there could be baby spiders on it. Didn't you see the thousands of baby spiders that exploded out of the spider after I killed it? I can't go back in there. It's disgusting."

Austin jumped and threw the sandal down. "Why the hell didn't you say that to begin with?"

He looked down at his hand and saw a microscopic spider scurry across his thumb. "Ahh! Disgusting."

He started to swipe at his hand, then all over his body, as

if suddenly they were swarming him. He continued to make a fool of himself when he glanced over at Sophie to see her laughing and smiling like he had never seen before.

She had laughed lightly, given small glimpses of a smile here and there, but never anything like this. It personified her beauty like nothing else ever could. He loved her smile, and at that moment didn't care it was his foolishness that was making her smile.

"All right, miss funny pants. Let me shower and then we'll call an exterminator," Austin said with a devious grin.

Sophie stopped smiling. "I don't have the money for that, Austin. Why do you need to shower?"

"Are you kidding me? I walked out of the basement with the killer sandal and they could be—" Austin shook his body. "Roaming all over my body right now. I have to wash them off. I'm not a fan of spiders. For you, I was willing to be the hero and kill it. Don't worry. It's my cousin Emmett. He won't charge you."

"Well, I don't know, Austin..."

He braved moving toward her. She made no slight movement of stepping back as she normally did. "Sophie, there are probably a million baby spiders loose in your house right now. You just said you couldn't go back in there. We have to kill them all. But I have to shower. I have to."

She sighed heavily. "Okay. I'll wait right here for you."

"Good." Austin looked at Axel. "Wait with Sophie, buddy. Keep her company."

She smiled another glorious smile at him as he walked to his house to clean off the grotesque feeling of spiders inhabiting his body.

AUSTIN COULD SMELL the heavenly scent of Sophie, she stood so close to him. Ever since she ran into his arms fleeing the house, she had felt more comfortable next to him than she had the entire time he had known her. Her frequent steps backward when he came near, or her subtle moving to the side to make space, familiar to him, seared in his brain as a normal part of who she was. He respected her space, knowing she felt uncomfortable, perhaps even a little afraid as well.

When Emmett arrived at her house and put his hand out to greet her, Austin saw the hesitation to shake it. He knew Emmett saw it as well but made no comment on the fact. Sophie had quickly shaken his hand out of politeness, then immediately stepped closer to Austin. He could get used to this. He liked having her near him.

"Austin, I'm not an exterminator. I own a landscaping business and sometimes administer pest control, but that's it," Emmett tried to explain.

"Okay, pest control. Go control the spiders. Trust me, I don't want Sophie's house swarming with spiders. Do you?" Austin asked.

"Of course not. I still find it quite humorous you felt the need to shower. I can't wait to share that," Emmett said, laughing.

"Really, Emmett? Do we have to act like children and gossip?"

"Hell, yeah. I can't wait to tell Gabe and Ethan about this. You tease and rip on us all the time. How about that time when Gabe got on the mechanical bull down in the Twin Cities and he went flying off, breaking his nose? You couldn't stop for weeks teasing him about it. Spiders? That's just too funny not to laugh," Emmett said, chuckling. He glanced at Sophie. "You were braver than Austin here. You at least killed a spider."

"Yes, well, I wouldn't have if I had known it was carrying a whole family inside it," Sophie replied softly, edging farther by Austin.

"Look, I'll go in there, spray some chemicals, and try to kill as many as I can. It'll also help with prevention. I'll spray some around the outside of the house as well. I can't say it'll kill them all, but it'll help. That's the most I can do," Emmett replied, eyeing Austin with his brows raised sharply. "Because I'm not an exterminator."

"Yeah, yeah, I heard you the first time, Emmett. I swear if you tell your brothers, Gabe and Ethan, I will find something to damage you. Mark my word, Emmett," Austin said firmly.

"Not a chance, Austin. I'm even going to tell Zane," Emmett said, still laughing.

"You know, I appreciate your kindness, but I don't have the money to pay for something like this," Sophie quietly interrupted.

Austin looked at her. "Don't worry, Sophie. Emmett's not charging you."

"No, I'm not. I'm charging Austin," Emmett replied with a smirk to him.

"Oh, no, I can't have that," Sophie said with a delicate cringe that somehow personified her beauty even more. Or could it be because she was trying to stick up for him?

"I don't mean literally charge him for the services, Sophie. A friend of Austin's is a friend of mine. Plus, he never asks me to do stuff like this, especially for a woman. You would be the first in that sense. But I'm thinking good seats to a baseball game, maybe," Emmett said as he looked at Austin.

"What does *good seats* mean?" Austin asked with a groan.

"Behind home plate, first row," Emmett replied slyly.

"Are you nuts? Do you know what those cost?" Austin exclaimed.

"I do recall helping out at the farm a few weeks ago with the west field and helping with taking some of the hogs to the local market when Zane had to take Ava to a doctor's appointment. Oh yeah, and when baling hay comes around, who are you going to call? When are you guys heading to New York? I suppose you want me, Gabe, and Ethan to help with the farm while you're all gone," Emmett pointed out, as he ticked off each item on his fingers as he said it. "And you need to buy a ticket for yourself. I don't want to go to the game by myself."

"Which means I have to buy Ava one because she'd kill me if I went to a baseball game without her. And Zane won't want her going without him," Austin said, trying to process what the cost would be in his mind.

"Great. When does New York come to town? Might as well make Ava happy and go to a game with her team playing," Emmett said happily.

"Are you nuts? Do you know the kind of fanatic she is when it comes to them? We'd probably be kicked out of the stadium or something with her loose lips." Austin shook his head just thinking about it. "Although, she would love that. I know she misses New York quite a bit."

"Zane's a lucky man that he can keep her here. When are you guys heading to New York so I can figure out my work schedule?" Emmett asked.

"I don't know yet. We've talked about it, but nothing is set in stone. Zane keeps hedging because he doesn't want to go, but he will if Ava does. She mentioned around the Fourth of July. Every time we bring it up, he grumbles about it. New York is awesome if he just gave it a chance," Austin said with a smile, yet he could see Sophie's frightened expression every time they mentioned the words *New York*.

"Are you sure he'll go?" Emmett asked quietly.

"Yes, he will. Kicking and screaming, maybe, but he will. If it's last-minute notice, I'm sorry, but I seriously think it'll be around the Fourth. You know it means a lot to us when you pitch in at the farm. Thanks, Emmett. Even now, helping Sophie out. The tickets are yours, front row behind home plate," Austin said sincerely.

"That's what family does, man. I'm always here for you guys, just as I'm sure you'd be there for us if we needed it. I'll give you money to buy some Tootsie's to give to Jimmy," Emmett said as sadness touched his eyes.

Austin laughed. "Yeah, he loved his Tootsie's all right. I can do that. Enough of this stuff. Go kill some spiders already. The game is starting soon. Do you wanna come over when you're done for a beer and watch it?"

"Yeah. I don't have anything else going on. Is it okay I treat your house, Sophie?" Emmett asked, the sorrow slowly dissipating as he glanced at her for approval.

"Is it okay for dogs and humans alike? Axel sometimes runs around the yard, and I don't want him getting sick from the pesticides," Sophie said as she leaned down to comfort Axel, who had been sitting nicely by her the entire time.

"Yeah, it's safe for everyone. I would take him into Austin's house while I administer it, but after it settles, it'll be fine," Emmett replied.

"Okay. Thank you for your kindness. Austin occasionally gives me wood and such things to fix my house, and I bake him a pie in return. What's your favorite pie and I'll make you one?" Sophie asked shyly.

Emmett smiled brightly. "I love pie. Any pie will do.

That's really nice of you, Sophie." Emmett glanced at Austin, who frowned slightly.

"Good. Let me do that while you work, and I'll bring it over to Austin's before you leave," Sophie said, walking away before they could respond.

"She's sweet and very beautiful," Emmett said as soon as she stepped inside the house.

"Back off, Emmett," Austin growled.

"Oh, you like her then? Are you dating her?"

"She's a friend, nothing more. But she...she doesn't like men. At least, that's what she's told me and the impression I get. She likes her space and she likes her privacy. I don't want anyone upsetting that," Austin said with a serious glower, "including you."

"So, you like her," Emmett repeated, laughing as he did.

"I just said—"

"Austin, I know what you just said. You didn't specifically say it, but you like her. Maybe you don't want to, but you do. Since when do you give women things like you do with her? You date casually, but putting in an effort like this is very strange behavior for you. I'm just saying." Emmett rubbed his chin as Austin's frown deepened. "I know what you mean about the space thing. I'm surprised she stood so close to you. She's wary. You do know what that means, don't you?"

"She normally doesn't. She keeps her space, even from me, but she's known me a bit longer than you. Maybe that's why. Trust me. It's taken a lot for her to get to know me. She never accepts my help in fixing anything with the house, but she does a great job herself, so it's not like she really needs my help. She never invites me inside her house, and when I offer her to come inside my house, she declines. I'd like to say we're friends, but the most I can really say is we're friendly. I'm guessing someone abused her before. If I knew who it was, they would be the sorriest man alive," Austin said with a slice of venom in his voice.

"I don't know her that well, but I'd be right by your side if you ever find out. Just say the word."

"Yeah, well, I don't know. I'm not going to ask her or suggest to her that I know anything. I'm keeping it light here. I'm just trying to be her friend because it looks like she needs one. That's it." Austin glanced at the house.

Emmett slapped him on the shoulder. "Keep telling yourself that if it makes you feel better, but you like her. I think it scares you. Don't drink all the beer. I better go kill some spiders."

Austin scowled as he watched Emmett head for the house. Suddenly, he worried about Sophie inside the house as a man she barely knew was heading inside as well. Not that he didn't trust Emmett, because he trusted him with his life. Sophie didn't know him and could be very nervous.

Would she hate it if he came inside as well?

What the hell. She broke a small barrier between them today when she stood so close to him.

"Come on, Axel. Let's get you inside my house, and then I'm going to check on Sophie, okay?" Austin said as Axel happily followed him home. He swore Axel's tail wagged faster when he said her name, as if he agreed with Austin's worry.

8

SOPHIE BOUNCED AROUND THE KITCHEN, pulling ingredients out, trying to calm her nerves, but they refused to calm down, jumping with every movement. Her hands shook every time she pulled something from the cupboard or opened the fridge or a drawer. She'd burn herself, cut herself, or hurt herself in some silly way if she didn't calm down.

But a man was in her house and she hated it. She didn't even know why she offered him a pie. She only did that for Austin. It felt like a small betrayal, but she couldn't allow him to do it for free. Every man expected something in return. He would get nothing but a pie.

Not a grape nut pie either.

That was for Austin only.

She wouldn't cross that line. He would get a simple apple pie. She breathed a sigh of relief when she saw she had apples in the house, because she was out of every other ingredient for pie except for grape nut pie. He just wasn't getting that.

She stopped in front of the fridge to take a calming

breath when she felt another presence. Everything tight-ened inside, ready to take flight-or-fight mode into gear, when she heard a familiar, calming voice.

"Are you okay, Sophie?" Austin asked.

She turned around, pasting a small smile on her face. "Of course. Why wouldn't I be?"

"I would like to think we've become sort of friends in the past month. You said so yourself that you don't trust men. Emmett's a great guy, but you don't know him, and I don't want you to feel uncomfortable while he's working inside. If you want me to keep you company in the kitchen, I can. Or I can go back home because I know you probably don't want me in here either. You never invite me in and you never accept my invite to come into my house. Let me know what you want and I'll do it," he said with concern in his eyes.

"You're too perceptive for your own good, Austin," Sophie said, pulling open the fridge to grab the apples. "I would feel better with you in the house. I know he's your cousin, but you're right. I don't know him and it is slightly uncomfortable."

She closed the fridge door, set the apples on the counter, and noticed that Austin had stepped into the kitchen and taken a seat at the table.

"I can't help myself. What happened to you, Sophie? Why don't you trust men?" Austin asked softly.

She glanced at him. "I don't want to talk about it. Please don't ask me again, Austin."

"Okay. I won't."

She nodded, surprised he didn't pry further. "Thank you."

She turned back around and started peeling the apples and slicing them up in tiny pieces.

AUSTIN WATCHED IN SILENCE, enjoying the way she moved about the kitchen. Fast and efficient in every movement she made, especially slicing the apples. Although, she did have a handy tool to help her along. She would grab an apple, slide it onto a device he had never seen before, and then rapidly twirl the knob on the other end as it would peel the apple skin off and slice it at the same time.

Simply amazing.

Then she'd toss the apple slices into another bowl, grab another apple, and repeat the process. Before he knew it, she had finished slicing the apples.

He hated holding back his questions. The need to know more about her coursed through him every time he saw the slight fear in her eyes. Even though he saw that fear, she was still one of the bravest women he had ever met.

Ava, of course, would be the first.

Sophie never let that fear hold her back and bring her down. He admired that about her.

He had gained a small amount of her trust, but he wanted that full-fledged trust that came with a deep friendship.

That's how he saw her. A good friend. It didn't matter what Emmett said about him liking her.

He didn't. Not like that.

As he watched her bend slightly to toss the pie in the oven, her petite bottom wiggling, he realized he was kidding himself.

He did like her.

Talk about trying to suppress his emotions. He refused to go down the path of love again, no matter how much it killed him to ignore it. Not that he loved her, but he was on his way to a deep feeling he couldn't describe nor wanted to contemplate.

"All done. Now we just wait for it to bake. Do you think he's almost done? I would hate for you two to miss the beginning of the game." Sophie wiped her hands on a towel as she looked at him.

He grinned, knowing full well that was her polite way of saying she wanted them out of her house. "I can go see. But it takes time. You did say a thousand of those spiders escaped. It would be a good thing for him to get every single one."

Sophie shuddered. "I don't even want to go down there. It's gross. You're right, though, I do want him to get them all. Would you like something to drink? I don't have alcohol because I don't drink, but I have water, iced tea, or milk."

He wasn't surprised she didn't drink. Probably had something to do with the secrets she kept inside. "I'm okay." She nodded. "You ever been to New York?"

"Why would you ask me that?" she exclaimed.

Austin almost jumped in his seat by her response. "No reason. Just trying to make small talk. I take it, you don't like it."

"No. But I gathered from the conversation outside that neither does your brother."

"No, he hates it." Why did he even bring up the subject?

"Why does he hate it?"

"Why do you hate it?"

"Perhaps we should skip this conversation." Sophie turned her back to him and started to pick up the mess she'd created from preparing the pie.

The rigidness as she wiped the counter and the stiffness as she opened the cupboard under the sink to throw some trash away couldn't be missed. Austin wanted to apologize for opening his mouth, but he wasn't sure if bringing it up again, even for an apology, would be good. Agitated didn't begin to describe how much he upset her.

His mouth started to open to apologize when she whispered softly, with her back to him, "I lived there before I moved here. It wasn't a pleasant experience, and it brings back memories I wish to forget. That's why I hate it."

Austin stood up but made no move to approach her. "Ava was born and raised there. She's a New Yorker through and through. My brother Jimmy always wanted to be a cop, but it had to be in New York. He met Ava fresh out of the academy and they became fast friends. I'm glad he made friends with her because he probably wouldn't have survived otherwise. He could be extremely shy. Zane never wanted him to leave for the big city."

Sophie turned around when he stopped talking. "So he hates it because Jimmy still lives in New York. He isn't excited to see him?"

"No, he isn't excited. Because Jimmy died in the line of duty. We're going there to visit his grave because Ava wants to tell him that she's pregnant. Zane disliked the city when Jimmy moved there, but he definitely hates it now that Jimmy died there. He's only going for her, otherwise he would never step foot in that city again."

He suddenly pulled a grin from nowhere. "Well, that was a pleasant storytime. We all have difficult times in life, Sophie. I miss my brother every damn day. He was a hell of a guy. Sometimes, I hate talking about it, but mostly, I've come to find that it brings me a little more peace when I do. I can't keep it bottled up. Neither can you. Maybe I'm not the best person to talk to, but if you happen to pick me, I'm all ears. I'm a really good listener."

Before she could respond, Emmett walked in, oblivious

to the serious conversation. "All done. Boy, that pie smells great. I can't wait to taste it."

Sophie looked away from him. "Well, it won't be done for at least another thirty minutes. You two should head back to Austin's for the game, and I'll knock on the door when it's finished."

"You don't want to join us?" Emmett asked.

"No, thank you. I'm not a baseball fan," Sophie replied.

"I hope I get a piece. You're sharing with me, right?" Austin said to Emmett with a laugh, trying to ignore the rapid pulse of his heartbeat for speaking that way to her.

"I don't know, man, it smells pretty darn good. Depends how nice you are to me," Emmett said with a chuckle.

"I can be really nice. Or I can con Sophie into baking me my own pie." Austin winked at her.

Sophie shyly smiled. "Perhaps you can. I do need wood to replace a few of the basements steps."

"Yeah, I know. I noticed that myself. Wait to go down there until I bring some over tomorrow. I don't want you to get hurt," he said with concern. "No need to knock when the pie is done. Just come in the house. Okay?" She broke the barrier, and he would try his hardest to keep it crumbled to the ground as much as he could.

Sophie nodded.

He walked away before he tenderly pulled her into his arms to wipe the sadness from her eyes. He put that there. And he wanted to take it away.

As he closed her front door, he knew that she would never join them. She'd drop the pie off and run back to her house like she always did.

Distance would be better.

That wasn't something he wanted anymore. Just how in the hell could he bridge the gap between them?

"How's Sophie?" Ava asked with a sly tone as she came up behind him as he was mucking out a pig stall.

Austin turned to her, glaring a bit at the intrusion.

How was Sophie?

Good question. A very loaded question.

Vigorously trying to work off the sexual frustration of not pulling Sophie into his arms and Ava had to ask about her. He certainly didn't want to talk about her when his sole purpose was trying to forget about her.

Another long, insufferable week of seeing Sophie briefly here and there, but instead of that wondrous day when she had stood close to him, she had gone back to distancing herself. It made him mad.

"What, no response? Did she get the stairs to the basement fixed and are the spiders gone?" Ava tried again.

"Stairs are fixed. Spiders are gone. I'm busy, Ava." He turned back to his task.

"You know when you get irritated, you're just like Zane. You ignore the issue and get all testy about it. Why can't you just ask her out and see where the relationship could go? Everyone knows you like her."

Austin abruptly turned around. "Ava, please kindly leave me alone. I don't want a relationship with anybody. Even if I did want one with Sophie, she sure in the hell doesn't want one with me. She hates men. I am a man."

"Yes, you are. A very kind, loving, generous man who could show her what she deserves and what she's missing. Emmett stopped over the other day and told us about her. He said she's very beautiful and very timid. Perhaps abused at one time. Obviously, you have to treat her gently to crack open her shell, but you can't do that if you're not trying."

"I am trying!" he shouted, then cringed when he realized what he just admitted.

Ava smiled widely. "I knew you liked her. Try a little harder. Invite her to the farm. It helped me heal. Maybe it'll help her."

"She'll never come to the farm. She won't even come into my house for a slice of pie that she bakes me," he said with impatience. "Ava, I know you mean the best, but I'm not looking for love. I'm just trying to be her friend. How many more times can I tell you guys that?"

"Until I actually believe it. I see it in your eyes what she means to you and it isn't a simple friendship. I get it. You were burned before with love, but that doesn't mean if it suddenly comes back into your life you push it away because of one crazy bitch that probably didn't deserve your love."

"What? You don't even know who she was or if she was a bitch."

Ava scoffed. "I don't know when you started becoming this player persona you seem to have adopted and maybe you just fell into it right away. The examples I've seen you date are nothing to brag about. I have a good idea that this woman you supposedly loved probably falls into the same category as all these other ridiculous women. How old were you?"

"Why?" He hated this probing of his love life.

"Because it matters."

Austin sighed. "I was nineteen. She wasn't like the other women. I don't want to talk about it."

"Way too young to know what love is. Did you tell her and was she the same age?"

"Ava, you're killing me here," Austin muttered as he rubbed a hand over his face in frustration. "Yes and yes. She didn't say it back. I know what I felt and it was love, even if I was nineteen."

"Okay, mister smarty-pants. If it was love, then does it feel the same way you feel right now about Sophie? Is it as strong? And she was dumb. You're a catch, Austin. The woman who finally wins your heart will be the luckiest woman in the world. She isn't worth the pain. Why are you hurting yourself like this? I know the kind of man you can be."

Ava put her hand up to stop his interrupting arguments. "Maybe you don't love Sophie yet, but you have feelings for her. You're constantly trying to make her happy by giving her things from the farm—and things I've seen you buy claiming they're from the farm. I'm not stupid, and don't pretend I am. I'm asking you, for once in your life, to let go of that teenager pain and give a real relationship a chance. You deserve it, and I imagine she does, too. You're just the man to pull her from her own turmoil. I won't bug you again about it because, ultimately, it's your life. I just worry about you."

She walked over to him, jumped on the railing of the

stall, and leaned over lightly to kiss his cheek. "You're not happy. Going from woman to woman, as if that's fun, is starting to wear you down. I see a light shine in your eyes when you talk about Sophie. Just think about that. You stink, too. Take a shower before you bring those pallets I saw in your truck to Sophie. I know that's why you grabbed them from the meat market."

Ava hopped off the railing and walked away without waiting for a response. Austin watched her, wondering if his pain from the love he lost was really just teenage anguish.

"*THAT WAS SO MUCH FUN, AUSTIN,*" *Cara said as she slid her hand down his chest.*

"*I always have fun with you. I can't get enough of you, darling,*" *Austin replied, kissing her on the lips.*

"*I would love to do it again, but I should get ready for work. You know Mrs. Shiplay hates it when I'm late, and you tend to make me late...a lot.*" *She giggled as he tickled her.*

"*I can't help myself.*" *Austin sucked in a deep breath. "I love you, Cara.*"

She backed away, pushing him slightly. "What?"

"*I said I love you.*"

"*We're just having fun here, Austin. You're a great guy, delightful in bed, but I don't really see us going anywhere.*"

Her words skewered him to the bone.

Austin moved away from her, stood up, and grabbed his pants from the floor. "Fun, huh? That's all this was? A bunch of fun."

He tried to ignore the pain impaling his heart.

"*Austin, you're known for fun, not relationships, and...I don't see myself as the wife of a farmer. Sorry.*"

For a brief moment, he froze in place. "Wow. That was... brutally honest."

"I thought it was just sex. Why'd you have to make it more than that?"

"I don't know why. But I can promise it won't ever happen again."

Not with any woman.

He would never give his heart to another woman.

She started laughing. "Let's just forget you ever said the L word and we can keep having some great sex."

"Yeah, I don't think so." He grabbed his shirt from the floor. "Have a nice life, Cara." He walked out of her apartment, slamming the door as he went.

CARA HAD BEEN cruel and mean with the words she threw at him. He thought back to the so-called love he had felt for her.

Maybe Ava was right. Was it just teenage love?

He had enjoyed hanging out at the usual spots with her, laughing with her, drinking with her, and then ultimately falling into bed with her. At the time, he felt love. A deep, aching love.

Well, most of his body parts felt a deep ache. Maybe that ache wasn't so much love as it was lust. Cara was one of the best he ever had in bed. He always enjoyed women to the fullest extent, and he couldn't figure out what made Cara any different.

Damn. Ava was right.

Cara had been like all the other women he ever dated. Except she had been the longest he dated.

It came to him instantly and clearly.

Her words.

They hurt.

He was nothing but a farm boy, not good enough. He opened himself up to someone and they threw nasty words back. He was too scared to try again, afraid he would never measure up to what a woman wanted.

Just a simple farmer. Nothing fancy about that. He didn't make loads of money, and sometimes they struggled to make ends meet.

So, he took the easy way out. Definitely easier to skim by in life going from woman to woman than to open himself up to another tirade of horrible, damaging words. No woman was worth that sort of pain.

Just as suddenly, Sophie's face popped up. Her beautiful, shy, fierce face tingled his senses, awakening a yearning deep inside. Not just a sexual awakening either. A deep, soul-searching, connecting one. He wanted to hear her fears, her pains, why she shied away as she did. He wanted to simply pull her into his arms and hold her until it all went away.

Love wasn't just about fun. It also grabbed a hold of the hard times to soothe those pains away.

It did feel different with Sophie. He just wasn't sure he was ready to open himself up again, even to her. When he thought about her, the temptation was strong. But the pain that could possibly follow scared him. He had no doubt she could damage him more than Cara ever did.

He needed to clean out a few more stalls to get a good direction of where to proceed with Sophie. Should he try harder at cracking open her shell? Should he attempt to put himself out there for her to possibly rip his heart to shreds?

He was leaning toward yes. Yes, he should. Just thinking

about her sweet smile made him want to try. He had to think carefully before he did. It wouldn't be an easy road to tow.

Work always helped clear his mind and find a good decision. The shovel lifted to load more manure into the wheelbarrow when Ava came running toward him.

"Austin! I just got a call from the precinct. Your house was broken into and they caught the person. I have no idea if anything's missing. We should go."

Austin threw the shovel over the side, laid it against the stall, and hopped out. "What do you mean?"

"They got the person as they were coming out of the house, so they're still at the scene. Come on already. It was a woman, too. Quit dating trash," Ava said as she walked away.

He rubbed a hand over his face. How much worse could the day possibly get?

They made it to his house less than ten minutes later. He slammed on the brakes when he saw the commotion by the curb.

"What the hell, Austin? Do you need to drive like a maniac?" Ava exclaimed.

Austin pointed out the window as he hastily threw his seatbelt off. "Sophie. She's in handcuffs. Why?"

Austin rushed out of the vehicle, almost decking the officer who stood hovering over Sophie as she sat on the curb, head down and her hands cuffed behind her back. Axel sat next to her, baring his teeth, guarding her for all he was worth.

"What's going on here? Why the hell is she in handcuffs? Let her go now," Austin yelled at the officer.

Sophie jerked her head up. Austin cursed softly when he saw her tear-stained face, a few tears still running down as she sat dejected and lonely. He looked back at the officer when he made no move to remove them. "Did you hear what I said? Take the damn cuffs off her."

"Austin, I can't. She broke into your house." He cringed when Ava joined them with a glare that could peel his skin off without effort.

"She didn't break into my house. She wouldn't. Take the handcuffs off before I deck you," Austin said through clenched teeth as he glanced at Sophie, who looked surprised by his words. And scared. She looked so scared it killed him inside.

"We received a call that your neighbor across the street heard loud noises and saw someone in your house. When I arrived on the scene, I saw her at the back door and it looked like she just walked out. There's glass all over the porch and the kitchen door window is shattered to pieces. Says to me she did it."

"Officer Adams, take the handcuffs off. This is Austin's neighbor. She wouldn't hurt a fly nor break into anyone's house, least of all Austin's. She has a key. Why would she break in if she has a key? She wouldn't. Do it now before I get really angry," Ava demanded. "Did you secure the scene?"

Officer Adams shuffled his feet at her berating look. "I didn't know she was his neighbor, and Malley is waiting by the back door. We secured the scene. Nobody else was inside. I swear it, Ava. It was reasonably assumed she did it."

"Did you even ask her about anything?" Ava asked.

"Well...no," Officer Adams said.

"What the hell are you waiting for? Take them off," Austin said.

"I can't. Because the dog won't let me get near her, and I didn't want to shoot your dog, Austin. I tried putting her in the patrol vehicle and he started snarling and growling at me. I barely got the handcuffs on before he almost attacked me," Officer Adams replied.

"Give me the key," Austin demanded as he held out his hand.

Officer Adams grabbed his key and handed it to Austin, who immediately went behind Sophie, bending down and unlocking the handcuffs. Ava gave Officer Adams another irritated glare as Austin took care of Sophie. He took that as a sign to leave them alone and walked to the back of the house where Officer Malley stood securing the back door.

"I'm so sorry, Sophie. Are you okay?" Austin sat next to her on the curb after he had taken the cuffs off.

SOPHIE WIPED HER CHEEKS, trying to control the tears, but it was hard. So many scenarios had played through her mind. So many memories had flashed through her like a horrible movie reel that never ended.

Just a horrible nightmare. One she thought she would never make it out of.

She couldn't look at him. The embarrassment, the horror that he would believe she could do such a thing, made her tremor deep inside. She started to rub her wrists in a frenzy, the suffocating feeling that she still had her hands bound drowning out everything around her.

"Sophie? Please, I'm sorry. Are you okay? Why were you by my house?" Austin asked gently.

"So you do think I did it? Why take the cuffs off?" Sophie whispered.

"What? No, I don't think that. I would never think that. But someone broke in and you were on my porch. Geez, Sophie, don't you realize what could've happened? You could've been hurt by the intruder. That scares me so much, you have no idea." His words spilled out in a rough whisper.

Ava bent down in front of them. "Hi, Sophie. I'm Ava, Austin's sister-in-law. I also happen to work in the crime lab here in St. Joe. I need to go check the house, but did you see anything? I'm assuming since you were near the house that you were checking something out. Austin has a right to worry that you could've gotten hurt. Did you hear something?"

Sophie slowly turned her eyes to Ava, seeing compassion and concern. Sophie couldn't believe she worked for the police. She had never seen such emotion from anyone associated with the police. "I heard the noise, too. I wasn't sure what it was and went outside to look. I didn't notice anything until I got to the back door. I knew you weren't home, Austin, but I saw Axel in the kitchen. He wouldn't come at first when I called his name, so I had to go inside to get him. I didn't think about anyone being inside the house. I was just worried about Axel. I thought maybe he got hurt because he was sitting by the table and wouldn't move. When I got closer to him, I saw his paw was bleeding and he couldn't walk. Maybe he cut himself on the glass, I don't know. Before I went in, I thought I saw someone running in the woods behind our houses. I'm not sure."

Austin reached for Axel and lifted his paw where a few drops of blood fell down. "Hey, buddy, we'll get that taken care of. Good job, boy, taking care of Sophie."

"I thought he was at the farm," Ava said.

"He was. I take him every morning with me. I was busy in the barn. I guess the little rascal took it into his mind to come home without me. Maybe he knew Sophie would need him," Austin said, glancing at her.

She still couldn't look at him.

"Hmm. Dogs do sense things. He probably did, even though it's a long walk. Are you okay, Sophie? You never answered Austin. Did you happen to see any distinctive features of the person you saw running?" Ava asked.

Sophie wiped her cheeks again, sniffling lightly as she glanced at Ava. "I'm fine. I'm just a little shaken from having handcuffs on. It's a very unpleasant experience. I didn't see much. It was a man, I think. He looked younger, maybe in his twenties, and he had a red hoodie over his head. I couldn't see his face well because of that. That's it."

"Why didn't you try telling Officer Adams this?" Ava asked.

Sophie looked her squarely in the eye and said with a venom-laced tone, "Because the last time I tried telling an officer something, they didn't believe me. They threatened to arrest me, and I didn't really expect much from him either, since he already had handcuffs on me. I don't expect anything from any cop because they don't help people. If Austin didn't know me, I'm positive I would still be in handcuffs. I think you know I don't have a key to his house. I'm not sure why you said that."

"When I'm angry I blurt things out, but maybe you should have a key." Ava shrugged as if it didn't matter what she said earlier. "You and Austin are good friends. I was just as upset seeing you handcuffed as he was. I can tell by looking in your eyes that you have a kind soul. I can tell by looking into Austin's eyes that he cares about you. I'm sorry that you were ever in a position where you needed a cop and they let you down. I'm a cop's daughter. I've grown up around cops. I work with them. There are bad one's out there, and I won't deny that. You have to think of the true gems that shine through. They aren't all bad. Don't make one bad experience—scratch that—two bad experiences give you a bad impression."

Ava grabbed Austin's hand. "Jimmy, Austin's brother, was one of those true gems. Best damn cop I knew. He did it because he wanted to help people and put the bad guys away. He was a good man, a good cop, and I suppose he learned it all from his brothers."

"Oh, geez, Ava, please don't cry, too. I can't handle two women crying on me," Austin pleaded as the tears started to roll down her cheeks.

"It's hormones, Austin. I'm pregnant. And I miss him. Zane's cranky anytime I bring up New York, and it's hard because I miss him. I don't like that Sophie feels this way, and that's not right either. She's your friend, which makes her my friend. We all hurt together. That's the way this family operates. Moments like this, I need Jimmy." Ava let his hand go and rubbed her cheeks dry. "I need to process the scene. I'll be back."

"Maybe someone else should do it. I worry—"

"Knock it off, Austin. It's my job. I can handle a simple crime scene. I'd like to hang out sometime, Sophie. But if you don't want to, that's okay, too." Ava gave her a friendly smile and then abruptly walked away.

"We should look at Axel's paw. Clean it up. Can we do it in your house?" Austin asked tentatively.

Sophie nodded. He reached over to help her up, but she shied away from him. He sighed quietly and gently picked up Axel. "Come on, buddy. Let's look at that paw."

They walked into her house, making their way to the kitchen where Austin set him gently on the counter. Sophie stood near them, wanting to comfort Axel, yet nervous to be around Austin with no one else around. She had come to trust he wouldn't hurt her, but being near him always made her nerves jump like crazy.

Austin looked at his paw, then turned the water on, finding the right temperature. "Do you have a towel you don't mind getting dirty? I'd like to wrap his paw. It's not bleeding too badly, but just in case when he steps on it."

Sophie nodded, reaching into the drawer near the sink, and grabbed a towel, not really caring what one she chose.

AUSTIN SMILED SOFTLY at her as he gently wrapped Axel's paw after cleaning it. He picked him up and set him on the floor where Axel quickly sat down next to Sophie's feet.

"I'm glad you're okay. You shouldn't have checked that noise out or went inside my house. You could've gotten hurt. I'd go nuts if you got hurt, Sophie." Austin waited for her to look his way.

More words sat on the tip of his tongue, words that would probably make her go screaming from the kitchen in shock. Hell, the urge to pull her into his arms would probably make her go running from the kitchen. He steeled his emotions in a silent, deep breath to tamp down any urge that riddled his body. Hard didn't begin to describe the strength it took to do that.

"Axel was inside. I was worried about him. I really didn't do it. I swear it wasn't me who broke in."

He swore softly, then grabbed her hands. She jerked slightly at the touch, but he had to make her see. Make her feel what he felt.

"Listen to me, Sophie. I never once thought it was you. I still don't. I want to know everything about you, especially what happened to make you dislike and not trust cops. But I know you won't share it with me. I care about you. You're my friend, and I wish you would trust me more than you do. I feel you shaking as I hold your hands. Can't you feel mine shaking right with you? That's me worried about you."

"It's not easy trusting. I've given it so many times just for it to be broken once again," Sophie said quietly, almost in a whisper.

"I may make you mad, I may drive you nuts, but I will never break your trust. Just give me a small chance. Hang out with me a little more. You don't have to share anything you don't want to. Axel enjoys your company and misses you. If not for me, at least for him."

"You're using Axel to get me to hang out with you." She finally glanced at him, shyly smiling back when she saw his sweet grin.

"I guess I am."

"Hanging out means what exactly?"

"I don't know. Watching a movie, baseball, or something boring on TV. I know you said you don't like baseball, but I think I can convince you otherwise. I need another supporting Minnesota fan because Ava's a diehard New York fan and I need help bantering back with her. Or we can take Axel for a walk. Or you could come out to the farm. I'd love to show you around. Maybe we could go horseback riding." He suddenly hoped against all hope she agreed.

His uncertainty where to proceed with her vanished when he saw her sitting so lonely on the curb. The clarity of it all hit him so hard he almost staggered to the ground getting out of his truck. He was ready to take a chance on love, to see if he could have what his brother had.

What did Zane say that one morning to him...*companion-ship, love, a deep relationship with a magical woman*...that's what he wanted—a chance at that. He was just hoping she would give him the chance.

"Maybe I should leave Axel with you during the day. I don't like it that he walked home like he did today. He could've gotten hurt or lost."

"But he's your dog."

"I don't know about that. When I first saw him, he was on your front porch. I think that kind of makes him both of ours. He clearly loves you because he's very protective of you. I think he'd like it."

"Okay," she replied, glancing at their hands, as he had started to lightly rub his thumb on her palm.

"Okay on Axel and hanging out with me? Or just okay on Axel?"

She tilted her eyes back up to his. "On both."

Austin smiled wide as happiness flowed through his body, among other things. He should let her go, but the feel of her soft hands was making him come undone. She wasn't pulling away, and he wanted to enjoy her nearness as much as he could. He imagined he might not get it as often as he wanted, not without patience and time. "You have no idea how happy that makes me...and Axel."

A loud, booming knock echoed throughout the house.

"I'll get it. You hang out with Axel and baby him. He'll soak it up, and he deserves it. It's either Ava or another officer," Austin said, as he finally let go of her hands.

Sophie nodded. He winked at her and then walked out of the kitchen.

"YOU'RE THREATENING *to arrest me for a false report? I didn't do this to myself,*" Sophie exclaimed as she held her arm out, showing the bruise that was darkening more as each minute ticked by.

"That isn't what Mr. Dittmore said, ma'am. He said you've had some mental issues in the past and tend to hurt yourself sometimes. He's worried about you. Perhaps a psyche eval would be good for you. We can't make you, but we can help you get there if you like," the officer said in a soothing tone. To Sophie's ears, it came out more as an insolent tone.

She couldn't believe this was happening. Kevin had grabbed her, squeezing her hard, and bruised her arm. He even shoved her against the wall. Several times, in fact, but she had no marks to prove that. She waited until he left to call the police, but apparently, it hadn't mattered. He came home before they arrived, giving his side of the story, which was her harming herself. She had mental issues. They were right, in a sense. She couldn't believe she was still with Kevin or that she allowed him to treat her this way. She was weak. She had nowhere else to go, and Kevin knew that.

"That's not true. I didn't hurt myself. He—"

"Ma'am, I suggest you not further implicate yourself in that false report. I don't want to arrest you because Mr. Dittmore asked us not to," the officer interrupted her, holding his hand up in her face, making her step back from a potential slap.

She almost laughed aloud at the absurdity of an officer slapping her. A natural reaction to step back when a hand came toward her. What did that tell her? What did that tell the officer?

Apparently nothing, because he didn't believe her, didn't see the fear, the horror she lived with.

Why was she even trying to explain herself?

Kevin Dittmore, a prominent businessman, a man with money, power, and the influence to make the police believe she harmed herself. She was wasting her breath.

"I believe we have nothing more to say to each other, officer.

Good night," Sophie said, stepping farther back into the house and closing the door in his face.

She took a small breath to compose herself when bristling tingles of terror prickled her skin as she felt Kevin come up behind her. He wrapped his arms around her, pulling her against his hard frame, whispering into her ear, "That was dumb, Sophie. Don't ever be dumb again. You will never win against me. You're mine."

10

"OH, no, you don't, Axel. Get down from the table," Sophie said with a stern tone. She grinned at his attempt to snatch a piece of the meal she just set down to eat. Walking to the counter, she grabbed the bag of dog treats she bought earlier and pulled one out.

"Here. You can have a treat. Just one. If you eat some dog food, you can have another, but not until you eat your supper over there," Sophie said, pointing to his dog dish she also bought today.

Yesterday had been a day from hell in Sophie's book. She had been accused of breaking into Austin's house, handcuffed, and thoroughly embarrassed in front of the entire neighborhood. Austin believed she didn't do it, as did Ava. That made her feel slightly better, but she was still worried. Her last experience was hard to forget.

She didn't want to like Ava, her working with cops, but it was hard not to. The way she spoke so lively and lovingly about Jimmy, it was difficult not to believe he had been a good cop. Perhaps the world held good cops alongside the bad ones, but where were they when she needed help?

Austin insisted Axel spend the day with her, but looked guilty when he said he left around five in the morning to go to the farm. She wasn't much of a sleeper anyway, tossing and turning most nights from the memories she wished to forget. She insisted it was fine that he knocked on her door at that time to drop him off.

Later that evening, as she sat in bed, she thought it was strange sharing a dog as if he were a child. One parent dropping him off to the next. The more she thought about him coming in the morning, the funnier it became, soon putting her into a fit of laughter.

When Austin knocked on her door the next morning looking sleepy, yet delightfully alluring in a simple shirt and jeans, she was glad to have Axel. Just to see Austin. Funny or not, it was worth it just to see him.

She left for a short time to pick up some groceries and a few essentials Axel would need. Such as dog food, dog treats, dog bowls, some dog toys, and because she couldn't resist, a nice fluffy dog bed. She worked on her orders that were increasing daily to her wonderful surprise, while Axel lay next to her, giving comfort and peace for the day.

She chuckled as Axel chomped on his treat, even to the point of licking the crumbs off the floor when her timer went off. She pulled the pie out of the oven and set it carefully on the counter when a knock sounded on the door. She smiled, even as she nervously wiped her hands down her shirt trying to wipe the tension away.

She opened the door, holding it for support. Austin looked just as sexy as he had this morning. Even with the dirt, sweat, and hard day's work from the farm covering his body, he smelled divine. As always. Especially since she knew he hadn't showered yet. How could he smell good? She had no idea, but he did. She loved that farm smell and suddenly couldn't wait for him to offer to bring her to the farm. She wanted to see it.

"Hey, darling. How's Axel? Was he a good boy?" Austin asked with a tired grin.

"He was. We had a good day. I went shopping and I bought him a few things. When I got home, he helped me with my work."

"Good, I'm happy to hear it was a good day. So, I guess him and I will head home," he said, quietly as his eyes darted away with nervous energy.

Her eyes got wide, her hands started to shake, but before she lost her nerve, she spit out quickly, "I made dinner. If you want to join me, that is. Axel's eating, or he better be if he wants another treat."

Austin laughed, his eyes swiftly lighting up with happiness. "I would love dinner. I imagine he'll listen to you because I know I would if you were offering me a treat."

"Well, if you clear your plate as well, I made pie."

His eyes lit up with pleasure. "Grape nut pie?"

She blushed lightly. "Of course. I know that's your favorite. Come on in. It's done. I guess I timed it out perfectly to the time you roughly estimated."

"Yeah, you never know if you'll hit a snag, but we had a good day on the farm. Busy, but we got everything done we wanted to," he said as he stepped inside.

He followed her to the kitchen where Axel chomped away at his food. He looked at the table where she had laid out all the food. Meatloaf, mashed potatoes, green beans, rolls, and his favorite, grape nut pie.

"Man, do I feel lucky. This looks great, Sophie. Thanks so much for the invite," Austin said as he took a seat across from her.

"It's not much, but I hope you enjoy it."

"Not much? Are you kidding me? This is a feast. Looks like a meal Eleanor would make for us," he replied, digging in as his stomach started to gurgle in hunger. "I do miss those meals, although half the time I still eat there because I'm too lazy to cook once I get home."

"I'm sure you work hard during the day. You deserve a good meal once you're done. How did you two decide on having a farm?"

Small talk, especially with a guy, wasn't her forte. She had no idea what she was doing, but she knew in her heart she was taking a chance. It felt different this time. Austin made her feel different.

"Grew up there, actually. We inherited it from our parents. Not sure how long it's been in the family—a few generations. Jimmy's the only one to branch out and do his own thing. I thought about it for a while, but every time I thought about saying something to Zane, I just couldn't. He needed me, and I guess I needed him. I'm a farmer and I wouldn't trade it for anything," Austin replied genuinely, but with a slight hard tone at the end.

Something about his last statement struck a chord with her. His pain could be felt all the way across the table. What had happened for him to say such a simple thing about being a farmer so rough, so painful?

Not wanting to talk about her own pain, she glossed over it as if she never heard it.

"Do your parents still help?" she asked, immediately regretting the question when the sadness covered his eyes. She sucked at this small talk. She couldn't seem to get anything right.

"My dad died in my early twenties, my mom when I was just a kid, and we lost Jimmy last year. It's just Zane and I now. That's another reason I never left. When Jimmy left for

New York, I could see the pain in Zane and didn't want to add to it. Now I can't leave him because he's all I have. Well, and Ava, too. She's been a great addition to the family. I have my cousins and whatnot, but I think you know what I mean. He's all I got in my immediate family. How about you? Where's your family?"

She looked down at her plate and started to push her food around. How did she answer that? He opened up so easily, but she saw the struggle tangled in his eyes. If he could do it, she could, too.

"My mom died just after I graduated high school. My real father owned this house. He left when I was five without a backwards glance and, for whatever reason, decided to leave this house to me. I now appreciate that thoughtfulness because I needed it. I don't have any other family. I don't have anybody."

She glanced up when she felt his soft hand cover the top of hers. His touch always made tiny tingles spread throughout her body. Just a simple contact anywhere on her made her wish he would pull her into his arms. His touch made her want him, and that in turn scared her.

Why did she open her mouth? Confess a small part of herself? The tiny tingles were starting to intensify to raging flames of desire. She should really pull away from his touch.

"You have me now. I'm glad I met you. Why did you need this house?"

"Because I had to get away," she whispered.

"Get away from what, Sophie? Please tell me," he whispered back.

"I think you know. I can't say it out loud. It's too terrifying. It's too much. My whole life has been too much, and I finally had to escape or die," she said as the tears started to lightly fall.

Austin immediately stood up, grasping her hand more firmly, and pulled her gently into his arms. She sank into his frame as the tears fell in the quiet confines of the house. No sound echoed back, except her soft cries of pain and heartache. He held her tenderly, rubbing her back in a soothing manner, and wished with all his heart that he could take the pain away.

"I can only imagine what you went through, but I can't know for sure until you tell me. I won't pry or beg or demand, but wait for when you feel the moment is right. For as long as you let me, I'll be here for you. Even after you tell me to hit the road, I'll be there for you. You're special, you're beautiful, and you deserve the world, Sophie. Don't let anyone tell you different," he whispered softly into her ear.

He had wanted so much to come in and enjoy the evening with her, but figured he had to move slowly. That's all he thought about over the course of the day, wanting to spend time with her, how to go about doing that, yet scared to push her. He couldn't have been more surprised when she asked him to come in. Now, here he was. Making her cry. Bringing up painful memories.

She squeezed him tighter, but no words entered the quiet room. He took her embrace as a small answer to his turmoil. She had needed to release some of her pain. Let it out for once.

Talk about new territory for him. He never got this deep or emotional with women before, suddenly clueless where to proceed. Did he keep giving encouraging words, or hold her until she let go? Did he pull away first?

He ached to swing her up into his arms, carry her slowly to her bedroom, and show her exactly how he felt. Or simply lay with her in his arms as she cried the pain out of her body. That would be okay, too. He just wanted her pain to disappear. He wanted to see her bright smile and loving laugh.

His prayers were answered when he heard her chuckle into his chest. He looked down to see Axel with his front paws clinging to her leg, and if Austin wasn't mistaken, a goofy grin on his furry face.

Sophie pulled away, ruffling Axel's head with a tender hand. "You either wanted to join the hug, or you ate your food and want that treat now. Which one is it?"

"I vote for the hug. It was a nice hug." Austin received another smile in return from her. "The treat is a high possibility, too. I know I want mine."

Damn smart dog. He knew a good woman when he saw one. If Sophie promised a treat, Axel knew he would get one. Austin wished his treat was more than just pie, but he suppressed the urge quickly. He'd frighten her if he made a move in that way. A little light flirting couldn't hurt. She hadn't completely stepped away from him yet. That had to be a good sign. Or, at least, his heart hoped so. She still hadn't said anything to him. Just an uncertain look directed his way that he couldn't exactly decipher. No fear, though. He didn't see any of that.

"Well, then I suggest you eat your food like Axel did. You know the rules," she finally replied. She glanced at Axel's bowl that sat clean and empty. He had licked away every last remnant of food from the bowl. She wiped her face of the tears and walked over to the counter. Grabbing two treats this time, Axel wasted no time gobbling them up.

"You want that pie?" Sophie asked, as she made her way back to the table.

"Yes, darling. Don't have to ask me twice." Austin sat back down in his seat.

"About that silly meltdown there, I—"

Austin put his hand up. "Sophie, you can melt down on me anytime. It wasn't silly. Your feelings and emotions aren't silly. I'm here for you. We're friends, right?"

She took a swallow of her milk. "Yes, we're friends."

"Good. In my experience, friends talk to each other about their troubles now and again. It was no big deal and I didn't mind."

"Do you use the word darling to your friends as well, or just your women?" she blurted.

He paused with his fork halfway to his mouth, the delicious meatloaf hanging in the air. "You don't like it when I call you darling?"

"No. Not if that's what you call the women you date. I don't want to be lumped in that category." She tossed her fork around her plate again.

"I'll try not to do that. I do call most women that. Not just women I date, but all of them. It's just a natural thing for me to do, I guess. I'm sorry if it bothered you," he replied, finishing the trek of food to his mouth.

He chewed, trying to enjoy the flavors washing over his taste buds, but the energy dissipated. He'd finally decided to pursue a full-fledged relationship with someone and she didn't want anything to do with him. She didn't want to be one of his women, but she failed to realize he would never clump her into that category.

She was so much more. A true treasure hidden away, waiting patiently for him to find. It figured she wouldn't want him that way. He shouldn't be too surprised. He hadn't given her a good impression of himself.

"Thank you." Her eyes dropped back down to her plate. "I hope you like the food."

"I love it." He shoveled another fork full into his mouth before he said something he would regret.

Would she ever see him as more than a friend? Did he ruin his chances when he explained what he wanted in life?

He changed his mind. He wanted a relationship.

How did he show her that his heart had changed?

11

"How's Sophie?" Ava asked Austin. She joined him by the fence, grabbing a hold of the top railing to watch the horses that were enjoying themselves in the corral.

He glanced at her, and then trained his eyes back on the horses. "She's fine. Why do you ask?"

"Just curious. It's been a week since the break-in, and I wanted to make sure she was okay. You haven't been staying for supper either. Are you okay?"

"I'm fine, Ava. I haven't stayed for supper because Sophie has been inviting me over when I pick up Axel. I enjoy the evenings with her," he muttered under his breath as he stepped away from the fence. He swung a glance back at Ava. "She sees me as a friend. How do I get her to see me as more than that without breaking her fragile state? Or so she doesn't think she's just another woman on my list of women, because she's not. I'm ready to try this whole relationship thing."

Ava smiled tenderly. "I'm glad you finally came to your senses. I like her. She's a good choice. You'll know what to do. Just take it a day at a time. She's different from every other woman you've dated, especially because she has a disturbing past. You'll have to take it slow, and she'll eventually see how you feel. Or just tell her."

"I don't think she would believe me. I never noticed I called women darling, but she doesn't like that, and I find myself almost saying it a lot. She's different, and this is new for me and I don't know how to act."

"You're worrying too much about it, Austin. Just be yourself and she'll fall in love with the man that I know you are. Of course, she doesn't want to be called darling, if you call every other woman on earth that. When are you going to bring her to the farm? I think it would be nice," Ava said, rubbing a hand over her belly.

"Why would she wanna come here? It's a farm. I'm a farmer. Why would she want that?" His brows burrowed in torment.

Ava slapped him on the shoulder. "Knock it off. I'm married to a damn farmer and I love it. What's wrong with you? I've never seen you bring yourself down."

He grimaced in mock pain. "That hurt, Ava." He glanced at the ground, shuffling his foot around the grass as embarrassment flooded his cheeks. "I don't know what's wrong with me. I just don't want to screw it up. I love the farm, and I would hate to see disgust or something like disapproval in her eyes if she came here."

"If she did, she's not worth your time. You deserve better. Love's scary, but you can do this. If you're acting like this, thinking such dumb thoughts because of what another woman said to you, well, knock it off. They aren't worth the trouble or your thoughts because you are a good man. Be proud of who you are. I'm proud of you and I'm proud of Zane. Do you think I would've moved all the way from New

York if I wasn't?" she said, rubbing her hand on her belly again.

Austin smiled. "I suppose not. I'm glad you did because Zane's the happiest I've seen him in a long time. You're right. I am proud of who I am."

"Good. Now that we have that settled, invite her over tomorrow. It's Saturday. Come early so we can spend the day together."

"I'll try, but I can't guarantee she'll agree. Just because you want her to come doesn't mean she will. Any news on my break-in?"

"No, not yet. I didn't find any useful fingerprints. I went down the list of the prints I did pull, including some of your women, but everyone had alibis for the time of the break-in. I'll figure it out, but sometimes, the sad reality is we can't figure it out."

"Yeah, well, I'm glad they only got some cash that I had upstairs in my room and nothing else. Maybe if they had taken some electronics or something you could have traced it that way."

"Might've been easier. I'm glad Sophie's okay, but it would've been better if she had gotten a good look at the guy."

Austin's expression hardened. "No, Ava, it wouldn't have been better. I'd be worried they could hurt her if they knew they were seen and could be identified. I don't want her involved in any way. Don't ever say that again."

"I'm sorry. Go home already. Zane and I can handle the evening chores."

"Well, that's not fair, especially if I don't come over until late in the morning tomorrow."

"No, it's not, so take advantage when I offer."

Austin pulled her into a brotherly hug, kissing her on

the head. "You're the best sister ever. I'm leaving before my brother disagrees with you. Gives me more time to convince Sophie to come over. I have no idea what I'm doing with her. I hope I'm not screwing up."

"You're not. I have every faith in you that it'll all work out in the end," Ava offered with a gentle smile.

SOPHIE STOOD in the middle of the kitchen wracking her brain on what to make tonight for supper. It became a simple routine where Austin would pick up Axel, automatically staying for supper. She enjoyed the routine, but now she was running out of impressive meals to make him.

Why did she torture herself with impressing him?

She couldn't compete with the other beautiful, well-endowed women who graced through his door frequently. They walked with confidence, dressed like seduction, and spoke with a voice that curled your toes into oblivion. She displayed none of those sexy characteristics and wouldn't even know where to begin. Why should she? He would never see her like that anyway. She was nothing but a ball of pain and a walking disaster. She had baggage that wasn't worth sifting through.

He called every woman darling. She had liked the way it rolled off his tongue, wrapping her into a sweet embrace, but when she thought of him using it with other women, she didn't like it so much. She knew she hadn't been special to be the only one called that. She wanted to be considered special when it came to him.

The sensation of feeling sorry for herself almost consumed her when she heard a noise in the backyard.

Walking over to the back door, barely moving the

curtain to peek out, shock vibrated as she looked upon the familiar red hoodie from the day of Austin's break-in.

She inhaled a deep breath, frozen in her spot. What should she do?

He stood rigid by her shed, darting furtive glances every second or two, trying to break in with a tool of some sort. It looked like a tire iron, but Sophie wasn't positive as she tried not to open the curtain any farther.

She hated her privacy being disturbed. The small chance someone could peek in on her when she was unaware sent tingling shivers of horror through every vein. Every single window in her house was blanketed in a curtain of some variety. She enjoyed the sun shining, sending whispering pockets of brightness, but she never enjoyed it as she should. Because she never opened the curtains, the fear so ingrained inside.

She pulled the curtain open a titch farther, trying to make out more. The man slumped his shoulders in defeat and sagged to the ground. She wanted to shout out, "Of course a tire iron won't work! You should've brought a bolt cutter to get the lock off!" She certainly didn't do that but watched in fascination as the man's shoulders started to shake violently.

He was crying. Why in the world would the burglar cry?

There wasn't anything in her shed worth stealing. It held your normal mundane supplies, like a shovel, rake, gardening tools, gloves, and of course, her new lawn mower from Austin. But it wasn't that new as it sat covered in dirt, scrapes, and dents mingled all over the machine. She figured of all the supplies littered in her shed worth any money, it would be the lawn mower.

A strange feeling zapped into her bones, stripping her bare as she watched the young man continue to shake from the tears wracking his body. She couldn't explain the sudden emotion, or the foolishness, as she unlocked the kitchen door and stepped outside.

The young man heard the noise, jerking his head toward her. He jumped up with quick precision, but before he ran, Sophie yelled with desperation, "Please. Don't run. I didn't call the cops nor have any intention of calling them. Trust me. I have no desire to be handcuffed again for breaking into a house I didn't break into."

The man shielded his face with the hoodie, hanging his head down, poised in a position to run. Sophie knew how insane it was as she carefully walked toward him. She had no weapon and the man did. He carelessly held the tire iron in his hand as she stepped within swinging range.

"Why are you stealing? Austin, the man's house you broke into, is a nice man. He didn't deserve that. Why are you trying to steal from me? I have nothing in there worth much," Sophie asked softly as she scrunched her toes in anticipation of running away. She reminded herself daily she wasn't dumb like she had been told numerous times, but right this instant, she was dumb. Why was she talking to this man?

She wrung her hands nervously together. "Why were you crying?"

The man whipped his head up in surprise, a pair of bright-blue eyes staring at her in humiliation. Sophie dropped her jaw in astonishment. "You're a woman. I thought you were a man."

"Just forget you saw me. I'm sorry about your neighbor," she whispered, turning around abruptly to leave.

Sophie grabbed her arm gently, surprised by her own bravery. "Don't go. Please, talk to me."

The woman turned back toward Sophie, glancing at the

hand resting on her. "Let me go before I hit you with this tire iron," the woman said in a low voice as she raised the tire iron, the intent clear in her eyes.

Sophie swiftly let go, taking a step back. "I don't wish to be hit. I've been hit enough times in my life, thank you." Why that came out, Sophie couldn't explain. She always held herself in check, even with Austin. She found herself slipping in his presence, but she always managed to pull back before the words fully left her mouth. She saw something in the woman's eyes. A kindred spirit, an understanding, a pain as fresh as Sophie's. Perhaps that's why the words fell from her lips.

The woman's eyes bulged at the omission, and then quickly pulled the emotion out of her face. "I don't want to hurt you. Why didn't you just call the cops?"

Sophie gave a strangled laugh. "Last time they came, they handcuffed me for your crime. The time before that, they threatened to lock me up when my boyfriend hit me, claiming I was lying and hit myself. I'm not exactly a fan of the cops. I don't generally trust people. It's taken me a while to trust Austin, but I do. I don't appreciate you stealing from him. I won't call the police on you because I don't like them. But you shouldn't steal. Why were you crying?"

"Why do you care?"

"I have no idea, to be honest with you. I guess I see a wounded soul like myself. Nobody was ever there for me. Is there anyone there for you?"

"There's never been someone there for me. I don't trust easily either. Why should I trust you?"

Sophie shrugged. "I think you must be a little otherwise or you would've run by now. Who says I didn't call the cops?"

The woman burrowed her eyebrows in contemplation as

her piercing blue eyes dug deep into Sophie. "Two wounded souls, huh? Is that what we are?"

"Yeah, I guess. I've never stolen before. What brings you to a point where you need to?"

The woman glanced away, the shame evident in her posture. "When you have nowhere to go, no one to turn to, no food to eat, no place to sleep, you do what you have to. I don't like stealing, but I—never mind. I had a job, but I refuse to do that anymore. I'd rather steal."

"Well, if that's the problem, we can fix that. I have a spare room and I have food, but you'd have to find a job," Sophie said before she could stop the words.

She shouldn't trust this woman, and yet, she did. She left with no help, with no hope, and with no guarantee everything would work out well. Maybe all this woman needed was a little something she never had.

The woman turned her ocean-blue eyes back to her. "Why? Why would you help me after I stole from your neighbor? Or just tried stealing from you? What's in it for you?"

Sophie sighed, wondering the same exact thing. "Because no one was there to help me and I wished every day a savior would swoop in and help me. But no one ever did, and I had to save myself. I'm not saying I can save you, but I'm offering a gesture of help. Sometimes, one small gesture of help will make all the difference. Take it or leave it. But please, don't steal from Austin or myself because next time I will call the police."

Suddenly, Sophie felt drained. The idiocy of it all sinking in, making her realize how truly stupid she was being. Even as that horrible feeling washed over her, she waited for the woman to respond. When she didn't but kept staring at Sophie as if she had horns on the top of her head, Sophie turned around and walked back to the house.

She opened the kitchen door, locked it quickly, and stood in the middle of the room. She wouldn't call the police, but if that woman tried stealing again, she wouldn't hesitate.

Would Austin understand why she didn't call the police? Or would he be mad at her?

Sophie was in no mood to cook anymore. Perhaps Austin wouldn't mind ordering pizza.

A tentative knock sounded on her back door. Sophie pulled the curtain back a little and saw the woman standing with apprehension on her steps. Releasing a small breath to blow away the absurdity of her actions, she opened the door.

Sophie glanced at the woman's hand. The tire iron was gone.

"I hid it." The woman shifted uneasily on her feet. "I'm Deja. I've never met someone who would so easily overlook my indiscretions and give me a chance. I've been alone, lost, and scared for so long that I'm even frightened right now to trust you. But I do. I guess we are two wounded souls. I would like to accept your offer of help and maybe become a friend."

Sophie smiled lightly. "I'm Sophie. I can't say I'm not upset by what you did because I am. If you stay here, I have to tell Austin and you have to pay him back. It's only right. I would very much like to be friends."

Sophie stepped back and gestured her inside. It was the right thing to do to make her pay Austin back. If she couldn't accept the terms, it was her choice to leave right now. To Sophie's satisfaction, Deja stepped inside, looking around. Axel immediately jumped on her, begging for a loving head rub.

Deja chuckled, obliging Axel as Sophie closed the door.

"That's Axel. He's Austin's dog. He's a real sweetheart," Sophie said a bit wistfully.

"Which one? The dog or Austin?" Deja asked with a wry smirk.

Sophie cleared her throat and walked to the fridge. "Well, if you must know, both of them. Would you like something to drink? I have iced tea."

Deja glanced around, took a seat at the table, and nodded.

Sophie grabbed the jug of tea, snatched two glasses from the cupboard, filled them up quickly, and walked over to Deja. "Do you have any belongings?"

"I have what I'm wearing. I had a ton of clothes at one time, makeup, little treasures that meant something to me. Now all I have is my tire iron and my wits."

"Okay, well, we look to be the same size. You can borrow some of my clothes for now. No more stealing, though. You have to find a real job." Sophie took a sip of tea.

"You're not going to pry into my life? Ask what happened to me?" Deja asked, confused.

"No. Just as I expect the same courtesy. We may be two wounded souls living in this house, but it doesn't mean I wish to share it with you. I don't like talking about it. I don't know why I said anything. Austin says it would be good for me, but it's hard."

Deja raised an eyebrow when she said Austin's name again. "You must really like this Austin, especially since you have his dog. Is he gone on a trip or something?"

Sophie blushed. Was she that obvious? Did that mean it was obvious to him? Nothing but trouble would come if he learned she liked him. "He's my neighbor, my friend. Axel left his farm the day of the burglary and came home here. He hurt his paw on the glass. Austin was worried he'd run home again, thinking he was coming here to me, and asked if I would take him during the day while he worked. I don't mind. I like Axel. He's good company."

"He's a cute dog. I'm sorry for breaking into his house. I needed money for food. I didn't see Axel in the house. I'm sorry he got hurt."

"He's okay now. But thank you for the apology. I was thinking of ordering a pizza when Austin got here later, but if you're hungry now, I can whip something up." Sophie stood up from the table.

"I can wait. A shower would be nice. I imagine I smell. Not something I'm proud of."

"Of course, I can show you the bathroom upstairs."

Deja smiled warmly as she got up and followed Sophie out of the kitchen to the stairs. "I guess you want me to apologize to Austin when he gets here tonight?"

Sophie stopped, turning around on the bottom step. "He'll understand. He's a good man. And if he doesn't, I've lost all hope in men forever."

Sophie continued up the stairs, wondering where that answer came from. Probably deep down in the pit of her heart, she was nervous Austin would finally show his true colors, like every man always did. Or maybe she was just dumb for trusting someone who broke into his house, stole from him, and tried stealing from her. He probably wouldn't understand, the more she thought about it.

She held a small amount of hope he would see Deja for what she was: a woman in need of a friend, just as she had been in need of one. He happily became Sophie's friend. Why not Deja, too?

12

Austin pinched the bridge of his nose, releasing a heavy sigh. "Sophie, please explain to me one more time why you have a woman in your house that broke into my home, stole from me, and tried stealing from you? Why am I not calling Ava to have her arrested? She could've hurt you today."

Sophie wrapped her arms around her stomach as the brisk wind whipped around them on her porch. She had stepped outside the moment he knocked and explained the situation. He wanted to take comfort that she didn't hesitate once to lay a gentle hand on him when he wanted to burst into the house to confront the woman. But he couldn't because he still wanted to bust inside the house.

"She didn't hurt me because she's not like that. She'll pay you back for the broken window and the two hundred dollars she took. She will, or she needs to leave. That was part of the deal."

Austin whipped his hand toward the door. "You can't let her stay here. You don't know her. Maybe this is what she does and she's going to rob you while you sleep or...or worse! Kill you in your sleep."

"She won't hurt me. She—"

"Sophie, you don't know that. You don't know her. How can you possibly trust her when you just met her? You barely trust me and you've known me longer than an hour." The pain was laced in his tone.

"I trust you. If I didn't, I would've never told you about her. I was hoping you'd understand. What do you see when you look at me?" she asked with a tremor.

"What do you mean?" he asked, confused, yet shocked to hear the words *I trust you.*

"What do you see when you look at me? What impression do you get? I want an honest answer."

"Why? What does that matter?"

"It matters," she said defiantly, pulling her arms tighter around her.

Austin raked a hand through his hair, frustrated his early night off was going horribly from the onset. "I see a strong, courageous woman who has had to fight through life struggling. I don't know with what, obviously, because you won't share it with me. But I see the fight in you. I see the strength. You shy away from me, your space is important. I imagine it's because you—" He muttered under his breath, trying to find the right words. There weren't any.

"You were abused. Abused by the hands of a man, which is why you don't trust any and why you don't like them. It's why you back away when I get near and jump at the slightest noise or tremble at certain words. You said you had to escape or die, and I took that literally. I'm telling you right now, Sophie, if I knew who put one hurtful hand on you, I'd make him see the error in his ways. I can't stand to think of anyone hurting you. I won't let anyone hurt you, especially that woman inside."

"Is it that obvious?" she whispered.

Austin took a step toward her as she instinctively took a step back. He gave a small laugh in defeat. "Yeah, it's obvious. I still can't step toward you without you stepping back. Those other times you let me touch you must've been a fluke. You just said you trusted me. Do you honestly trust me?"

Sophie glanced at her feet, then glanced back at him. He couldn't keep the hurt out of his eyes. Maybe that's why she took a few steps forward, barely an inch between them when she finally stopped. "Yes, I trust you. I don't give it lightly either. When I saw her today, I can't describe to you what I felt because I can't explain it to myself. But when I look in her eyes, I see me. You knew I needed a friend and have willingly taken the time to be my friend. I know I haven't made it easy. She needs one now. I know how it feels to be alone and scared. She feels bad for what she did. Please, give her a chance, Austin. I told myself not to trust you. That all men are the same. You're not like any other man I've ever met. You're different, and despite my frequent hesitations, I trust you. Don't make me see how dumb I've been for trusting you, because that's how I will feel."

Austin had to clench his teeth from grabbing her mouth to his. Just a breath away. The temptation to wrap her up in a desired frenzy swirled around him like the night wind. He ignored all that as he muttered, "Fine. I won't have her arrested, and I'll let her pay me back. She took two hundred dollars and it cost two hundred to fix the window. Just how is she going to pay me back?"

Sophie shivered. Whether it was from their close proximity or from the wind, Austin couldn't be sure.

"She's going to find a job. I can help her get back on her feet. I have no clue how. I know this is stupid, but I have to try. I...I am dumb."

Austin put a warm hand on her cheek. "You're not dumb. You're a kind-hearted woman who wants to help another lost soul. I get it. I'll give her a chance, but we have to protect ourselves here before we fully trust her. I don't want her in this house with you."

"She has nowhere to go. That's the whole point here, Austin. I'm trying to help her."

"Stay with me."

"I can't stay with you."

She tried to take a step back, but he moved his hand from her cheek to her waist, stopping her movement with one gentle touch. No protest hit her lips.

"I may have dug myself a hole when I first met you, Sophie, but I'm going to attempt to dig myself out right now. I don't do relationships. I enjoy women and they enjoy me. We have an agreement upfront what kind of guy I am. I do this because I was hurt one time and I never wanted to feel that way again."

"I will not be one of your women, Austin," Sophie said, offended.

"I'm not doing a very good job of digging myself out right now. The damn dirt is suffocating me." He groaned and pulled her firmly against his body, cradling her perfectly to fit his frame in every delicious corner.

"I don't want you to be one of my women. I would never put you in that category. Never. You are special, so special. I can't even describe it correctly. I never touch a woman who has marriage written all over her, and you shine brightly with that. The problem I have now is, I want to try the whole relationship thing, and I want to try it with you. I told myself to take it slow with you because I know you have trouble trusting. I don't know what the hell I'm doing because I don't do relationships. This is totally new territory for me. I have no clue how to act with you or what to say. I asked you to give me a chance to be your friend, and what I really wanted to ask was for a chance to be your man. What are my chances here?"

"But I'm not—"

Austin put a finger to her lips, rubbing it softly back and forth, loving the way a sharp, quivering sensation jolted throughout his body. He felt himself getting harder each second he held her. "If you're about to say something I'm not gonna like, stop right now. I won't have you belittling yourself, damn it. You're beautiful. You make me come undone with the littlest thing. Just a sweet, tentative smile makes me happy. I love your smile. Do I enjoy sex? Hell, yes. Do I want that with you? Of course. Would I be happy just holding you like this all night? Definitely. What I feel for you goes beyond the physical stuff. That's why I want to try a relationship with you because you make me feel things I've never felt before. I'd be dumb not to see if we could work. I only hope you see that, too."

"You keep swearing, you know. You shouldn't swear."

"Fanuzeling just doesn't have the same ring to it as the other words, but for you I'll try harder to remember next time," he said with a sly grin. "You're ignoring everything I just said. I'm pouring my heart out here, Sophie, and this is why I hate doing this sort of thing. You're probably—"

Sophie cut him off by pressing her lips hesitantly to his. Austin needed no further response as he kissed her back, edging his tongue to make her open farther. As soon as she did, he dove in fiercely, tangling with her in sweet delight. She moaned as she wrapped her arms around him, clinging to him with desperation. He grabbed her tighter, trying to seep in as much pleasure from her as he could. He loved feeling her in his arms.

One of a kind. No woman would ever match his beautiful Sophie.

She was his. He wasn't letting her go without a fight. She was giving in to him now, but he had his doubts, knowing she would pull away again with fright. Patience was his new middle name.

His hand slid to her bottom, pressing her gently into him, even as he did, knowing he needed to slow down. But he had difficulty pulling away as she felt more delectable in his arms than he could've ever imagined. When he felt himself wanting to reach higher for her breast, he finally pulled away. "Sophie, we need to take it inside. But later. We do have other pressing issues at hand. I want you so badly, you have no idea."

Her heavy breaths took a while to slow down as she adjusted her senses back to the problem they were discussing. "Right. You're right. I can't stay with you."

"Damn it, Sophie. I won't—"

"You're swearing," she said with a smile. God, he loved her smile.

"Well, when you talk such nonsense, my memory of not swearing flies out the door. I said I would give this woman a chance, but I refuse to let you stay alone in this house with someone you just met an hour ago. She could hurt you."

"You're not my keeper, Austin. I will not allow a man to run my life any longer, including you."

He inhaled a patient breath, knowing this was where he needed to tread lightly with her. "I'm not trying to run it or tell you what to do."

"That's exactly what you're doing. You just said you *refuse* to let me stay alone in this house. It's my house. You have no say."

"Okay, wrong choice of words. Will you pretty please stay with me so I know this woman will not hurt you?"

"No."

He ran another frustrated hand through his hair. "Can I please stay with you in your house so I know you'll be safe with an unknown woman who could possibly hurt you? We don't know anything about her."

Sophie glanced down at his chest. Could she see the way his heart beat madly at the fear he held for her? Could she feel his worry as he held her in his arms?

"I can't sleep with you."

He lifted her head gently, her soft cheek falling into his hand. "I don't expect anything to happen. I enjoy having you in my arms, but I would never force you. I can sleep on the floor if it makes you feel better. Until we get to know her better, we need to be safe about this. Please, Sophie. Pretty please."

She giggled at his goofy grin when he said the last part. "Why do you make me laugh?"

"Because I'm adorable, irresistible, and oh so charming. And because I love your smile and your sweet, sweet laugh."

"I'm scared, Austin. I do trust you, but I'm also apprehensive. Everything you say is valid and I should be smart about letting her in my home. I honestly don't fear her."

"But you fear me?" he asked, the pain lacing his voice again.

"No, I don't." She bit her lip, silent for a moment. "Okay. Until we get to know her better, you can stay with me. I feel better being in my own home. I can ply the floor with blankets so it's not uncomfortable."

Austin sighed inside. She took his offer for the floor to heart. Yet, he instantly felt better knowing he would be there if this woman tried anything. "Then it's settled. I'll sleep on the floor in your bedroom just to make sure she tries nothing. And about us? Just so we are clear, because I found with Zane and Ava, well, they were never very clear about their feelings in the beginning. Is there an us? Will you give me a chance at a real relationship? You can set the pace."

"Yes. I would like that very much," Sophie said with a shy smile, blushing slightly as he grabbed another quick kiss.

"Good. I thought this night was going to end horribly. It's starting to look up now. Let's go meet this woman." Apprehension mingled in his tone.

She nodded, stepped out of his embrace, and took a deep breath as she opened the front door. He decided he needed a deep breath as well.

He wanted to make Sophie happy as much as possible, but trusting this woman—not really something he wanted to do. Twenty minutes later, he still didn't want to trust her.

"I really am sorry. I've never done anything like that before. I'm not proud of it either," Deja said, avoiding eye contact like the plague as she sat at the kitchen table across from Austin and Sophie. The pizza had arrived, but it sat in the middle, getting cooler by the minute as they tried clearing the air.

"Sophie seems to have a very kind, trusting heart, but I can't say mine is that great. If you hurt her in any way, I will not hesitate to report you. My sister-in-law, Ava, works for the police department, and she's quite a shark when it comes to her work. She'll take care of you with a snap of her fingers. That all being said, I'll give you the chance Sophie asked of me. I expect to be paid four hundred dollars. How do you imagine you're going to do that?" Austin asked, trying to keep his anger in check.

Sophie trembled next to him, and he hated that it was

because of him. But he couldn't help it. He wasn't about to trust this woman because of a few heartfelt words and apologies.

"I'm not sure. I guess I'll look at the ads tomorrow for any jobs around town," Deja said quietly.

"I'll help you. I told you Austin would understand. Everything will be okay." Sophie glanced at Austin when he grabbed her hand, squeezing it in reassurance.

"What kind of jobs have you had? Maybe I can help, too," Austin said begrudgingly.

For the first time, Deja whipped her head to him, her bright-blue eyes searing into him. "Jobs I refuse to do anymore. I'll find something and pay you back. I can tell you don't like me, not like Sophie does. I'm still a little leery myself here. I've never met anyone so nice. I'm taking her for her word, just as I hope you take my word for what it is. I'll pay you back."

Austin stared for a moment, letting her eyes bore into him. He finally saw what Sophie did. "Okay. I believe you."

Sophie's hand trembled within his. Why was she still concerned? He raised her hand to his mouth and lightly kissed it, hoping to take the pain away. "Let's eat, huh? I'm starving, and I imagine so are you two."

SOPHIE FELT the change in him, the acceptance mingle in with the distrust. It was Deja's eyes that did it. She knew that.

She glanced back at Deja, appreciating her beauty for the first time. Long blonde hair that ran down to the middle of her back. An oval face with fine, dainty lips, and the bluest, deepest eyes imaginable.

A gorgeous woman sat across from her. A woman like so many who had crossed the threshold of Austin's door. Deja was exactly his normal type. Nothing like plain Sophie.

Was his change in demeanor attraction? What would she do when he left her for Deja? Would he do that to her?

Sophie glanced at him, treasuring his comforting touch, the tingling pleasure his soft kisses did to her. The more he touched her, sat near her, held her in his arms, she became that much more comfortable with him. She wanted this man so much. Even as she wanted him, the thought of letting him in her bed, in her heart, scared her.

She grabbed a piece of pizza to move the conversation away from Deja. The less he paid attention to her, the better. He crinkled his mouth into a smile and took a bite of his pizza. They ate in silence, everyone leery of where to take the conversation.

Sophie had grabbed a second slice when she decided the silence needed to end. "I can help you look through ads tomorrow, Deja. Austin goes to the farm quite early, so I tend to get up just as early to take Axel. Whenever you want to get started is good with me."

Deja had gobbled down three slices already. She wiped her mouth from the frenzied pace. "Okay. That's really nice of you. I suppose I'll look for waitressing or something simple like that."

"Oh, actually, did you have plans tonight, Austin?" Sophie cleared her throat, looking down at her plate. She didn't want to see Austin's face when he broke the news of his plans. "Normally, you go out on Fridays and sleep in on Saturdays. Not that I watch what you do or anything. I mean, that one Saturday I knocked on your door for the lawn mower and that woman was—"

"Sophie, stop." Austin pulled her hand closer to his

chest that had been wobbling horribly. "Yes, I have plans tonight. They're hanging out with you. Yes, I plan to sleep in tomorrow. With you. The only woman for me is you. Remember what we talked about outside? I meant every word. I only want you. I've been wanting you to come to the farm, and Ava even asked if you would come. I was hoping you'd want to come tomorrow. I can help look at the ads with you both. And if Deja wants, she can also come with to the farm as well. Do you want to see it?"

Sophie's hand rested on his chest, the rapid beating of his heart plain and clear to the touch. Nervous. It surprised her to think he was nervous of her. She raised her eyes to his and gave a small smile. "I would love to see the farm."

Deja sat quietly through it all, until Austin glanced at her. "Does that sound like a plan, Deja?"

"Oh, I don't think you want me at this farm you're talking about, especially since I heard you mention the name Ava. Isn't she your sister-in-law who works for the police?"

"Yes, she is, but she won't do anything unless I ask her to. She'll understand...for the most part. You're welcome to come with."

"Because you want to be around me, or you don't trust me in Sophie's house alone?" Deja asked.

Austin chuckled. "I suppose the latter. What can I say? I don't know you and you did break into my house. I can't learn to trust you if I don't get to know you either, can I? So the former applies as well."

"Nonetheless, I'll pass. Sophie's kind enough to offer help, and I'm gonna use it. I'll be finding a job tomorrow if it takes all day." Deja grabbed another slice of pizza.

"That's fine," Sophie said before Austin could say

anything else. She wanted Austin to trust her, but she also didn't want him to *want* to spend time with her.

Austin squeezed her hand again, perhaps knowing instinctively that she needed some sort of reassurance from him, and stood up from the table. "Well, I'm full. I'm going to go grab some things from my house and I'll be right back. I'll let Ava know that we'll be there tomorrow. She really is looking forward to hanging out with you, Sophie."

"I hope I don't disappoint," Sophie replied with a stiff laugh.

Austin set his plate down on the counter, turning to her with annoyed anger. "Sophie, please don't put yourself down like that. Don't be nervous about anything. No one blames you for the house, and no one will pry into your background. Just be your beautiful self. Just please, don't put yourself down. I hate it."

Sophie nodded, hating the self-doubt that always entered. A lifetime of put-downs, hatred, jealousy, and constant fear made it difficult to change how she reacted.

Austin nodded back, then left the kitchen.

"He cares for you. In a positive way. That's rare to find, Sophie," Deja said, filling the silence within the room. "Does he normally stay with you, or does he just not trust me with you alone?"

"I'm slowly coming to see that, but a lifetime of otherwise unsavory incidents makes it difficult to transform overnight. The reality is, I don't know you that well, and yes, he doesn't trust you. He wants to stay here until we get to know you better. I hope I'm not hurting your feelings or seeming insensitive." Sophie stared at her last piece of uneaten pizza.

"I don't believe you have a mean bone in your body, Sophie. You would be dumb to trust someone like me, and you don't strike me as the dumb type. I swear I mean no harm, but those are just words. I'll prove to you what kind of person I am. I won't disappoint either of you. I'll give you your space, and I'm really looking forward to a real bed now anyway." Deja stood up from the table. "Is that okay?"

"That's perfectly fine. I hope you sleep well."

"You, too."

Sophie sighed as Deja walked out. Would she sleep well? Her sleeping patterns ranged from a nice restful sleep to nightmares plaguing her every waking minute. Would she feel comfortable with him in the room? Or would the mere presence of a man twist her tighter than a coiled snake feasting on its prey?

TRUE TO HER WORD, Sophie had plied the floor with blankets, creating a makeshift bed for Austin. He graciously accepted her homemade bed, even though deep inside he craved to dive into her bed with her warm body pressed against his. He was a man true to his word, though. He wouldn't push her or press her. Letting her set the pace was the utmost importance. He might die of starvation and thirst of the lust running rampantly through his veins, but patience was his new virtue. He wouldn't do anything that could ruin his chances.

She shyly said good night, tensing at first when he locked the bedroom door. He gingerly smiled. "I don't trust her yet, Sophie. At least she'd have to break a barrier before getting in. I swear I'll stay on the floor." She must have believed him because she simply nodded and rolled away to her side.

He sensed Sophie's movements all night, her tossing and

turning, creating an agitation inside him. He remembered his brother speaking about Ava and her nightmares, how he would comfort her, bring her back to a peaceful sleep.

Not that Sophie was having a nightmare, but he could feel her tension, her fear, her restlessness. He ached to climb onto the bed and calm her down with one sweet touch. Clamping down his urge kept him awake most of the night.

He prayed that this moment in time would end swiftly and she would happily accept him into her bed. He wasn't positive how many torturous nights he would be able to endure.

But he'd stay nicely on the floor if that's what it would take to make Sophie trust and believe in him.

13

"BEAUTIFUL, AREN'T THEY?" Ava commented as she joined Sophie by the corral.

Sophie smiled at the horses, breathed in the fresh farm air, and nodded softly. "They are. I've never been on a horse. I was apprehensive the whole time we were riding earlier. Austin was very patient with me. So was the horse."

"Austin told me about that woman, and I'm not too sure I like what's going on," Ava said without warning.

Sophie looked at her. "Please don't have her arrested. Austin's willing to give her a chance, can't you, too?"

"I wouldn't necessarily say he's willing. He's only doing it for you. He's concerned, just as I am. We don't know this woman."

"You don't know me either."

"Austin knows you, and that's enough for me."

"But does he really know me? I don't know her, you're right. I see something in her that I can't ignore. Nobody was there for me, Ava...nobody. I refuse to turn my back if I can help her. Don't you believe in reform?"

Ava sighed, pulling her hair out of her face as a slight

breeze swept in. "He knows enough to be willing to give his heart to you. Make no mistake. He's never given it to any woman before. I insisted that woman be arrested and he put his foot down—for you. Because you asked him to give her a chance. Of course, I like to think people can be reformed. Do I think they should be doing it in your house? Absolutely not. If anything happened to you, Austin would go crazy."

"Nothing's going to happen. Deja means no harm. I know I'm probably crazy, but it's not something I can explain. She'll pay him back. She'll hopefully have a job today. She found an ad in the papers for a waitressing job at some diner." Sophie glanced away from Ava's piercing stare.

"I still don't like it. I'm glad you're at least letting Austin stay with you. He'll be a perfect gentleman, I swear. I'll have his hide if he isn't. You just let me know."

Sophie swung her head back at her. "He was a perfect gentleman last night. He slept on the floor in my room, and I couldn't help it, but I was worried he wouldn't stay on the floor. I've never met a man I could trust. This isn't easy for me. He's wormed his way inside me and...I don't know what he sees in me. Thank you for giving Deja a chance. You'll be the first to know if she does anything."

Ava grabbed Sophie's hand, squeezing reassuringly. "He sees a beautiful woman, a strong woman. Don't sell yourself short. If you're even trying to compare yourself with any other woman you saw walk into his house, don't. They were all trash, and trust me, I let him know that on numerous occasions. I also let him know how much I approve of you."

Ava looked embarrassed. "That came out wrong. My approval is not a requirement." Ava gave a small smile to mend the mishap of words. "He's just as nervous as you. He's never given a relationship a chance, so give him leeway if he acts like an idiot sometimes."

Sophie smiled slightly. "I can't imagine him acting like that. And your approval means a great deal to me. I saw the same trash walk out of his house as you did."

Ava laughed with Sophie as a small chuckle escaped. "I'm glad I wasn't the only one to think so."

"Oh, no, I gave them a few glares I think you would be proud of," Sophie said, laughing a bit more.

Ava busted out laughing. "I bet you did. Thank you."

Ava let go of her hand, casually swiping her hair behind her ear as the wind whipped around them again. "There's something else I wanted to talk to you about."

"Austin always says I don't hold back when I speak to him. You don't either."

Ava laughed lightly. "No, I don't hold back. New Yorker in me, I guess. I would say, maybe that's why you don't either, the New Yorker in you."

Sophie glanced away, suddenly focusing intently on the horses. "I guess Austin told you I moved from there. That's territory I won't be speaking about, Ava. So don't bother. I know how to hold back my words. The things that can happ —" Sophie abruptly stopped, refusing to finish what had been on the tip of her tongue.

"We just bought our tickets to New York for next week. We'll be gone for five days. I'm worried—Austin's worried about leaving you with Deja alone. We bought the tickets before he told me about Deja."

"I'll be fine. Neither of you should worry."

"Fat chance on that. You could come—"

"If you're about to suggest that I come with to New York, I'll be leaving this farm right here, right now," Sophie exclaimed.

Ava held her hands up. "I'm sorry, I won't say it. Don't leave because Austin would kill me. Who are you afraid of? What cops—because I'm assuming that's where your first bad experience came from—made you hate cops? I want names."

"You're from New York, but not anymore. You work for the police department here. You have no influence there. He would crush you," Sophie said with a tremor. "He nearly crushed me."

"Who?" Ava demanded. "Don't think I can be easily crushed. I can't stand bad cops, and I want them punished for whatever they did. I want this man who hurt you. Tell me."

Sophie met Ava's penetrating stare and then just as suddenly caved, looking away.

Enough.

She turned to walk away when Ava stepped in front of her. "I can help you. I'll take care of it while I'm there. I want to."

"I don't want help. I want to disappear. I want to live in peace, not fear. If you dredge things up, he could find me." Sophie shivered from the thought.

"Who is he?"

"I want to like you, Ava, but you're making it difficult. If Austin had you come out here and—"

"Stop. Austin has no idea I'm talking to you about this. He'll probably be just as pissed as you are right now." Ava sighed heavily. "Look, Sophie. I can't begin to imagine what horror you've lived. Unless you tell me. My dad's the police commissioner. I imagine you can't get much more authority than that within the police department."

Sophie stepped back, shocked. "It doesn't matter. Please, don't ask me about this again."

Sophie turned around and walked away. If Ava wanted to stop her again, then so be it. She needed to leave. She needed off this farm. She didn't want to hear the questions, the concern, or see the compassionate look in her eyes, the understanding. Ava meant the best, but she had no idea what hell would be opened if she got the answers she was looking for. She couldn't believe Ava's father was the police commissioner, but would that be enough? Sophie didn't think so.

She quickly made her way to the house and found Austin in the kitchen with Zane.

"I'd like to leave now, Austin," Sophie said quietly, avoiding eye contact with both of them.

Austin pushed himself away from the counter, took two steps toward her, and stopped when she retreated two steps back. "What did Ava say to you? What's wrong?"

"I'm tired. I'd like to leave."

"Look, I know she wanted to talk to you about Deja, and I'm sorry. I told her—"

"It's not about Deja. We came to an understanding on that. I think, anyway. Austin, I want to leave. You can call it whatever you like—running, tiredness, fear, maybe all of that. I don't want to talk about some things. If I choose to talk to you about it, how do I know you won't go telling Ava? How can I trust you to keep things between us? You told her I'm from New York." Sophie finally looked at him. She saw Zane out of the corner of her eye, still leaning casually against the counter, yet his face hard with an expression she couldn't describe.

"I didn't think that was a secret. From now on, what you say to me is between you and me. Nobody else, I swear. What happened?" Austin asked, as the nerves could be heard clear in his voice as he braved a step toward her.

"I guess I didn't say it was a secret, but I didn't even want to tell you. There are things I don't want you to know. I don't want you to see—" Sophie paused, afraid to continue. What was she doing exploding her emotions out in the open like this? Especially in front of Zane, who she just met.

"See what? You wanna know what I see. I see a courageous woman, a fierce woman, a strong woman quite capable of taking care of herself. So please, tell me what you don't want me to see."

"A weak, broken woman who took the abuse until the day he nearly ended it all. I was so weak. I let him do those things to me. I made sure to do everything right, yet still couldn't manage to do anything right. I don't want him to find me." The last comment barely left her mouth in a whisper.

"Geez, what the hell did Ava say to you out there?" Zane asked.

Austin ignored Zane and walked up to Sophie, grabbing her hands before she could walk away. "You let no one do anything. You survived and then you broke free. I refuse to let you think anything else. I have no idea what Ava said to you, but she's going to get an earful from me. I won't let anyone hurt you, least of all the creep who dared to put his hands on you. I'm so sorry if telling her you're from New York was bad. I'm sure she was only trying to help. Please, don't shut me out now just when I felt like we were making headway."

"I know she didn't mean it in a bad way, but I'll never step foot in New York again. Don't ever ask me to," Sophie said.

"Hear, hear," Zane muttered under his breath. He looked guilty when Austin turned around and glared at him, realizing he must've spoken louder than he intended.

"I won't. I also won't say I'm not worried about leaving you with Deja alone. You can stay here on the farm with Eleanor while we're gone," Austin suggested.

"I'll stay in my own house, thank you," Sophie said firmly.

Austin grinned. "And you say you're weak. You continuously stand strong with your beliefs and your words when you speak to me. Or is it just me?"

Sophie paused, thinking it over. "It is you. I guess, for once in my life, I don't fear a man will hurt me for talking back. I guess I sensed that immediately when it came to you. Strange."

"Na, I'm just that irresistible," Austin said, suddenly pulling her into his arms.

Sophie smiled for the first time since walking into the kitchen, his magical essence pulling her into comfort, security, and a powerful feeling she never wanted to lose. "Irresistible, huh? I don't know, maybe—"

Austin cut off any other words she may have uttered by kissing her lightly on the lips. "Let's stick with irresistible and speak no more. We can go home if that's what you want, but I need to know you're okay first. That things between us are okay?"

"Yes, we are. I don't want to come between you and Ava and—"

"Don't worry about Ava, Sophie. She always sticks her nose where it doesn't belong, says things she should keep to herself. Trust me, that's how I met her for the first time. Sticking her nose where it didn't belong. Austin will have words with her for upsetting you, and then they'll both move on," Zane interjected.

Austin glanced at Zane again. "Do you mind?"

"No, not at all. Continue on," Zane said with a grin.

"Ignore my brother, but he does have a point. You'll never come between us because we will have words and move on. She's my annoying little sister who needs to mind her own business. I'll be sure to let her know. And I'm sure she won't listen to a dam—nuzeling thing I say," Austin said, catching himself at the last minute, earning another small smile from Sophie.

"What strange language you speaking over there?" Zane asked, confused.

"Why are you even still in the kitchen? Can't you see I may want to kiss Sophie a little more fiercely without you looking on? Go find your wife and holler at her for me for upsetting Sophie," Austin said with a pointed glare, begging Zane with his eyes to leave.

"Sure, I'll go holler at her for you. I love when she gets all fired up, hot in the face, fists clenched and angry with me. She's so adorable when she gets mad." Zane winked at them as he walked out.

"He's not really going to yell at her, will he? I didn't mean to come in here upset like I did. She just touched a sore spot," Sophie said.

"He won't yell at her. Care to tell me what she said?"

"I thought you asked him to leave so you could kiss me more fiercely. I'm dying to find out what that entails," Sophie said, hoping to change the subject. She didn't want to talk about her past anymore. Never again, to be exact. Deep inside, she ached for his lips to touch hers softly.

Austin raised a brow as a delicious grin formed just before he swooped in for a kiss. The minute his mouth touched hers, she was on fire. She opened for him immediately, joining in the journey he led. He pulled her closer, her molding instantly to his body in all the right places. His hands moved down her back slowly, cupping her butt lightly as he pulled her closer.

She felt his hunger, moaning into his mouth as the touch sparked something new inside. She never felt such passion, such tingling sensations absorbing her body. Kevin always took what he felt he was entitled, never giving in return. She never knew she could feel like this, that a man could invoke such desire.

Then the horrible thought, the embarrassment of someone walking into the kitchen to find them embracing as they were, consumed her. She shivered, but that brief thought vanished just as quickly as he pulled her even closer, if that was even possible, his touch igniting another moan from her.

AUSTIN'S MIND WENT BLANK, except for the beautiful woman in his arms. He slowly backed her up to the counter, pressing into her lightly but firmly, eliciting another beautiful moan from her lips. Not once did he let go of her mouth, exploring, taking, begging for more. His hands moved from her bottom and slowly made their way up her back where he was about to venture to her chest when his brain came back into focus.

Instead, he grabbed her face softly, kissing her deeply, hoping for one more delightful moan as he moved his hips against her one more time. As soon as he heard the glorious moan, he pulled his lips away but still held her face gently.

"That was a little more fiercely than I intended. I'm pretty sure I could take you, right here, right now, with absolutely no regrets," Austin said, trying to find his breath and his heart that soared away within that madness.

"I'm pretty sure I would have let you. Oh dear. We're in the kitchen, Austin," Sophie whispered.

He grabbed another quick kiss. "Can I ask you a question?"

"You just did," Sophie said with a small grin.

He chuckled as he moved his hips a little, receiving a small gasp from her. "I want you, Sophie. Unless I'm mistaken, you want me, too. I said I would let you set the pace, and I will. But...can I sleep in the bed with you? I'll behave if you really want me to. Knowing how you taste, it makes it hard to resist you."

Sophie bit her lip as the indecision soared across her face.

"You know, when you bite your lip like that, it kinda turns me on," Austin said with a grin.

"You always do that," she said with a small laugh.

"Do what?" he asked innocently.

"Make me laugh, forget what I was thinking. Make me happy when it's hard to be."

"Then I'm doing something right."

"I can't make any promises, Austin. When I'm in your arms like this, I feel things I've never felt. That's saying more than you can ever realize."

"No, I think that says everything I needed to know," he replied, wishing like hell he could find the man who ever laid a hand on her. He'd kill him right now if he could.

14

SOPHIE STOOD IN THE HALLWAY, beaming with happiness at Deja. "I'm so excited. When do you start?"

Deja shook her head slightly in disbelief. Sophie's excitement for her clearly showed, and she didn't think it was because she'd be able to pay Austin back.

She'd been offered *help* before. Of course, with it came a million questions, accusations, and knowledge with what they thought was best for her. Not once had Sophie, or even Austin, tried to dig deeper into her background. That alone made her like Sophie even more.

She couldn't believe her luck falling into the perfect place to rebuild herself, finding a friend, a woman who understood what she was going through. Disgust and disgrace still impeded her happiness. She couldn't believe she ever stooped so low to break and enter into anyone's home, least of all a nice man who was willing to overlook her crime.

She understood why Sophie got all dreamy-like when she spoke about Austin. He seemed like a good man, but like Sophie, she was also weary of men. But if she had a man like Austin begging for her affection, she'd pay attention.

"Tomorrow. Can you believe it? I went in with an application and walked out with a job. They must be really hurting for a waitress."

"Or they really liked you and your qualifications. This is good, Deja. It's a good start to a new beginning."

"A new beginning. Yeah, I like the sound of that. Did you have a nice time at the farm?"

Sophie hesitated for a brief second. "Yeah, I did. I've never been on a farm, and it was neat. Lots of pigs and cows. And the horses were just sweet. I was nervous the whole time riding one. It's a beautiful place. I can see why Austin loves it."

"Good. Ava was there?"

Sophie looked away, cringing slightly. "Yeah, she was."

"She's gonna have me arrested, isn't she?"

Sophie looked back at her, shocked. "What? No, no, she's not. You have nothing to worry about, Deja. She won't have you arrested. She may try prying into your background." Sophie gave a strangled laugh. "That's what she did to me. I know she was doing it to help, but I just want to forget it all. I don't even want to talk about it now. That part of my life is over. New beginnings."

"I'll cheers to that, Sophie. Good night." Deja didn't want to talk about painful memories either. She understood Sophie's torment and the need to keep it closed inside from anyone.

SOPHIE NODDED and watched Deja walk to the master bedroom, shutting the door quietly. She stood there for a moment, gathering strength, then turned toward her own door. She jumped back in surprise when she saw Austin and Axel curled up on her bed.

He patted the empty spot. "Waiting on you, Sophie."

"I never said you could sleep in my bed, Austin," she said apprehensively, glancing at Axel wagging his tail expectantly.

"You didn't say I couldn't either. You said you couldn't make any promises. You also said when you're in my arms you feel things you never have before. Let me just hold you. I like holding you. Axel slept up here last night and I felt left out," Austin said with a goofy frown.

"You always try to sucker me by using Axel, you know that."

"Hey, if it works." He patted the spot again as she struggled with the decision.

She wanted him, there was no denying that. He made her feel things she had never felt before. He had said last time that it would be like making love with her, not that he was insinuating it would happen if she let him in the bed. But she didn't know what that felt like and desperately wanted to find out.

The thought frightened her. It hurt when Kevin took her. He was never gentle. She shouldn't compare the two, it wasn't fair, but the fear was so embedded inside her, it was impossible to let it go.

"I won't hurt you, Sophie. I promise. I would never hurt you. You trust me, you said so yourself. Trust me by coming here and knowing that I won't do anything but hold you." Austin patted the spot one more time.

Sophie zoned in on the spot he kept patting and shivered. He was asking a lot of her right now, and she didn't know if she could. She did trust him, but it scared her.

Suddenly, she whipped her head away to her dresser and focused on her angel. Its beauty wrapped around her and instantly filled her with peace.

That's all the courage she needed.

She heard movement on the bed and turned back to see Austin sitting up and scooting to the edge.

"What are you doing?"

"You're scared. I can tell. I don't want you scared of me. I'll sleep on the floor," Austin said, looking at her with pain in his eyes.

"I trust you," she whispered.

"Enough to let me stay in the bed?" he whispered back.

"Yes."

He moved back to his original position and patted the spot next to him for the last time. "Come here, my pixie angel."

"What did you call me?"

"You don't like it when I call you darling, and with good reason. I'll never utter darling to you again, or any woman, for that matter. You're the only one for me. When I saw you look at the angel on your dresser—" Austin glanced at the broken angel and sighed heavily. "I can't compare you to any woman, and I don't even want to try. You're one of a kind. You're special. Everything about you makes me feel things I've never felt. You're not the only one feeling new things. I love your pixie haircut. I love your laugh. I love your kindness. I love your smile. When you smile, you shine just like an angel. I guess when I saw you look at the angel and then I looked at you...it just came to me. My pixie angel. I guess I can just call you Sophie. That works for me, too."

Sophie glanced at her angel, then back at Austin. "I think I like that. That angel means a lot to me."

"I know it does. Maybe someday you can tell me why.

Right now, because I know you don't want to share, join me in this bed. I'm dying to hold you."

She nodded shyly, locked the bedroom door, and glanced at her angel one more time before tentatively climbing on the bed. Her angel still gave her a calming peace. Hearing Austin call her his pixie angel, strangely, also gave her a calming peace. He was right. She couldn't share why the angel was important right now. Moments like this, him just knowing how she felt, made her emotions fall deeper for him.

Axel sat in the middle of them. Sophie ruffled his head and looked at Austin. "He's a bed hog, you know."

He grinned at her, shoved Axel to the end of the bed, and pulled her into his arms. "Not tonight, he isn't. He'll sleep at our feet because you are sleeping in my arms. I love how you feel in my arms."

She snuggled deeper into his embrace, breathing in his wonderful scent. "I don't know when I'll be ready for anything more than just holding. I enjoy being in your arms, kissing you, but I'm scared, Austin."

He lifted her chin. "I don't want you to ever be scared of me. One day at a time, Sophie. Sleeping like this will get you more familiar with me. I don't know what that bastard did to you, but don't ever be afraid of me. I swear I'll never hurt you like that. When we make love for the first time, you'll feel nothing but pure bliss. I promise."

"You sound so sure I'll give in eventually."

"Let's not pretend you don't want me. I've already made you moan in delight," Austin said with a grin as she smiled, conceding what he said was true. "If I really put my mind to it, I could probably convince you right now. I don't want to take you on my terms. I want it on your terms. I want to make you feel good, just like how you make me feel. You have no idea what you do to me with a simple smile directed my way. When you're ready, let me know. Or when you're ready for me to convince you, I'll start my wicked way on you."

He grinned again, kissing her lightly on the lips. He moved his soft lips from her mouth, peppering a few on her chin, and made a trail of kisses down her neck. "How does that make you feel, Sophie? Do you like that?"

She moved slightly in his arms, but made no sound in response. How could she when his touch immobilized every part in her body as she waited desperately for more? Such a small taste he bestowed upon her.

Without notice, he slowly kissed his way up the side of her neck to her ear, lightly nibbling. Shivering from the contact, she waited for more kisses to touch her delicate skin. He moved his sweet lips across her neck again, giving each kiss its own undivided attention, taking his time to love every part of her skin that he touched. When he made his way back to her lips, he nibbled on the bottom one.

Sophie shivered in his arms, the tingling sense of pleasure running all over her body. His light, feathery kisses did more to her than anything else possibly could. She didn't say anything in response as he continued to nibble on her lip. She tried to lay still, to enjoy every ounce of his touch, but when he brought his kisses back down her neck, she shivered again in anticipation.

To her delight, he didn't stop, but repeated what he did the first time. He slowly kissed his way back up her neck to her ear and lightly nibbled again, gliding his tongue around spots she had no idea were so sensitive.

He kissed her just below her ear. "Do you want me to

stop? Tell me what you feel, Sophie. I feel you shake within my arms. Is that fear...or pleasure?"

Sophie couldn't speak and closed her eyes as he continued to pepper small, delicate kisses back to her mouth. Instead of lightly kissing her on the lips, he deepened the kiss, demanding she open up to him. She opened willingly as she pressed closer to him, eliciting a delicious moan from him.

She could feel he wanted her with a passion, and yet, all he did was kiss her. He was showing her what they could experience together but wasn't forcing it on her. That alone made Austin special, made him stand out from all the rest.

She shivered again in his arms, the tingling pleasure deepening into a burning desire. She moaned in despair when he pulled his mouth away from her.

"You need to tell me what you feel. You keep shaking in my arms. I won't force myself on you," Austin whispered.

"It's pleasure...not fear," she whispered back. His eyes shined brightly at those words, yet made no move to kiss her again.

That made her mind immediately switch off from the pleasure back into fear. She had no idea why, when it felt so good with his arms around her.

She glanced away from his penetrating look.

"He wasn't gentle with me. When I say I've never felt things like this, it's because I never truly have. This feeling is new. I never knew what pleasure felt like. It always hurt. He always took from me. It was never about me." She gasped in shock and put a horrifying hand to her mouth. "I can't believe I just said that."

She tried to move away, but he held her firmly in his arms. "You'll never think about him again. When you're with me, I'll make you forget him. I'll make you feel things you couldn't possibly imagine. I'll do anything to wipe those memories away, Sophie." Austin gently pulled her face back to his and lightly kissed her, nibbling gingerly on her bottom lip.

"I like that," she said as he lifted his head to look into her eyes.

"Like what? What I just said?"

"Yes, but I meant you nibbling on my lip. I...I like that," she said tentatively.

"Well, I like it when you bite on your own lip. It makes me wanna nibble on it myself. Seriously turns me on. I like you telling me what you like. I'll keep doing those things. What makes you happy is what makes me happy. So just keep whispering what you like, and I'll keep doing it," he said softly, nibbling one more time on her lip.

"I like your kisses, everywhere you put them. That's why I shiver in your arms. A burning desire just courses through me," she whispered, as he trailed more kisses down her neck. She shivered again from the soft caress each kiss made.

"Oh, I like this. Keep whispering what you like, Sophie. You have no idea the pleasure I feel hearing that from your lips," he said, trailing kisses back up toward her ear.

In all the time he held her in his arms, he always kept his hands near her head. Surprising her, he slowly brought one down her arm in a gentle caress at the same time he peppered kisses back to her mouth. He took his time to feel her soft skin, weaving his hand over her fingers, rubbing a few gentle circles on her palm as he devoured her mouth.

She shivered again as he let her hand go and made his way back up, caressing her side, stopping just short of touching her breast. He lightly moved his hand back and forth under her breast, enticing her, teasing her with what was to come.

She moaned in his mouth at his torturous touch. He bit her lip as he cupped her breast and stroked her nipple. She arched into him, grabbing his back in delight. "Oh, I like that, Austin."

He deepened the kiss, caressing her breast in a playful wonder. He squeezed her nipple tenderly and made his way back up to her lips where he cradled her face as he kissed her deeply, drawing another delightful murmur from her.

"I think this is me having my wicked way with you. I have to stop before I completely devour you from head to toe. I want it on your terms, not mine. Remember?" he said, pulling away.

He rested his back against the bed and pulled her to his side. She rested her head on his chest as the desire from his touch still lingered in every corner of her body.

"I want you, Sophie. That was never in question. Do you know why I stopped?"

"Yes. I thank you for that. I like how you make me feel, but I'm not sure I'm ready for it all. He—"

"Did you think of him while I kissed you?" he interrupted her.

"No...but I can't help it when he pops into my mind afterwards. It's hard to forget about that horror in my life. You make me feel good, but the pain is still there."

Austin gently grabbed her cheek and looked into her eyes. "I'll make you forget him. When you finally forget everything but me, then I'll know you're ready for it all. I guess I'll just have to torture you every night with sweet kisses and light caresses. Each night, I'll move my hands a little further, a little longer, and you'll forget. You'll forget everything but me."

"You're already making me forget just by your sweet words," she whispered.

"Then we're making headway. Just wait until I make you forget it all," he whispered back, pulling her closer into his arms.

15

"HOW WAS YOUR DAY?" Sophie asked as Deja walked into the kitchen. "Get down, Axel. You know the rules. No treats until you eat your food." She pointed to his dish and shook her head as she smiled.

Deja laughed. "He's at it again. I guess I shouldn't fib. I snuck him a treat before I left this morning."

"Why am I not surprised? He's such a beggar. Just like Austin."

"I know I've only been here four days, but I've never seen Austin beg for anything," Deja said, confused.

Sophie blushed, thinking of the nights when they ventured to bed. The sweet way he held her in his arms and begged her to whisper what she liked as he kissed, caressed, and touched her in more ways than just physically.

Each night, Kevin's hurtful words and actions slipped deeper out of her mind as Austin's delicate touch and beautiful words took over. She wasn't quite there, but he was making his way quicker than she ever imagined.

"Oh, he does little things, I guess when you're not around," Sophie said, turning to the fridge and pulling it open, even though she didn't need anything. "How was your day?"

"It was good. My feet are killing me. I haven't been on my feet like that in a long time. Who knew waitressing was so backbreaking? I can help cook. What are we having?"

"Lasagna. It's cooking in the oven and not much to do but wait," Sophie said, finally grabbing the iced tea so she didn't look like a complete idiot. She closed the fridge and went to the cupboard to grab a glass. "You want some iced tea?"

"Sure." Deja sat down at the table. "So, Austin leaves for New York in two days. About me—"

"Stop, Deja. I trust you. He...maybe doesn't as much. But he has no say in the matter. We'll be fine, right?" Sophie set down the iced tea in front of Deja and took a seat across from her.

Deja lightly smiled. "Right. I just wanted to make sure. I know he doesn't trust me."

"Did he say something to you?"

"No. I see the way he looks at me sometimes. You mean a lot to him, Sophie. He wouldn't be so generous about me if it weren't for you."

"That might be true. Don't worry about it, Deja. Do you work this weekend? Maybe we can do something fun together," Sophie said, lightly tracing her glass as her nerves went haywire. She never had many friends growing up. It was easier to stick by herself than explain things about her homelife. She really wanted a friend for once.

"I do, but only a short shift. What do you wanna do?" Deja asked excitedly.

Sophie looked up from her glass with a small smile. "I have no idea. I hadn't thought that far ahead."

Deja laughed. "Well, we'll figure something out. Boy, that lasagna smells great."

"Thanks. It'll be done in about thirty minutes. Austin should be home soon."

Home.

She felt like she truly had a home for once, and Austin was slowly weaving his way into it. She liked that feeling.

AVA WALKED into the small white building they made for their offices and saw Austin typing away at his computer.

"Having fun?" she asked, taking a seat across from him.

"Inputting numbers and figuring out how much chicken feed to order. So no, not what I would call fun. I just want to get this done and go home," Austin said, barely glancing at her.

"Are you still mad at me?"

Austin stopped typing and looked at her, the pain clear in her eyes. "No, Ava, I'm not. I'm just busy."

"You haven't talked to me much this past week. Feels like you are. I'm sorry for butting in. I just want to help. I can't stand that Sophie was hurt and I could possibly help her."

"I would love nothing better than for you to take care of that piece of shit that hurt Sophie or the despicable cops that turned their backs on her. Trust me, Ava. I almost lost a lot of ground with Sophie. I can't say anything to you because I promised her I wouldn't. I won't break my promise. She's said some things to me, and every time a small piece of her old life leaves her mouth, it breaks my heart. It makes me want to pummel the man to death. I've never thought of myself as a violent person, but for him, I would be the most violent man in the world."

Austin pushed his chair away from the desk, looked down at the floor, and sat there taking small, deep breaths. "Maybe I'm still a little mad. Remember the first time you met Zane? The intense rage and anger he had toward you." He glanced at her.

"Of course I do. It's hard to forget."

"You butted into our family business and it pissed him off. I didn't understand his anger about it because maybe I saw a little bit of your side. Not this time. I understand his anger now because that's what I feel. You butted in where you shouldn't have and it pisses me off. I know you did it out of love and concern, but it's still there in the back of my mind. I've since mentioned your name a time or two, just in casual conversation, and I saw Sophie shake. I've gotten to know how her body moves, reacts to certain things. I know what shakes come from delight and what ones are from fear. I don't think she wants to come around the farm anymore because of you, Ava. She's afraid of what you might do or say to her. You're like my sister and I love you, but Sophie's coming to mean a lot to me, and I have to think about her feelings. Maybe I've kept my distance from you because it's easier on me."

"Damn it, Austin. I'm sorry. You know I can't help myself. I didn't mean to make her that upset, or you, for that matter. What can I do to make it up to you? I don't like this bridge between us. You don't have to come to New York with us. You can stay here with Sophie. I know you're worried about leaving her alone with Deja. I am, too."

Austin ran a frustrated hand through his hair. "I'm coming with, Ava. It's important I see Jimmy, too. Sophie's not budging about staying on the farm when we're gone. She's staying with Deja, and I can't stop her. She's very independent on that account, and I can't fault her for it. That's one of the things I love about her. Her fierceness and independence to know what's right for herself. It's important to her. I'm going to ask Emmett to check on her every day. I haven't mentioned it to Sophie yet, but I have to do something to make myself feel better. I know you're sorry. I'll get over it, and I do forgive you. It's just hard when I know Sophie's apprehensive."

"Maybe if I talk to her—"

"Damn it, Ava, don't you dare try talking to her again. It didn't work last time."

"Okay, but how can she feel better around me if she won't come around the farm and you won't let me talk to her?"

"Just butt out of my love life right now. I'm handling it fine myself. I don't want to be mad at you, and I don't want to fight with you. When Sophie is ready, she'll come around here. For now, leave it to me. Leave her alone, okay?"

"Okay."

Austin scooted back to the desk. "Please, let me finish this so I can leave."

Ava nodded and stood up. "Can I at least get a hug or something? You still seem mad at me."

Austin looked at her. "I'm really not. It's just a sore spot with me right now. Is this pregnancy hormones talking right now? You normally aren't in my face like this."

"We normally don't fight either."

Austin stood up and circled the desk. He grabbed Ava in a hug and squeezed her tightly. "I love you, Ava. I always will, no matter how mad I get at you. Just please leave Sophie and her issues to me. I'm begging you."

Ava squeezed him back. "I will, I swear. I was just trying to help. Make her come back here. I won't say a word, I promise."

He pulled away and kissed her forehead. "I will. After New York. Let's get through that trip first. I want to go to New York, but trust me when I say I'm kinda scared to leave her alone. Not just because of Deja either. I don't want to talk about it, so don't ask me. Go on to the house. Let me finish up here. We're good."

"Okay. I'll see you tomorrow." Ava grabbed another hug from him and then left.

CREATING tension in the family again. She obviously did a good job of it. She just wanted to help because she couldn't stand thinking about what happened to Sophie, and no one was paying for their crimes. Not the horrible man who abused her, or the cops who turned a blind eye. She wanted to know everything that happened, and it tore her up inside that she couldn't.

She walked toward the house and saw Zane swinging leisurely on the porch swing.

"Come grab a seat by me, sweetheart." He patted the spot next to him.

Ava sat down and fell into his embrace as he wrapped his arms around her. "How did it go with Austin?"

"He's still mad. He's trying not to be, but she's afraid to come around me. I didn't mean to make her feel that way." Ava sighed, leaning closer to him. "Why do I always screw things up?"

Zane tilted his head toward her and lifted her chin to meet his eyes. "Because you care. You have so much love and devotion inside that sometimes you just can't help yourself. Sophie didn't say a lot in the kitchen that day, but she said enough. Whatever that man did to her, well, it was rough. She's in good hands with Austin. He'll help her in any way he can. It's his job, not yours. I'd like to think it was me that helped you through the pain last year, not Austin. Maybe it was both of us. But—"

"It was you. He helped, but mostly it was you. I get what you're saying. We all have that one person to help us through something. Sophie has Austin, not me, is what you're saying."

"Yes. If there's a small chance down the road she needs your help, she'll let you know. She's a strong woman. She thinks she's weak, but anyone who can escape a horror that she did is strong in my eyes. Austin is trying to help her see that. Just let him take care of it. Stop worrying so much. It's probably not good for the baby." Zane placed a tender hand on her belly. He started rubbing soft, slow circles.

Ava covered his hand with her own and smiled. "I can't help but worry. I'll try harder for you, though." She rested her head onto him. "I love you, Zane."

"I love you, too, sweetheart. It'll all work out in the end. It always does."

Ava smiled, taking comfort in his words, and squeezed his hand tighter.

"HEY, AUSTIN, CAN I HAVE A WORD?" Deja said, popping her head out of her room.

Austin stopped and turned around. "Sure. What's up?"

Deja held her hand out. "Fifty bucks, so far. I've been making decent tips."

Austin stared at the money, then glanced at Deja. Her bright-blue eyes sparkled back at him, pulling him in. She was sort of like Sophie in a way. Trying so hard on the outside to appear strong and unafraid, but he saw the slight tremor in her hand. He definitely understood what Sophie saw in Deja. She had secrets, fears, and horrors hidden within those bright-blue eyes, but it didn't mean he liked her or fully trusted her yet.

He stepped forward and grabbed the money. "Thanks, Deja."

"You look tired."

Austin laughed lightly. "I am tired. We have a lot we need to do before we leave. Even though our cousins help out, Zane and I hate leaving too much work for them."

"I know you think I'm a horrible person and don't like me. I don't blame you either. I won't hurt Sophie. She'll be fine while you're gone," Deja said, making eye contact the whole time.

Austin sighed. "We all make mistakes, Deja. I've even made a few in life. Not so far as breaking into someone's home, but I've done dumb shit, too. I'm a little apprehensive leaving Sophie, but...she's a tough woman. She wouldn't be here in this house if she wasn't. Trust doesn't come easy, but I'm getting there little by little with you."

"Sophie has no idea what a true gem she found with you. She's lucky," Deja said, a small smile forming from his words.

"I like to think I'm the lucky one," he replied with a small smile back. "Good night, Deja."

"'Night, Austin." Deja stepped back into her room and closed the door quietly.

Austin glanced at the money in his hand. He had been more apprehensive leaving Sophie than he let on to Deja. The minute she handed him the money, it dissipated slightly. Sometimes, you had to show what you meant, instead of using just words. Her handing money over right away showed him that she was trying.

Plus, those eyes. Every time he looked into them, they said so much.

He shoved the money into his pocket and walked into Sophie's room. Axel sat on the foot of the bed, already snug in his position. Sophie looked cozy on her side, eyes closed and her hand resting on his spot. He smiled at her beauty and the way she curled into bed.

He already anticipated feeling her glorious body next to his, wrapped in his arms. He ached to have her whole body, to connect as one, but surprisingly, he was just as happy holding her at night. For the first time in his life, he enjoyed holding a woman. His woman. He liked the sound of that.

He quietly closed the door, locked it, and walked over to his side of the bed. He quickly undressed, and as lightly as he could, he climbed into bed and scooted toward her. She opened her eyes when she felt him cradle her cheek in his hand.

"What took you so long?" she whispered sleepily.

"Deja stopped me in the hallway. Paid me some money." Austin pulled her closer into his arms.

"Did she? Good," Sophie said, a slight shiver running through her body.

"Hmm...I haven't even touched you much. Why the shiver?"

She bit her lip, a small frown forming.

Austin dove in, biting her bottom lip. "You know how I get when you bite your lip. What's the matter?"

"What do you see when you look at Deja?" Sophie asked in a soft whisper.

"What kind of question is—" Austin paused, the obvious

finally dawning on him. "You don't think I'll leave you for Deja, do you?"

When Sophie made no move to answer but bite on her lip again, Austin knew. "You do think that. Geez, Sophie. No, my beautiful pixie angel, never. No wonder you shiver every time I talk to her or mention her name. Why didn't I see this sooner? Sure, she's pretty, but she's not you. Nobody compares to you. I will repeat that until you trust it. Trust me, please."

"So I was being silly?"

"Yes, you were being silly. Tell me these silly things right away. I don't ever want you to shiver over something like that. I want you shivering over something like this," Austin said, as he moved his mouth over her lips.

Sophie did tremble as his tongue tangled with hers. He pulled away, making her groan in sadness. "Do you believe me?"

"I do. She's just so beautiful. I just thought...I trust you. I'm glad she paid you some money already. Now you know you can trust her. See, there's no reason to worry while you're on vacation."

"Sophie, I'm gonna worry regardless. Not just because of Deja either."

She looked at him, confused. "What do you mean?"

Austin lightly rubbed her back. His fingers were like feathers, brushing her in small, tender strokes up toward her shoulders and back down softly to the edge of her pants.

He liked their honesty, their openness to talk about everything. He wanted to share it all with her. He didn't want secrets or the deep worry that had settled in his stomach to fester while he was gone.

He lightly stroked up and down again, this time hooking the end of her nightgown. Brushing his hand back up underneath the silky garment, he treasured every time she trembled from his soft touch. That's the only kind of trembling he ever wanted to feel coming from her.

Every small movement she surrendered made him harder to the core. It turned him on in a dizzying rush. He wanted this delicate, beautiful woman so badly it hurt.

He kissed her lips lightly. "You like how I touch you?"

"Of course I do. Your hands can do the most amazing things with just one light touch," she said nervously. "If it's not Deja, what are you worried about? You didn't answer me."

"I feel so close to you when you're in my arms. I feel a slight change in you every night. Like tonight. This is the first time I walked in and you had your eyes closed, just leisurely waiting for me. That's progress. Every other night, I was always in the bed first, patting the spot next to me. I'm happy with you, Sophie. Are we gonna go two steps back when I come back? Am I gonna have to work my way back into this bed? I'm scared that with me leaving, you might go into your shell a bit. I don't know why I feel that way. I just do. It worries me. Not that I won't work my way back in here, because I will. I need you, Sophie. Geez, I don't know what's wrong with me." He kissed her soundly on the lips, then turned his head away.

"Time away for my mind to play games with me is what you're worried about." She grabbed his cheek for once and made him look at her.

"Maybe. Am I being dumb? Am I being silly now? Do I have to worry? I'm gonna miss you like hell, you have no idea."

She rubbed her finger over his mouth. "You swore."

He opened his mouth and grabbed her finger with his lips in one smooth move. She slowly pulled her finger out as a smile formed on his face. "I did swear. Forgive me, my pixie angel?"

"It's not hard to forgive you. I'm going to miss you, too, Austin. Especially at night," she whispered tentatively. "You make me forget a little more each night, faster than I thought possible. You make me want you so much. I'm almost ready, but not yet. I hope I don't take two steps back, but if I do, I can't wait for you to convince me back into your arms."

She bit her lip lightly, but before he could say anything, she mumbled, "I even went to the doctor."

He looked confused. "Why? Are you okay?"

"I want to be ready for when you completely erase my mind," she said, sucking in a quick breath. "Birth control. I want to feel you completely. I'm so close to giving in, but there's that small fear that lingers. I don't know why."

"Getting ready for me...I like hearing that, Sophie. You have no idea how much I like hearing that. That's good. Even if you didn't, I would protect you. That's what condoms are for," he said with a tender smile. "I'd never intentionally hurt you."

"But I want to feel you completely. I've never felt so connected to someone before. I want that full connection," she whispered.

He smiled and grabbed a kiss. She immediately opened for him, tangling her tongue with his. He meant for it to be a quick, sweet kiss. When she responded like that, he couldn't help but kiss her back with a matching pace. He held her in his arms, kissing her deeply, and couldn't believe how lucky he truly was to have found this beautiful, sweet woman.

Without thought, he rolled to his side, making her roll with him. Almost lying on top of her, he pressed lightly into her as he continued to kiss her into madness. She moved beneath him, igniting a fire instantly, making him push into her a bit harder. She moaned into his mouth at the contact.

He suddenly broke the kiss. "Do you see how easily you get me going? One little kiss and I lose my mind."

"I like it when you lose your mind. It helps me lose mine," she said with a grin.

"Oh, Sophie, you always surprise me with the things you say. I like that." He kissed her lightly this time, rolled onto his back, and pulled her closer to rest on his chest. "Deja's worming her way into my trust, but not completely. Is it okay if Emmett stops by a few times to check on you? I'd feel better knowing he was."

Sophie trembled. Austin immediately recognized the difference. "Please, Sophie. You know Emmett. I need to know you're safe."

"I met him once, Austin. I wouldn't say I know the man."

"True, but he's family. You can trust him because I do. He's a good guy. I would seriously feel better about it. You don't have to let him in. Just open the door, flash a beautiful smile of yours, and tell him you're all right. We can make a safe word, in case something's wrong, so he knows there's trouble. How about sexy beast?"

She laughed into his chest. "How in the world would I use the words *sexy beast* in a sentence to tell him I'm not okay?"

"I don't know. Say something like...I talked to Austin, that sexy beast. That would work, don't ya think?" he said, laughing.

"Who said you're a sexy beast?"

Austin looked at her in mock surprise. "You don't think so? We already established I'm irresistible. I would assume sexy beast is right alongside that."

Sophie laughed even harder. "You're something else,

Austin. I guess he can check up on me and we'll use that as a safe word. I won't have to use it, but I can't wait for you to tell him what the safe word will be. He's going to tease you. Just like he did about the spider."

"That's okay. I can handle the teasing. I just wanted to hear you laugh," he said sincerely. He pulled her closer and kissed the top of her head. "Good night, my pixie angel."

Sophie snuggled deeper into his embrace. "Good night, my sexy beast."

Austin chuckled, already missing her like crazy, even as he held her in his arms. This would be the longest vacation he ever had.

16

AVA SUDDENLY STOPPED and inhaled deeply. A pair of arms wrapped around her and squeezed hard.

"Sweetheart, I nearly fell over running into you. What are you doing?" Zane whispered in her ear.

"Can't you smell it, Zane?" she said with a huge smile, inhaling another deep breath.

Zane glanced at Austin, who shrugged in confusion, and brought his attention back to Ava. He leaned his head closer to her ear, wiggled his nose in a sniffing excursion as Ava chuckled. "I smell the pretty flower in my arms, but that's about it."

Ava turned around in his arms, smiling. "New York, Zane. Can't you smell the wonder of the city? It's beautiful."

"It's called pollution. I do smell that now," he replied dryly.

"Sure smells better than the plane. You two weren't stuck by a smelly teenager and a dad with gas. I'm telling ya, he had gas. He was just too damn lazy to get up and use the toilet," Austin said, earning another chuckle from Ava.

"Yeah, sorry about that, bro, don't know how our seats

got mixed up like that. I'm thankful you had the smelly dad, too," Zane said.

"Wait until you're that smelly dad. Not gonna sit by you on a plane, that's for sure," Austin said, laughing.

"Just because I'm going to be a dad doesn't mean I'm going to pass gas on an airplane. It's called manners," Zane said with a touch of irritation.

"Stop arguing, children. Don't tease Zane, Austin. He's sensitive right now. You're going to be a wonderful dad. I'll sit by you, even if you do pass a little gas," Ava said, grabbing a quick kiss.

"Hey, what happened to stop teasing me? I'm sensitive, remember?" Zane said with a wounded face.

"That's why I kissed you. To soften the blow a bit," she said, grabbing another kiss.

"You're both going to make wonderful parents. Sorry I'm late. Traffic is especially horrible today. A holiday looming always means more tourists, which means more traffic. You think I would have realized that when I left," Peter said from behind them.

"Dad!" Ava ran out of Zane's arms into Peter's.

Peter grabbed her in a fierce hug, picked her up and twirled her around as he laughed with delight. "You're going to hurt yourself twirling me like that, Dad." Ava laughed in his ear, as she held on tight. Suddenly, she didn't want to let him go and wanted one more twirl.

"I'm never too old to hold my little girl and give her a hug." He squeezed tightly and twirled her one more time. When he came full circle, he stepped back and held her by the arms. "Let me look at you. You're beautiful. I see that wonderful pregnancy glow that women have. Yours is beyond the most beautifulest."

"Dad, beautifulest isn't a word," Ava said with a grin.

"Sure it is. When my daughter is pregnant and glows like an angel, it's a damn word. I missed you. You need to visit me more often." He pulled her in for another hug. In the tiniest whisper he could manage, he asked, "How's Zane? Is he doing all right? I didn't mean to say that last part so loud. I know it's hard for him here."

"He's fine, Dad. A little tension, but he'll be fine. Just don't make a big deal about it. I'll try to visit more often. Let's show Zane how wonderful New York can really be."

"Good plan." He let Ava go and looked over at the two men who had become his family with little effort. "Boys, where's my hug?" Peter asked with a grin.

"You're not gonna twirl us, too, are you?" Austin asked with a horrified expression, his smile hiding just below the surface.

"I just might. I may look old, but I'm fit as a fiddle. My three favorite people in the whole world are finally visiting me. It's cause for some twirling," he replied jovially.

"Twirl me all you want, sir. Just maybe, no more twirling Ava. What happens if it's hurting the baby?" Zane asked, concerned, grabbing a hug from Peter.

Before Zane could let go, Peter picked him up and half twirled him. He couldn't manage the gracefulness as he had when he twirled Ava, but it got the job done. Zane laughed, backing up a few steps after Peter finally let him go.

"Son, that's not going to hurt the baby. I can see you're going to be a worrywart, just like I was. I was a mess until Ava popped out, and then my worry increased tenfold. It doesn't get easier...the worry. Trust me. She's how many states away, and my worry is ten times worse than when she lived here. I know she's in good hands with you, Zane. I can tell already how wonderful of a father you're going to be. I can't wait for my grandchild to get here. Boy, you're going to have your hands full."

Zane groaned. "Don't I know it." Then he glanced at Ava, her beautiful smile shining at him, and glanced back at Peter. "Thanks for the twirl."

"Anytime," Peter said, laughing. He turned to Austin.

"Man, I'll just feel left out now if I don't get twirled," Austin said with a mock frown.

"Get over here," Peter said, tossing his head back in a come here gesture. He grabbed a hug from Austin and did another half twirl like Zane. "You boys are just too heavy for a full-on decent twirl. That's the best I can do."

"Best twirl I ever had," Austin said, clapping a hand on Peter's back. "What's on the agenda for today, Dad? Oh, wait...Grandpa."

For a brief moment, panic settled on Peter's face. "Grandpa?" he muttered in disbelief.

He kept his eyes on Austin the whole time, finally bringing his mouth into a deep smile. "Grandpa. I think it's starting to sound better each time I hear it. Don't scare a man like that, Austin. A little warning next time."

"I thought the announcement of Ava's pregnancy was enough warning," Austin said with a grin.

"You know what I mean."

"Sure, I do...Grandpa," Austin said, laughing again.

"I see how this trip is going to go," Peter said with a laugh. He gestured for them to follow, pulling Ava into his arms as he walked by her. "Let's hit the road. I thought you guys might be hungry and figured we could swing by O'Hares. I have a strong feeling there are some people who might be there. What do you think about that, Ava?"

"Sounds like the best plan...Grandpa," Ava said, glancing

behind her to see Austin laughing. She smiled at Zane, who smiled back, but she saw his apprehension. His tension.

They made it to O'Hares twenty minutes later, surprisingly, considering traffic was still hectic. They were about to step inside when Austin pulled his phone out. "I'll meet you guys inside."

Zane nodded in understanding and held the door open for Peter and Ava.

"Everything's all right, I hope?" Peter asked.

It wasn't hard to mistake the brief worry that filtered into Austin's face before he covered it up with a smile.

Zane walked in behind him. "Yeah, everything's fine. He met a woman. Well, he always meets women. I mean, he met a good woman he truly cares about. He's worried about her back home in Minnesota."

"Why?" Peter asked, confused.

"I'll explain later, Dad. Maybe you can help somehow," Ava said. A huge smile formed on her face when she saw her friends.

Zane grabbed Ava's arm before she could rush off in excitement. "Ava. Remember what happened last time you butted in? You can tell your dad, but don't go trying to fix anything. Sophie wouldn't like it, and neither would Austin if it hurts Sophie."

Ava sighed. "I know. I can't help myself."

"Well, try really hard. You saw the way Austin acted after what you did last time. He practically ignored you," Zane said with a warning in his tone.

"I know. I swear I won't do anything to hurt either of them. Can I get all excited now, Zane?" Ava asked with a beaming smile.

"Yes," Zane said, just as Markus came up and grabbed Ava in a hug without asking.

"Where have you been hiding? Man, I missed you, Ava," Markus said, squeezing her hard.

"I missed you, too," Ava said, squeezing back.

"Maybe not so hard. You could hurt the baby," Zane said with a cringe as Peter put a comforting hand on his shoulder and chuckled.

Markus let Ava go, laughing, and walked up to Zane, grabbing a quick hug. "I know what you mean. I was like that the first few months. I forgot she was pregnant because she's not that big yet. Wait 'til you see Ashley." A chorus of screams sounded in front of the two men. "And there she is."

Zane laughed as Ashley waddled up to Ava and grabbed her in a hug, both of them screaming in delight. "She's beautiful, Markus. How far along is she now?"

"Seven and a half months. It goes way too fast, man. Enjoy every little minute. Even the annoying ones where they complain, cry, demand you go get them food and crap. It's worth every minute, though. I love when the baby moves around and kicks. That's the best," Markus said, smiling. Julie had joined them in the hug. They gushed over one another, touching each other's bellies and talking pregnancy. Julie wasn't pregnant, but she wasn't shy about gushing over the two of them.

"I haven't felt the baby move yet. I can't wait. I can't help but worry over every little thing. You know Ava. She doesn't slow down for anything. Still the same old Ava. Do you know what you guys are having?" Zane said.

"No, we decided to keep it a secret. It's killing me, but Ashley really wanted the element of surprise. It's just crazy to me. Tell me already, you know?" Markus said, shaking his head in annoyance.

"Women have all the control. Haven't you learned that, Markus?" Peter said with a grin.

"Oh, I know, sir. Hence why I have to wait to find out what the sex of my own baby is," Markus said.

"They have us wrapped around their finger...and I think they know it," Zane said.

"Damn right, they know it," Peter said with a laugh. "Seems to me...Sophie, is it? She seems to have Austin wrapped around her finger, too. He's been outside a long time. Real curious about that story."

"Oh. Austin's seeing someone? Like a real woman?" Markus asked, surprised.

"Yes, a real woman. What the hell you think she is...a blowup doll?" Austin asked from behind Markus, a slight chuckle escaping.

Markus turned around with a grin. "Hey, Austin. You know what I meant. I thought you were destined for bachelorhood."

Austin grabbed a quick hug from Markus. "Me, too. Guess that's what happens when a great woman comes outta nowhere. I can't imagine being without Sophie."

"How's she doing?" Zane asked.

"Good. No problems," Austin replied.

"Are you expecting problems? Ava made a cryptic comment that has my curiosity piqued," Peter said in a fatherly tone.

Austin glanced at Ava with an annoyed look, then turned back to Peter, sighing heavily. "It's a long story. I never thought I'd fall for a woman, but I have. She's everything I could ever ask for. She doesn't have a pleasant past, and part of it actually comes from New York. I can tell you later what Ava knows, but anything beyond that stays a secret. Sophie would hate me to pieces if I broke her trust, and I promised not to speak about it."

"New York, huh? Now you got my curiosity piqued," Markus said, raising an eyebrow in eagerness.

"If the time ever comes I need you, Markus, or you, Peter, you'll be the first to know. Trust me. But for right now, let's celebrate Ava being home. Please?" Austin said.

"Son, you know I'm always here for you. We will talk later, that's a fact," Peter said sternly, with no room for argument. Then he grinned slowly. "What happened to calling me grandpa?"

"Grandpa. Now ain't that something. You're getting old," Mahone said, joining the circle they had formed. "Those three are driving me bonkers already talking baby crap. Let's talk some baseball or something."

Peter laughed. "Watch it, Mahone. You still work for me. I'm not that old. Being a grandpa doesn't make me old."

"Yeah, but it's too much fun not to rub it in a bit," Mahone replied. "What the hell you all standing over here for? Let's sit down. We ordered appetizers until you guys got here. What do you want to drink, Zane and Austin? It's on me?"

"Oh, that's not necessary," Zane said.

"But it is. Never refuse a drink from Mahone when he's offering. He's stingy like that. It's a real treat when he treats ya," Markus said with a laugh.

"It's true. I am a stingy bastard. What'll you have?" Mahone said with a grin.

Zane sat next to Ava. The ladies had already sat down to munch on the appetizers. "Well, damn. I'll take the most expensive drink they offer," Zane said with a devious grin.

"Now we're talking," Markus said.

"What's going on?" Ashley asked, looking around at all the men laughing.

"Mahone offered Zane and I a drink. Guess we're getting

top-shelf drinks in honor of that gracious offer," Austin said, clapping a hand on Mahone's back. "Right, buddy?"

"I did offer," Mahone groaned.

"Wow, that's nice of you, Mahone. You feeling okay?" Ava said with a smirk.

"That's my Ava I know and love. Glad to have you back in town for a while. I'm feeling just peachy. I can splurge now and again, especially when the McCords are in town. Gotta show 'em a good time. Just like we did for Jimmy. The first toast is on him," Mahone said with sincerity.

Ava smiled wide. Zane grabbed her hand and nodded in agreement. "That sounds like a great plan. I'll always toast to Jimmy."

"Hear, hear. Where's my drink?" Austin said, putting his hand up to signal any waiter. He looked over at Zane. "What are we having in honor of Jimmy, bro?"

"Whatever his favorite drink was here, I suppose," Zane said softly.

"Perfect...especially for me. He always got beer. Nice and cheap," Mahone said with a laugh.

"Well, there goes your chance of emptying his wallet," Markus muttered.

"Damn. Next time, for you, Markus, I'll empty it," Zane said with a chuckle. "But if it's honoring Jimmy, I gotta go with what he'd drink."

"I'm holding you to it," Markus said as their waiter walked up to the table finally.

"Yo, Ben, the whole table will take a round," Mahone said, holding up his bottle of beer.

"All of us?" Ava asked, surprised.

"Why the hell not? I'm feeling generous. Plus, it's for Jimmy," Mahone said with a tender smile.

"Thanks, Mahone. That's sweet of you. Ben, make two

non-alcoholic strawberry daiquiris for Ash and me here. Pregnant and all," Ava said, reminding Mahone.

"You got it. Coming right up." Ben walked away to the bar.

"It's so good to be surrounded by all of you again. You have no idea how much I miss this," Ava said sincerely. She squeezed Zane's hand and leaned into him. "But I also love Minnesota."

"We've missed you. It's going to go so fast. You'll be gone before you know it," Ashley said with a frown.

17
_____

"Come on up, Axel. Sit by me," Sophie said, patting the seat next to her on the couch.

Axel jumped with a graceful move, circled twice by her side, and then plopped next to her thigh, scooting his body as close as he could to her. Sophie chuckled, grabbed the blanket next to her, and covered them both up, keeping his head out from under the covers so he could see the television as well.

"What should we watch? What are you in the mood for?" Sophie asked, getting a look from him, but no response.

She didn't expect one, but knowing for the first time that Austin wasn't going to walk in the front door tonight had her feeling down. Talking to Axel made her feel slightly better. She knew she would miss him, but she never thought she'd feel this miserable. He had wormed his way through her defenses easier than anyone had.

It suddenly struck her.

If he left her for good, this was how she would feel. But ten times worse. She didn't want to lose him. He had become important to her. Making her feel things she had never felt in her life. Sitting on the couch, curled up with Axel, she couldn't feel an ounce of regret for meeting him and letting him into her life.

Hearing his voice a few minutes ago had brought her a few moments of happiness. He made it safely to New York. She didn't know why she sweated bullets until she received his phone call. So many things could've gone wrong from leaving the house to landing in New York.

And what waited for him when he landed.

No. She was silly for worrying. Kevin knew nothing. Just because Austin was in New York didn't mean anything would happen to him.

But she couldn't help herself. She tried to keep her worry for him out of her voice, but she was positive she didn't do a very good job. He never mentioned it, but his tone of voice told her she didn't cover her worry well.

Nothing would happen in New York. There was no way—

No! She wouldn't think about it. Austin would never run into the horror of her old life. He was safe. She was safe. Nothing to worry about.

Axel lifted his head and licked her hand twice. Sophie looked down and smiled. "Hey, buddy. You're right. Quit worrying, huh? I just can't help it. I hate New York. I hate the thought of Austin there."

Axel made a small woof sound and licked her hand two more times. Sophie bent down and hugged him tight. "I heard you the first time, Axel." She held him for a few moments and then sat back up. "Did you decide what you wanted to watch yet?"

He continued to stare at her with his goofy grin. Sophie laughed at her own silliness for talking to the dog and grabbed the remote. She swore Axel understood every word she spoke, though. He understood her pain, her worry. He was comforting her in the best way he knew how.

She turned the television on and started surfing the channels. Nothing looked appealing. She didn't watch much TV, even when Austin was around. They always found something to do. He taught her how to play cards and every time he pulled out the cards, he taught her a new game. She swore he made each game up, but he promised they were real and his family played them all the time.

They sat on the porch swing and talked about nothing. She enjoyed just swaying in the evening breeze with him. They didn't even need to talk and she would've enjoyed it. She couldn't be happier that they fixed the swing. She couldn't imagine not being able to swing with him at night.

Sometimes, he even helped with her projects. His hands were somewhat big and sometimes clumsy, but the effort he put in to help her made her stomach quiver with bliss. His thoughtfulness spoke straight to her heart. She treasured every little thing he said and did for her.

He seemed too good to be true. When would it all fall apart? When would the horror, the pain, the cruelty start to show itself?

Axel moved against her, looking his furry face up at her. She realized he could sense when her mood changed. "I'm being silly again, aren't I? He won't ever get mean. He's a good man. Right?"

Axel sat up, jumped on her lap, and started licking her face like crazy. Sophie started giggling. "Axel! I hear you. I hear you, I swear. It was a silly question. Of course, he'll never turn mean."

Sophie glanced at the TV and saw in the midst of Axel's delightful attack, the channel had changed again. She smiled as she saw a player in blue hit the ball towards third and it flew past the third-base player faster than the speed of light. Axel turned toward the TV, gave a small woof, and laid back down by her side staring at the TV.

"Baseball, huh? That's what you wanna watch. I suppose Austin would enjoy this. I just don't understand the game. I've never really watched it, and it just seems so slow. I'll give it a try, Axel," Sophie said, leaning back and pulling the blanket back over them. She grinned at the TV, automatically thinking of Austin. He would like knowing she's watching his team. That alone made her not change the channel.

They sat there a few minutes. Sophie finally figured out Austin's team was in blue. "What just happened there? Do you know what just happened, Axel?" she said, glaring at the TV. Axel lifted his head, glanced at the TV, and if Sophie wasn't mistaken, shook his head no.

"Well, what just happened? Why is he out?" Sophie muttered with confusion. The runner touched the bag and she thought that meant he was safe. But the announcers stated he was out without providing an explanation.

"Why!" she screamed at the TV.

"You okay, Sophie?" Deja asked, standing by the front door.

Sophie whipped her head toward her, putting a hand to her chest with alarm. "Oh, geez, Deja. Go and scare me why don't you. I didn't hear you walk in."

Deja smiled, chuckling as she walked into the living room. "Clearly. What are you screaming about?" She looked at the TV. "You're watching baseball? I thought you didn't like baseball."

"I don't. I'm trying to get into it, but I just don't get it. The guy is out and he touched the bag. He should be safe. The other team threw the ball to the wrong bag in the first place," Sophie said, confused, throwing her hand at the TV in annoyance.

"Where did the ball originally go?" Deja asked.

"Umm…the outfield. The guy in the middle caught it and threw it to first. But the runner made it to second. So why is he out?" Sophie asked.

Deja sat down on the couch, laughing a little. "Oh boy, do you have a lot to learn. Did the runner tag up on first base when the outfielder caught the ball?

Sophie looked at her utterly confused. "Uh?"

"So, the outfielder caught the ball. The runner was on first and he ran to second without waiting for the outfielder to catch the ball. He needs to wait on first base until the ball is caught, tagging up, and then try running to second. Sounds like he didn't stay on first base. The other team knew that and threw to first and got him out."

"That sounds very complicated. How do you know so much about baseball?"

Deja cringed, covering the look up quickly. But not quick enough. "My brother's a baseball fanatic. I used to watch it with him all the time."

"Where's your brother? How come—"

Deja stood up from the couch, interrupting her. "He's in prison, Sophie. Don't wanna talk about it."

"Okay." Sophie turned her attention back to the TV.

Deja turned around just outside of the living room. "How about I grab us some drinks and popcorn? I'll teach you some finer points about baseball. Rules and whatnot. I bet it would impress Austin the next time you two watch it together."

Sophie looked at her. "If you're sure. I don't—"

"It's fine, Sophie. My brother may be behind bars, but I

love him. I love baseball because he does. I would like to watch the game with you. What do you say?"

"I say hurry up. I'm confused again. I thought swinging and missing was a strike out when there were two strikes already. Why did the batter run to first? They threw the ball to the bag as well."

Deja smiled. "Oh yeah, we have a lot to learn. The catcher didn't catch the ball on the third strike. No one was on base, so the batter had a chance to make it to first. But they threw the ball to first, which made him out."

"Yeah, you're right. We have a lot to learn. You're going to have to explain that one to me again."

Deja laughed as she walked away.

Sophie smiled, gave Axel a friendly scratch on the back, and trained her eyes back on the TV. She couldn't wait to learn everything about baseball. Deja obviously knew what she was talking about. Sophie could already see Austin's surprised expression the next time they watched a game together. It made her happy just thinking about making him happy.

Deja came in a few minutes later with two glasses of iced tea and a bowl of popcorn. For the next two hours, they sat watching baseball. When something confused Sophie, which happened frequently, she would glance at Deja. Just a simple glance got the point across she was confused. Deja would get a huge smile on her face and gladly explain the many intricacies of baseball.

Time flew by.

Sophie sat perched on the edge of the couch when a knock sounded on the door. "Ugh! Who could that be? I don't have time for this."

She stood up and slowly walked to the door backwards as she kept her eyes on the TV.

She made it to the door, cringing inside that she still didn't have a door with a peephole and pulled it open. "Oh, Emmett. Hi. What are you doing here so late?"

Emmett shuffled his feet, embarrassed. "I'm sorry it's so late, Sophie. My last job ran over really late because one of my lawn mowers broke down, had to wait for one of my employees to get done at his job to bring me another lawn mower. I was filthy as could be and wanted a quick shower before I got here."

"But why are you here?" Sophie asked, glancing behind her to the TV.

EMMETT NOTICED her distraction and the lack of nervousness around him.

Weird.

Last time she barely spoke to him, and now she seemed eager to get rid of him, but he didn't think it was from fright. "Austin asked me to check up on you. He told you, right? To make sure you were okay with this Deja woman in the house with you."

Sophie frowned. "Oh, yeah, I remember now. We're fine. But I gotta go. It's the bottom of the ninth, two runners on, two outs, and we're down by two runs. I have to see how it ends."

Emmett looked surprised. "You're watching baseball?"

"Yes," Sophie said with hesitation.

"Can I come in and see the ending? That's the best part," Emmett asked.

Part of him wanted to see the end of the game. Part of him wanted to meet this Deja woman and make sure Sophie was truly all right. And part of him was testing Sophie to see if she would let him in.

"Fine. Something's going on, though. I can hear the stadium getting loud," Sophie said, walking away from the door.

Clearly shocked that she would let him in so easily, he didn't say a word as he stepped inside, closed the door, and heard Sophie say, "What happened? What did I miss?"

"Oh, man, you should've seen it. Just a foot over to the right and it would've been outta the park. Three-run home run and we would've had this game, but it was a foul ball. Full count now. We just need a base hit or a walk to stay in the game," Deja said, glancing at Emmett. Her eyes widened with surprise, but she didn't say a word to him.

"Playing Chicago. These games are the most important, too. We can do it." He thought about taking a seat next to Sophie, but decided against it. She might come to her senses he was actually in her house if she felt him near her. He stood near the couch and tried to stay focused on the TV, but his temptation to glance back at the woman he assumed was Deja consumed him.

Austin, in all the times he talked about her, never once mentioned how beautiful she was. Never once mentioned her eyes and the way they sucked you in with one simple glance. She had glanced at him, just a flicker of her eyes, and then looked away. He didn't need more than a flicker. Her beauty, her eyes grabbed a hold of his senses and pulled him in. How could Austin not mention any of that?

Sophie shouted at the TV. "Straighten the ball out. Quit hitting it foul!"

Oh, yeah. That's why Austin never mentioned it. Because his eyes only saw Sophie and her beauty. Austin was a lucky man.

"I thought you didn't like baseball," Emmett said, glancing at Sophie, also catching a glance at Deja. She wouldn't look at him.

Sophie never moved her head from the TV. "I don't."

Emmett chuckled. "You seem deep into the game right now, Sophie. Doesn't seem like someone who doesn't like baseball."

She took her eyes away from the TV and looked shyly at Emmett. "Maybe it's growing on me."

Emmett smiled. "I think so. Austin will love to know that."

"Oh, don't tell him," she said nervously.

"Wanna surprise him, huh?" Emmett asked.

"Something like that. I've learned a lot tonight. Deja's an expert," Sophie said.

"Oh, geez. I'm no expert, Sophie," Deja said with a soft snort.

"Oh, there we go. Keep going, keep going," Emmett said, as he watched the ball soar through the sky.

The moment the ball flew over the fence, Sophie and Deja started screaming in delight. Emmett watched as they stood up and hugged each other, still screaming in excitement. Who knew watching Minnesota win a game could make him smile as it was now. The win meant nothing, not compared to seeing these two rejoice. He imagined they didn't get this excited about much. He almost felt bad for intruding on the moment.

"Did you see that? What a game! Is it always this exciting?" Sophie said, sitting back down.

"No. We were lucky. Walk-off home runs don't always happen, but it sure is exciting when it does," Emmett said.

Sophie looked at him and smiled. Her smile slowly

dipped. Emmett knew right then she had finally realized he was in her home.

"I see you're good, Sophie. I saw them win and I'm bushed from the day, so I'm gonna head out."

Sophie stood up. "Right. Thanks for stopping by, Emmett." Sophie glanced at Deja. "I'm sorry. That game really sucked me in. Deja, this is Emmett, Austin's cousin," Sophie said, gesturing at him while looking at Deja. Then she glanced at him. "Emmett, this is Deja."

Deja finally looked at him again.

"Nice to meet you, Deja," Emmett said softly.

The longer he stared into her deep-blue eyes, the more he understood why Austin was giving this woman a chance to correct her mistake. He had sided with Ava originally to have her arrested, but now he understood Sophie's side of it. She displayed that same nervous energy as Sophie. Not the same exact kind, but nervous, nonetheless.

She had a hard life. The question was, what kind? Like Sophie? Or was it something else entirely?

"I'm assuming it's not a social call and you're not good friends with Sophie. It's to make sure I haven't harmed her in some way, right?" Deja asked, standing up, her posture stiff, her face hard with strength.

Emmett smiled. "Yes. I'll be checking in every night because Austin asked me to. I'm sure once we get to know you better the worry will go away. Give us time. We're a fair family. I haven't seen anything in this short amount of time to suggest you'll harm her. Austin asked and I deliver. That's what we do in this family. We look out for each other. I hope you're not mad at him for it, Sophie." Emmett glanced at Sophie.

"No, I'm not," Sophie replied.

"Hell, me neither. I expected nothing less. He's been like

a hound dog since I first met him. It's good he looks out for Sophie. I did break into his house. I'll never harm Sophie, though. She's my friend now. I guess we'll see you tomorrow, Emmett." Deja looked at him, the steel in her expression still there, yet an underlying softness that he didn't miss.

Definitely not nervous anymore. She built a wall and firmly put it in place. "Good. I'm glad we settled all that. I'll see you ladies tomorrow. Austin gave you my number, Sophie. You obviously won't need it because of Deja, but in case something else pops up and you need me. Don't hesitate. I'll be right here. I swear."

"Thank you, Emmett. Everything will be fine," Sophie said.

Emmett nodded, walked to the front door, and left them without another word.

DEJA RELEASED a stringent breath as soon as the door closed.

The heat of his glare. It had almost made her fall off the couch when she first looked at him. She couldn't be more thankful that her butt had been firmly planted on the couch. She never had a man make her come unbalanced with one simple look.

Then Sophie just had to introduce them, making her feel obligated to glance his way. The same rush of heat had hit her with force again.

The resemblance to Austin had been obvious, but whereas Austin was pleasant looking, Emmett was downright handsome. He had instantly made her nervous and couldn't be happier he was out of the house.

Did he notice her nervousness?

She hoped not. Life knocked her down so many times,

she hated to reveal any weakness. Her strength and determination always pulled her through. If she started to lose that, she'd lose herself altogether.

He might speak to her body, but she would never let him in. Perhaps she misunderstood his eyes. Why would he see anything in someone like her anyway? She was nothing but a thief to everyone in the McCord family.

He didn't matter. But Sophie did. A slight tension and awkwardness still lingered in the room.

"Are all the men in that family handsome as can be?" Deja asked, trying to lighten the mood.

Sophie chuckled. "Well, I've only met Emmett and Austin's brother Zane so far, but...yeah."

They both dropped back down on the couch giggling like a bunch of teenage girls.

Tension erased.

18

EMMETT KNOCKED AGAIN, louder this time. He had knocked three times now, and not once did his loud bangs perforate through the music blaring from inside.

Sophie didn't strike him as the loud music kind of person. Apparently, she was. And she couldn't hear him knocking.

He didn't want to worry, but the horrible thought the music was a diversion slipped in.

That couldn't be true. Deja wouldn't be that dumb.

Three nights had gone by. Every night went well, Sophie harm-free and looking rather happy, he might add. He could tell she was enjoying her time with Deja. Girl time, as she put it last night.

Two more days. He blew a small breath and knocked again. Only two more days and Austin would be home. He called Austin every night after he left Sophie's house. He heard the worry in his voice, and the longing. Austin missed Sophie.

Emmett wanted to laugh. He couldn't believe his cousin, the player of all players, finally fell hard for a woman.

He didn't want to break down the door, but he would. He had to make sure she was okay. He couldn't leave without knowing.

He knocked again, as loud as his fist would allow, and waited. Another knock loomed when the door finally swung open.

Sophie stood in front of him looking out of breath, a smile on her face and dressed cute and comfortable in her pajamas. "Oh, hi, Emmett. We didn't hear you."

"Clearly. How can you hear yourself think with the music on so loud?" Emmett asked with a grin.

"Isn't it great? I think it could go a little louder, actually."

"What are you two even doing?" Emmett asked, intrigued. Her excitement with whatever they were doing was obvious. She was having the time of her life, and Emmett couldn't fault her for it. He imagined Sophie was doing a lot of things for the first time in her life. He didn't know that for sure, but it was a strong inkling that tickled his gut every time he saw her face light up with a smile.

"Having a sleepover," she said matter-of-factly.

"A sleepover? Really?"

"Yeah, why so surprised?"

"Have you ever had a sleepover, Sophie?"

"No."

No. Such a simple word, yet held a world of meaning. He almost wanted to cry in that moment for her. Even he had sleepovers when he was a young boy. It brought him to the edge of sadness, but at the last moment, he pulled away. She was beaming with excitement and happiness. She never had a sleepover when she was younger, but she was sure having one now.

"Well, turn the music up if it isn't loud enough for you.

Your first sleepover should be the best," Emmett said with a smile.

Sophie smiled back, lighting up her face to the point of wanting to drop him to his knees. "I just might do that. Thanks for stopping by, Emmett. I'll see you tomorrow night."

"'Night, Sophie. You girls have fun. Stay up real late. It's not an official sleepover if you don't."

"Will do, Emmett." Sophie closed the door.

Emmett turned around with a smile still on his face. He couldn't wait to tell Austin. He'd be just as shocked when he told him.

His smile wavered when he caught a glimpse of the black car still sitting a few houses down.

He hopped in his truck, nonchalantly glancing in the car's direction. A guy sat in the driver's seat. Why was he still sitting in the car? He hadn't moved since Emmett pulled up to Sophie's house. Why did he appear to be positioned with a good view of her house? He didn't like the funny feeling entering his gut.

He saw the car last night, too. Seeing it for the second time, the funny feeling became larger. This bugged him too much.

He whipped out his phone, but instead of calling Austin, he called his brother Ethan.

"Yo, man, what's up? You hit up Sophie's house yet?" Ethan asked, answering the phone in his usual chipper self.

"Yeah. She's good on all accounts. They're having a sleepover of all things."

"A sleepover? Little old for that, don't ya think?"

"She's never had one."

"Oh."

Emmett knew he didn't need to say any more. Sophie

wouldn't like it, but the whole family knew she had a troubled past with abuse mixed in it somehow. Austin accepted her in his life, which meant they all did, too. They would do whatever they could to help her, be there for her, protect her, and above all, love her. If Austin did, then so did they.

"Look, I'm not calling because of that. I'm still in front of her house. There's a car a few houses down and it's bugging me out. It was here last night doing the same thing. Just a guy sitting in it. I don't like it, Ethan. You know some of the guys in the police department. Can you have someone run the plates to see who this guy is? I'd call Ava, but I don't want to cause mayhem if there's no need for it. I'm not even gonna tell Austin unless something pops up. He'd worry to death if I did."

"You got it. Give me the plates and I'll get back to you ASAP. Are you going to wait around in front of the house?" Ethan asked.

"Yeah, definitely."

"Give me the plates."

"Thanks, bro. I knew you'd understand."

"I always got your back."

He hoped not to have a problem with Deja, but he never imagined he would have a problem with an unknown enemy. As he waited for his brother to call him back, the funny feeling got bigger and bigger.

***

"How was E-man?" Deja asked as Sophie came from the kitchen after grabbing more drinks.

"Who?" Sophie asked, laughing.

"You know, Emmett? E-man. Has a nice ring to it, don't ya think?" Deja said, taking the drink Sophie offered.

Sophie laughed again, sitting down on the makeshift bed they had made in the middle of the living room for their sleepover. "You never fail to surprise me, Deja. He was good. He said we had to turn the music up if it wasn't loud enough for us and that we stay up as late as possible, otherwise it's not an official sleepover."

"Since when is he the expert on sleepovers?"

"Well, I don't know. I've never had one. You've never had one. He had that look in his eyes like he did have one before. So, I guess that does make him the expert."

"I suppose you're right. I think we're doing a pretty good job right now with ours." Deja waved a hand around the mess they already made in the living room.

They had rounded up every blanket Sophie owned, which wasn't a whole lot, and tossed them all on the couch. Why they didn't just have a sleepover in one of their rooms, well, it never crossed their minds. They hadn't wanted to sleep on the hard floor, so that meant they needed a mattress.

They had grabbed Deja's mattress and wielded the heavy thing down the stairs in an utmost graceful form as they could manage. The trip consisted of frequent stops of laughing and trying not to lose their grip with it tumbling down the stairs in a wrecking ball manner.

They had set up Sophie's small radio near a table by the entrance to the living room, jamming the music from the very beginning. They had also put the baseball game on in the background. They couldn't help but stop and watch frequently in between dancing and having fun with getting their sleepover set up.

Deja had stopped at the store after work, grabbing goodies galore for the night of fun. Chips, candy, cookies, ice cream, and the mixings for strawberry daiquiris—non-alcoholic, of course. Deja indulged with alcohol, but Sophie didn't. Deja was fine abiding by Sophie's terms for the sleepover. Sophie's face lit up when she told her they were having strawberry daiquiris. "It'll be like a smoothie" were her exact words.

"So what's next, do you suppose?" Sophie asked, taking a sip of her daiquiri.

"I haven't a clue. Maybe you should've asked E-man for more ideas."

"I have his number," Sophie said with a giggle.

"If we're truly desperate, maybe. If we do, it should be at like one in the morning or something. Hey, E-man, it's really late, but we're running out of ideas," Deja said, laughing.

"That would be so bad." Sophie laughed with her, taking another sip of her drink. "I like that idea."

Deja's eyebrow rose in amusement. "Okay. I bet back in the day as teenagers, girls would talk about boys. When was your first kiss?"

Sophie almost closed up at that question. "Fifth grade...Todd Brack. It was a very sloppy kiss."

"Tongue?"

"Eww...no. He just was sloppy. Almost like there was drool coming out of the sides of his mouth. Austin is a much better kisser, tongue or not."

"I like how you threw Austin in the mix there." Deja busted up laughing, almost spilling her drink in the midst of it. "So, did you date sloppy Todd?"

Sophie laughed. "Wow, you're on a roll tonight with nicknames...sloppy Todd." Her expression got serious. "No. I just kissed him once. It came out of nowhere. Maybe that's why it was so sloppy. But sloppy or not, I enjoyed it. It's the only kiss, besides Austin, and he doesn't count, that I wanted for myself. I even kept it a secret from my mom. I never did that. I didn't want that special moment to be ruined by anything. I knew my stepfather would've found out somehow if I told my mom, and then he would have—"

Sophie looked up at Deja, taking her eyes off her drink, not wanting to hide the pain when she spoke. Deja would understand. "He would have taught me a lesson in the etiquettes of dating."

"Is there any man in your life that hasn't beaten you?" Deja asked.

"Austin."

Deja nodded and smiled.

"Your turn. First kiss."

"Brad Grance. Oh, and there was tongue," Deja said, eliciting a giggle out of Sophie. "We dated until he wanted more than a kiss. I wouldn't give it to him, so he dumped me. He decided he didn't want to look like a loser and told all his friends he scored even when he didn't. His nickname originally had been Brad-bear. After his lie, it became Brad the ass."

"How come you like to give nicknames?" She didn't know what else to say. Their first kiss stories weren't much to talk about.

Deja smiled. "It's something my brother and I always did. It was our thing. I haven't done it in a while. A very long while. When I said E-man earlier, it kinda popped out of my mouth without thinking."

Deja started playing with her drink, then looked up like Sophie had when she shared a private memory. "I was known in school as the slut. Slept with every boy that attended. When in reality I was still a virgin. I don't know how that happened, but I'm guessing it started with Brad the ass. I still haven't had that drop you to your knees kind of kiss that I assume you've had with Austin."

"When the right man comes along, you'll get it. I've never thought in those terms until I met Austin."

"I hope so. I was really running out of hope...until I met you."

Sophie smiled warmly. "Well, aren't we a lovely pair? I imagine this isn't how share and tell goes in a normal sleepover."

"Maybe not, but I'm enjoying myself more than you could possibly know."

"Me, too." Sophie raised her drink toward Deja. "Cheers. To new beginnings and to my new friend."

Deja clinked her glass with Sophie's. "I'll cheer to that."

"How's Sophie? Emmett call yet?" Zane asked, adjusting his bow tie.

"No. Still waiting. If Ava sees you adjusting that tie one more time, she's going to give you an earful," Austin said with a grin.

"Enough to get mad and take me home because of it?" Zane said seriously, adjusting the tie again.

"Not quite. So stop messing with the tie," Ava said, walking back up to them.

"Why are we here again? This isn't our kind of scene, Ava. We're out of place here. We don't—"

"Austin, stop talking. If you're about to say you don't belong in this crowd, you're dumb. I don't ever want to hear out of your mouth that you're just a simple farmer and not good enough here."

Zane gave Austin a funny look. "Why do I have this feeling you two have had a similar conversation before?"

"I have no idea," Austin said, looking around the room.

He didn't care what Ava said. They didn't fit in here. He saw the powerful people roaming in this room and he hated being here.

"Look, my dad is ecstatic you're both here. If he didn't think you were worthy, he would've never asked us to come with to this charity dinner. And I think you both look very handsome in your tuxes and bow ties."

"We don't know anybody," Austin said.

"So. Who cares about these people surrounding you other than the wonderful money they are donating to the city. Children programs that need more funding, homeless shelters, rec centers...this money will help out some areas of the city that really need the help. We leave in two days. I know you're missing Sophie. Is that why you're cranky?" Ava asked with a warm smile.

Austin glanced away from her tender look. "Maybe. I just don't feel comfortable here. I know it's for a good cause. Hell, we didn't even pay for our own plates. I don't even wanna know what your dad had to donate to get us in."

"It doesn't matter, Austin." Ava sighed, grabbing Zane's hand. "Please tell me you're at least enjoying this trip a little."

Zane squeezed her hand and lightly kissed her on the lips. "It's been good. Better than I thought it would go. I had fun touring the hot spots around the city. I even felt a little better visiting Jimmy. It's almost like I felt him there with us. I didn't so much enjoy the boat ride to the Statue of Liberty. Never gotten seasick in my life, but that boat ride did hell on my stomach."

"Please. It was probably those burritos we had before we took the ride," Austin said with a chuckle. Zane laughed with him. "My stomach was a little queasy as well."

"That's my boys. I like it better when you're smiling and laughing," Ava said.

"I need another drink. You guys need one?" Austin asked.

"No. We're good," Zane said, speaking for both of them, eyeing the full glass already in Ava's hand.

Austin walked away, heading toward the bar when he veered toward the right to use the bathroom first. He took his time using the facilities, washing his hands, and just stared in the mirror for a while.

He didn't want to go back out there.

No matter how many times Ava said it, he didn't feel comfortable here or like he fit in. All he heard were Cara's words run through his mind. He couldn't help it.

What he wouldn't do to see Sophie right now. He missed her more than words could express. These next two days needed to go faster. He enjoyed his time so far, but he was ready to go home. To Sophie.

He left the bathroom and started to walk back into the ballroom when he decided he needed air, not a drink. Just one small breath of fresh air and he would be better. He started to walk down the hallway and turn the corner when he heard someone on the phone just around the corner.

"Look. I want you in front of that house until I get there. Do not let her out of your sight. I want to know who that man is knocking on my Sophie's door. And I will find out. That man will pay and so will my Sophie. She thought she could leave me and run to Minnesota, like I wouldn't find her. Like I wouldn't come after her. She's mine. She'll learn her lesson. I'll be there soon."

Austin inhaled a deep breath and slowly backed up. That man was talking about Sophie.

His Sophie.

He knew it. He said Sophie, and he said Minnesota.

What were the odds he was talking about a different Sophie? He couldn't be.

Heart pounding, he pulled his phone out. He needed to know she was okay. That man said a car was outside her house.

His contacts pulled up on the screen when the man turned the corner. He glanced up as the man walked by him.

Rage consumed him. The urge to slam the man into the wall and beat him to death nearly overwhelmed him.

He had hurt Sophie. He still wanted to hurt her.

Over Austin's dead body would he ever lay another hand on her.

Austin didn't stare, not wanting to draw the man's attention, but he made sure to get a good look before he glanced back at his phone.

Shaking, he scrolled through the contacts looking for Emmett's number. He'd call him first. Emmett hadn't called him yet, so he knew he hadn't checked on her.

Emmett needed to get there now. As soon as the man walked back into the ballroom, Austin hit dial.

"Hey, Austin. Just the man I was gonna call. How's New York going?" Emmett asked.

"You need to get to Sophie's now. There's a car in front of her house, and they aren't there for a good reason." His voice cracked as he spoke.

"Shit. How the hell did you know?" Emmett asked, surprised.

"You see the car?"

"Yeah, it bugged me out. I already checked on Sophie about thirty minutes ago and she's fine. I had Ethan run the plates. It's a rental, but the driver...let's see...Tony Delgani. His license indicates he's from New York. I just put two and two together that he was here because of Sophie."

"I don't care what she says, you do not leave that house until I get there. I'm taking the first flight home," Austin said, his voice getting a little stronger.

"What happened there? How did you know?"

"We're at a charity event. I took a breather and I heard a man talking on the phone. He said things...he'll hurt her if he gets to her. It's him. The man she ran from. I'm about to find Peter and ask him who the hell the guy is."

"Austin, listen to me. I hear the venom in your voice. Keep your cool. I know you want to hurt him, but let Peter and...and whoever the hell has the power to make arrests take care of him. Sophie needs you here, not in a jail cell."

"I will, Emmett. I swear...well, I hope. Just watch your back. He knows you knocked on the door, and he didn't like that either. Watch your back, man."

"We'll be fine here. They're having a sleepover. Sounds like fun. Never had a sleepover with girls before," Emmett said, laughing.

"A sleepover? Good. Keep her mind happy. Don't let her dwell on this asshole and what he's going to do. I'll call her and give her a heads up. I have no idea how she'll react. Make it the best damn sleepover she's ever had, Emmett," Austin said forcefully.

"I plan to."

Austin hung up and walked back into the ballroom happy to see Peter by Ava and Zane. As he made his way over to them, he scanned the ballroom, immediately spotting the man from the hallway. He was standing with a group of gentlemen, laughing, drinking, and acting as if he wasn't going to hurt the woman Austin loved.

"Hey, where's your drink?" Ava asked.

Austin ignored her. "Peter, please, don't be obvious about it, but who in the hell is that man over there to our left? Black hair, laughing like a jackass, third from the left in the circle of men."

Peter glanced where Austin described as his brow rose with surprise. "Odd question and quite concerning how angry you sound. That's Kevin Dittmore. Why?"

"What's going on, Austin?" Ava asked, just as concerned.

"I heard that man talking on his phone. I just talked to Emmett, who confirmed it. There's a car sitting outside Sophie's house. He sent that car to watch her until he gets there. He's the same man who hurt her." Austin glanced over at him, unable to help himself. The urge to walk over there and confront the bastard overwhelmed him.

"Are you sure, Austin? He's a very prominent business-man. He donates to these charity events all the time. Clean record—"

"Pillar of the community. Enough influence to make the police turn a blind eye when Sophie needs them the most," Austin interrupted him. "I don't think you need to say any more, Peter. Maybe that's the reason Sophie wouldn't tell Ava or me who he was, because she knew people wouldn't believe her. All I need to do is call her and say his name and I think we'll have our answer."

Before Peter or anyone else could say anything, Austin hit dial on his phone and waited for her to answer.

He laughed when she answered the phone. "Wow, Emmett didn't lie. You are having a sleepover. The music's pretty loud."

"What's a sleepover without loud music?" Sophie asked, laughing with him. She must've heard the strain in his laugh. "Is everything okay?"

"Sophie, I don't want to scare you or upset you. I swear

it's the last thing I ever want to do. I have a question. It can't be avoided."

"You're scaring me, Austin. What is it? Oh, there's someone at the door."

"Let Deja get it. It's Emmett. Is Kevin Dittmore the man who hurt you?" Austin blurted it out before he lost his nerve.

She gasped, then silence answered back.

"Sophie?"

"How did you...you butted in where you aren't welcome."

"That's not true, Sophie. It's not. We're at a charity event right now, and I heard him on the phone. He said your name. He threatened you. He has a car parked outside your house, watching you. I just happened upon it. I would never break your trust like that."

He heard her sniffling in the phone. "Please don't cry. I'm coming home. First flight out of here, I'm on it. Emmett's going to stay with you until I get home. Please don't argue about that. I don't trust whoever is outside the house."

"Emmett can stay. I'm scared, Austin. He'll kill me," she whispered.

"Listen closely, Sophie. I will not let anyone hurt you. I'll kill him first. He won't hurt you again. I'll make sure of it. I'll be home soon." He needed to be home now. He certainly didn't want to blurt anything else out that would frighten or upset her. "Everything will be fine. See you soon, Sophie."

"Okay. Good-bye, Austin," Sophie whispered.

"I told you it was him. She immediately started crying. If you only heard the fear in her voice. I need to be there. I need to go home." Austin chanced another quick glance at Kevin.

"Don't go killing anyone, Austin. We'll all keep her safe. I'm sorry for questioning you and doubting you," Peter said, glancing over at Kevin again. "I'm just shocked. I'll take care of it. When you guys told me about Sophie a few days ago, you didn't give me much information. I need to know what those cops did wrong. Can you get the exact story from Sophie?"

"Yes, but when I get home. I need to be with her...not over the phone. I gotta go—"

"We'll all go home. Ava can call Chief Tanner and update him on the situation. If this Kevin Dipshit thinks he can waltz into our hometown and hurt one of us, he's got another thing coming," Zane said, clapping a hand on Austin's shoulder.

"Dipshit?" Ava asked, raising an eyebrow as a grin formed on her lips.

"Seems fitting, sweetheart." Zane grinned, squeezing Austin's shoulder in encouragement as the anger rippled throughout his entire body.

"Sophie's in good hands here. Let's go back to Dad's and pack. Austin, you get us a flight, and I'll call Chief Tanner. First thing we'll do is take care of the car in front of her house," Ava said with a smile.

"Let's go. I need to see Sophie. I need to see she's okay with my own eyes," Austin said, leading the way out, not daring a glance at Kevin again. He knew if he did, he would march over there and start beating the shit out of him.

It took all his restraint, all his willpower not to walk that way. It also helped that his brother kept a hand on his shoulder the whole way out. It grounded him more than anything else could have.

19

DEJA SWUNG THE DOOR OPEN, glad she held it firmly. The impact of his look caught her off guard, but she managed to seal it up quickly. "Emmett? Sophie's okay, you know. And here I thought you were starting to trust me."

"I do. It's the car a few houses down I don't trust. Don't go looking and making it obvious. Consider me a new member of the sleepover because I'm staying the night," Emmett said with a sly grin.

He said not to make it obvious, but Deja couldn't help trying to catch a glance. She and her brother used to play many games when they were younger. Spy, as they called it, happened to be one of them. She managed a quick glance without giving it away.

"What's going on? Full details, E-man. I'm not afraid to beat them out of you either," she said with a hard glare in her eyes.

"E-man?" Emmett asked, confused, looking around the porch as if someone else was with them.

"Nickname for you. Do you like it?" Deja gave him a quick smile, then brought the hard glare back to her eyes.

"Start answering my questions. Does that car have something to do with Sophie?"

"Yeah. I had my brother run the plates. It's a rental car with the guy sitting in it from New York. Talked to Austin as well. The man who hurt Sophie...he found her. The dude in the car has eyes on her until that bastard gets here. Sophie isn't getting hurt on my watch. I promised Austin I'd keep her safe, and that's what I'm gonna do. He's on his way home now, trying to get the next flight out of New York. I'm coming to this sleepover whether you like it or not." Emmett's statement left no room for argument. "And give me a while before I decide whether I like my nickname. Plus, gives me time to think of one for you."

Deja smiled, stepped farther inside the house, giving Emmett permission to enter. She started to walk away and then turned around as he shut the door. "I'll be right back. Lock the door, E-man. Of course, you probably know that, smart guy you are."

EMMETT CHUCKLED as he watched her walk away into the kitchen. He locked the door, glanced around the area until his eyes landed on Sophie sitting in the living room on the couch. He slipped his shoes off and walked over to her, taking his steps slowly. He didn't want to scare her by sitting next to her on the couch, but he also didn't want to stand over her while he tried talking to her. Next best thing he figured was to have a seat on the bed of blankets sprawled on the floor.

"Sophie, are you okay? I know you don't want me in your house, but—"

"You'll stay all night, Emmett?" Sophie asked, looking at him with the fear plastered in her eyes.

"Yeah, I will. Until Austin gets home—"

"Good. Please don't leave. The last time I saw...saw him...he...he..."

"Sophie, please stop. You don't need to say anything. I can only imagine what the bastard did, but he'll never do it again. No one—not me, not Austin, not one person in this family— will let a hair on your head be harmed. Hell, I imagine Deja has a mean right hook just by the hard glare I see in her eyes sometimes. You have a lot of people on your side."

"He's a powerful man. You have no idea. He'll...he'll destroy you all. No one will believe you," Sophie whispered, almost trance-like.

"I'd like to see him try. I'd be more than happy to use this on his head," Deja said from the entrance of the living room. She held a tire iron, clapping it in her hands, just waiting for any sort of action to begin.

"You disappeared to grab that?" Emmett asked, amused.

"Hey, E-man, you gotta be prepared for an assortment of things and scenarios. If you're otherwise occupied with something, at least I have my tire iron." Deja walked farther into the living room.

"And your wits," Sophie said, glancing at Deja with a small smile.

"Damn right, my wits," Deja said, smiling back. She walked around the couch and took a seat on the bed of blankets.

"Am I missing something here?" Emmett asked with a grin. "Because I feel like I'm missing something here. E-man can't be left out of anything. Not at a sleepover."

A small chuckle escaped from Sophie's lips as Deja

replied, "First time I met Sophie, she asked if I had any belongings. I told her all I had was my tire iron and my wits. What else does a girl need?"

"Can of hairspray?" Emmett asked with a devilish smile.

"I don't use hairspray," Sophie said softly.

"I don't either. Doesn't take much to make this hair shine with beauty," Deja said, pumping up some hair, exaggerating the beauty of it.

"Hmm...what else does a girl need?" Emmett sat there, tapping a finger on his chin like he was thinking real hard.

"It was a rhetorical question. I need nothing else, E-man." Deja rolled her eyes.

"Oh. I thought it was a question. Directed at me." He met Deja's eyes as they rolled back to him.

They shared a long look before Deja finally got the drift. He was trying to distract Sophie. He didn't want her to think about any of the worry outside.

"And a can of hairspray is all you can come up with? You're suddenly not living up to your nickname," Deja said, her eyes softening toward him.

"Oh, we can't have that. It's starting to grow on me. I am E-man," Emmett said in a deep voice, eliciting another chuckle out of Sophie.

"I know what you're doing," Sophie said.

"What am I doing?" Emmett asked.

"Distracting me, making me feel better. Thank you, Emmett. It's hard to bury that fear or make it go away when I've feared him for so long. He'll find a way around all of you, I just know it," Sophie said, wringing her hands nervously together.

"Look at me, Sophie." He laid a hand on top of hers to stop the mad twisting of her hands. She started to do it so violently it scared him. The tremors in her hands didn't stop when he touched her, but surprisingly, he didn't think it was because he held her hands. He waited until she finally raised her eyes to his.

"Not sure what's going on in New York right now, but I guarantee you plenty is. You say this man is powerful. Ava's dad can't get much more powerful. He's the police commissioner. He will do everything he can to help you. I know it. I may just be a landscaper, but I'm a damn fine one. You should see me wield my lawn mower and weed whacker." Emmett chuckled when he saw Sophie trying to hold in a laugh.

"I have one brother that works for the fire department. He's friends with so many police it ain't funny. Hell, Ava works for the police here. Oh, and did I mention that the chief of police here is like family to us? He was best friends with Austin and Zane's dad, and still is with mine. You say this man is powerful. So are we. We aren't just any family. We're the McCords, damn it. Not much gets by us. Nothing, as a matter of fact."

Sophie smiled, not just a small, wimpy smile she had been giving them, but a smile of all smiles. A smile so bright it would've knocked him to his knees in pain if he had been standing.

"Thank you, Emmett. I think I'm starting to actually believe that."

"As you should. I'd never lie. I'm E-man," he said with a serious expression.

Deja busted out laughing. "Now I think that nickname's going to your head."

"You're the one who gave it to me." He winked at her.

"I'm glad you're here," Sophie said.

"And I'm not going anywhere."

"Well, I'm not just glad you're here for that reason," Sophie said, glancing at Deja.

"Oh, what's the other reason? You two missed me?" Emmett said, pulling his hand away from her and put it to his chest.

"In your dreams. We kinda suck at this whole sleepover thing. We were gonna wake you up at, like, one in the morning to ask what we were supposed to do next," Deja said.

"Were you now? I can't imagine you suck at this sleepover thing. Looks like you were having fun until the party crasher came rolling in. Since I'm here, we can do all sorts of things. Spin the bottle, truth or dare, or—"

"Don't forget I still have my tire iron, E-man." Deja lifted it up to show him.

Emmett laughed. "Just kidding. Austin would have my hide if I kissed Sophie. Unless, of course, I'm more dashing than he is and you wanna." Emmett smiled wide at Sophie.

Emmett thought maybe he was pushing it in his teasing, but to his delightful surprise, Sophie smiled back. "Sorry, Emmett. Austin's the only man for me. Think of another game besides spin the bottle."

Emmett's witty reply almost rolled off his tongue when a knock sounded on the door. Deja instantly lifted her tire iron as Sophie cringed with fright.

"Settle down, ladies. It's okay. I'll get the door." Emmett stood up.

"Do you want my tire iron just in case?" Deja said seriously.

"I'm good, Deja," Emmett said, showing her a fist.

He walked to the door, making a note to tell Austin to get Sophie a new door. She needed a damn peephole to check who was standing on the other side before she opened the door. He took a small breath, so small so they couldn't see his nerves. He wasn't scared—more like, apprehensive. Yeah, apprehensive described much better how he was feeling. He grabbed the lock, twisted it quickly, and pulled open the door.

"Hey, chief. Good to see ya," Emmett said, resisting the urge to put a hand to his chest from the *apprehension* running through his veins.

"You okay, Emmett?" Chief Tanner asked with a smile.

"Never better. A man has a right to be slightly nervous when he's about to have a sleepover with two women who've never had one before. I have a lot to live up to. Make it the best damn sleepover ever."

"Sucks to be you. Can I come in?" Chief Tanner asked.

"Yeah, yeah, come on in." Emmett held the door open and shut it after the chief stepped inside.

"I hope you're not planning on using that tire iron on me," Chief Tanner said, looking at Deja.

Deja stood in front of Sophie, her tire iron firmly in her hand, although hanging down by her side. "Depends who you are and what you want."

"Stand down, Deja. This is the chief of police, Chief Tanner," Emmett said, realizing that nobody in this family had to worry about her anymore. She would never harm Sophie, especially considering how she stood in front of her ready to fight off anyone who dared to try and hurt her.

"Oh, okay." Deja loosened her grip on the tire iron.

"Where are your manners, Emmett? Introduce these beautiful ladies to me already," Chief Tanner said with a grin.

"My apologies. Fierce lady with the tire iron is Deja. And the sweet, quiet one is Sophie. Sophie took pity on Austin and decided to settle him down into a real relationship," Emmett said.

"Never thought I'd see the day. He's a lucky man. And you are a lucky woman. Best boys I know are the McCords," Chief Tanner said.

"Yes, they are, Chief Tanner. It's nice to meet you," Sophie said softly.

"I just got the full story, or what Ava knows anyway, from Ava herself. I had an officer take care of the car outside the house. Made it look like some of the neighbors called it in, not Sophie. He, not surprisingly, had no business sitting in the neighborhood. I'll have frequent patrols coming through the area from now on. Each officer will be given a picture of Mr. Dittmore. If he's spotted in this neighborhood, or near Sophie, he'll be stopped and questioned. Austin is still working on trying to get a flight out tonight, but it doesn't sound like it'll happen until early tomorrow morning," Chief Tanner said with a soft tone.

"You...you would have an officer stop him," Sophie said with a shocked tone.

"When it comes to Ava, I trust her when she tells me something. If she tells me this is a bad man, I believe her. I can't have him arrested, of course, unless he does something to warrant an arrest. No reason I can't have my officers put a little fear into him, though. It doesn't take much for me to see you're frightened, Sophie. Two questions, if I may. How bad did he hurt you? And what did the cops do to you?" Chief Tanner asked.

———

FOR ONCE IN HER LIFE, Sophie finally felt the fear leave her body. These people would truly stand by her and help her.

Here was the chief of police of this wonderful town telling her his officers would scare Kevin. For her. It just didn't seem possible.

Before she could stop the words, they left her mouth. "I could write a book on how bad he hurt me. Perhaps telling you what happened the last time would give you a small clue. He hit me. He hit me so hard that I fell into the dresser and dropped to the floor from the pain. He proceeded to kick me in the stomach. I thought it was over until he jumped on top of me and started to squeeze. He squeezed my neck so hard I knew I was going to die. A knock on the door saved my life. That was when I knew I had to run away."

The silence in the house should have deafened her, made her terrified to continue talking. She felt Axel by her feet, his nearness always a comfort to her. She felt Deja standing next to her, their new friendship a true strength to her. She could feel Emmett's eyes on her, his kindness and loyalty to Austin—support she hadn't realized she would ever get. She sensed Chief Tanner waiting patiently for the second question to be answered. No demands, no requirement for her to continue, just patience that if she did, he would do something about it.

Sophie rubbed a hand across her cheek to wipe the tears away. She couldn't look up, the fear overwhelming her to even try, but feeling their presence was enough. "The first time I actually tried to call the cops, he convinced them I hurt myself. He told them I had mental issues and I did it all the time. They threatened to lock me up for a false report. I never called the police again. He has money, influen—"

"That will do absolutely nothing for him here, my dear. You are in good hands. Not only with me, but most importantly, with Austin. I can't do anything about what happened in New York, but I'll do what I need to here if he comes anywhere near you," Chief Tanner said, interrupting her.

Sophie finally looked up. "I think I'm starting to truly believe that. Thank you, Chief Tanner."

"You're welcome, Sophie. You ladies be gentle with Emmett here. He can be very sensitive, especially when playing games. He likes to win. Don't let him get away with pouting when you beat him," Chief Tanner said with a grin, glancing at Emmett.

"I don't pout," Emmett said with a frown.

"Sounds like you're pouting now," Deja pointed out.

"What games you got, Sophie? I'll show you I don't pout when I lose. If I even lose," Emmett said.

"I don't really have any games. I have cards. Austin has been teaching me how to play card games," Sophie replied.

A slow grin formed on Emmett's face. "Perfect. I love card games."

"Me, too," Deja said, as a slow grin formed as well.

"Oh, how I would love to stay for this sleepover. I can tell this is gonna be one for the history books. But I gotta go. I just wanted to stop over personally and relay what I know on my end. Call me if you need me." Chief Tanner looked at Sophie with a tender expression. "Welcome to this family. I think Austin has chosen a wonderful woman to finally settle down with."

"You don't really know me, Chief Tanner," Sophie said, confused.

"I know enough. I can see it. You all have a wonderful sleepover. Remember, he pouts," Chief Tanner said with a laugh as he pulled open the door.

Emmett shut the door behind the chief, then turned to the girls. "I don't pout. I might cheat, though."

They all started laughing as Sophie walked toward the kitchen. "I suppose that means so you can win...so you don't pout. Deja, the cards are in the desk by the window, second drawer down. I'll make Emmett a daiquiri, and then we can play some cards to start out the night."

"Make enough to refill our drinks. Let's get this gaming on. I can't wait to see E-man pout," Deja said, walking into the living room.

"I said I don't pout," Emmett said firmly.

"You're pouting now," Deja and Sophie both said at the same time.

20

HE SWUNG the door open with a frenzy, his face etched with stress he had never felt in his life. "Sophie, are you okay?" Austin asked, dropping his bag by the door and walking into the living room where she sat with Emmett. She didn't appear to be in distress or nervous like he imagined she would be.

"Austin, you made it finally," Sophie said with a bright smile. She stood up, walking over their makeshift bed that was still laid out from the sleepover, and went into his arms.

Austin squeezed her so tightly he could have cut off her airflow. He should loosen his grip, and almost did, until she whispered in his ear, "I missed you."

He closed his eyes, kept squeezing her in the fiercest hug imaginable, and whispered back, "Oh, Sophie, I missed you, too. That was the longest flight I've ever taken."

"I'd say get a room, but I'm almost done with my string of beads here. I refuse to miss my praise from Sophie. I've worked hard on this," Emmett said from the floor as he picked up another tiny bead and carefully added it to his string.

Sophie chuckled in Austin's ear, the sound bringing joy to his heart, yet it surprised him. It obviously didn't take much for Emmett to gain Sophie's trust. Reluctantly, because he would have liked nothing better than to scoop her up into his arms and whisk her away to the bedroom, he let her go. She looked at him briefly, grabbed a quick kiss— too quick, in his opinion—and went back on the floor by Emmett.

"I've already praised you several times, Emmett," Sophie said with a grin as she picked up her string of beads.

"Yes, but not a full-on praise. One I expect to get when I finish. It better be a good one," he said, his eyes focused on his string as he put another tiny bead on.

"What are you doing?" Austin took a seat on the couch. Emmett sat on the floor not too far from Sophie. Really close, in fact.

"Beadwork. Sophie's making a curtain or something frilly and it needs beads. She made me help. It's hard as shit." Emmett held up his string of beads, the pride on his face. "It's not easy. These beads are tiny, tiny, tiny, and my fingers are big, big, big. Imagine the difficulties I've been having. Sophie's gonna be picking up these beads all day because I've dropped a lot of these damn things."

Sophie cleared her throat, glanced at Emmett with a look, and went back to her beads.

Emmett looked sheepishly at her. "Sorry, Soph. Those dam...nuzeling swear words just come out so easily."

Emmett looked at Austin with a grin. It slowly withered away as Austin's hard glare trained on him. "What?"

"I hope you aren't flirting with my pixie angel," Austin said with a frown.

At his words, Sophie quickly looked at him. He flashed

her a bright smile, which must've soothed her rattled nerves as she went back to her beads without an issue.

Emmett started laughing. "Jealous, are we? We had the best sleepover ever."

"You think you're funny, Emmett?"

Sophie glanced up again at Austin. He couldn't seem to remove the anger from his face, but his eyes softened when they landed on her. She tentatively smiled and let out a tiny breath as she lowered her head back to her beads.

"I'm very funny, Austin. I was told that several times last night by Sophie and Deja. I'm downright hilarious, actually," he said with a wide grin, as Austin's face got harder with anger. "Lighten up, buddy. If I was after your woman, I would've insisted on spin the bottle last night."

At those words, Austin almost jumped from the couch and decked him. Emmett slapped him on the knee, making him flinch. "Just testing ya, man. You passed. Good job."

"Testing me?" Austin asked, confused.

"Well, now, Sophie and I bonded last night. We're like this now," Emmett said, twisting his pointer and middle finger in a gesture that said they were close. "I had to make sure you truly want Sophie because I'm not going to let anyone hurt her. I had to make sure your player ways are behind you. They are. You passed."

"She needs protecting even from me. Did I hear you right?" Austin shook his head in disbelief.

"No, not anymore. I told you, you passed the test. I've never seen you get that jealous or possessive over a woman. She's special. Don't hurt her."

"I would never hurt her, you dumba...can you cover your ears, Sophie, so I can swear?" Austin asked with a small smile.

"No," she said, picking up another bead as a huge smile emerged. Her eyes slowly lifted to his.

No nervousness. No fear. No worry. He may have displayed his anger with clipped words and the fury etched on his face, but she knew he'd never act on it. Thank goodness she knew. He had her trust. That was the most precious thing in the world.

"You know what you are, Emmett, so I don't need to verbalize it," Austin said with force.

"A handsome, charming, dashing, sweep you off your feet kinda guy. That's what I am. Thanks for reminding me," Emmett said with a chuckle.

"You're a moron is what you are. You're lucky no spin the bottle was played. Only I get to play that with Sophie," Austin said almost in a whine.

"I never noticed before, but you pout, too. It must be a family trait. Does Zane do it as well?" Sophie asked.

"I'm not pouting," Austin said.

"That's the same thing Emmett said all night last night every time we pointed it out. He had that same pouty face you have right now," Sophie replied with a grin.

Austin glanced at Emmett. "I don't have a pouty face on, do I? I call this a grin." Austin raised the left side of his lip.

"I see no pout. I see a little of Elvis, but no pout. We McCords do not pout. I've told her this. She doesn't listen." Emmett grabbed another bead.

"I told him if he just admitted it, I'd make him a pie. He refuses to admit it," Sophie said, glancing at Emmett.

"I don't pout," Emmett said.

"Oh, that's the face." Austin pointed to Emmett. "Okay, I pout. When do I get my pie?" Austin said with a deep smile.

"I never said you would get one by admitting it," Sophie

said. His smile started to waver, when she added, "But I'll make you one anyway."

"That's because I do the pouting the right way," Austin said.

"No, she's just a sucker for you. Do you smell that?" Emmett said, sniffing.

"Emmett," Sophie exclaimed.

Austin sniffed, his eyes bulging in surprise. "You tricked me. You're already making pie. How did I miss that?"

"I have no idea. Let me go check on it. You boys behave," Sophie said with a stern look.

Sophie walked away, her steps steady and unwavering.

"She's putting on the bravest front I've ever seen. That's the first time she walked out of this room without shaky feet. It's gotta be because you're home. I've tried and tried to keep her happy and her mind off that bastard and what he's up to, but it's been hard. And that pie is for you. I refuse to admit I pout. I don't pout." Emmett nodded, confirming to himself that he didn't pout.

"I'm going to gloss over the pouting bit for now, since we all know you do pout. How did the night actually go?" Austin asked, concerned.

"She was fidgety as all hell, then suddenly she was like...I gotta make Austin a pie. Once she got done doing that, she went back to being fidgety. I couldn't take it anymore. I saw her crafty crap in the corner and suggested we work on that. She pulled these beads out, and here we are. I'm going insane doing these beads just to make her happy and get her mind off everything. Surprisingly, the night went well. We had fun and stayed up real late. The minute Deja left, her nervousness increased. I don't think it's because she was alone with me like you would think. Deja just has this way with her. They definitely are kindred spirits or some shit like that," Emmett said, waving his hand in the air at his last statement.

He looked at Austin, who couldn't manage to keep the concern or worry hidden. "Trust me, Austin. The night was good. We played cards, and damn! Don't play with Deja. She'll take all your money. Pretending like she doesn't know what she's doing and then wham! She's taking your money. Or potato chips, because that's what we bet with. We sang karaoke, told ghost stories, and laughed about nothing. I didn't lie...best sleepover ever. Sophie didn't start to worry again until this morning. She got anxious waiting for you to get home."

"Thanks for watching out for her, Emmett. And making it a good night. I knew I could count on you. I never expected any of this. I figured down the road she would finally share what happened. I never thought I would find out about him like I did. You should've seen him, the sleaze-ball. He thinks he's untouchable. He's about to get a rude awakening if he attempts to contact Sophie."

"Let me know when you need me and I'm here. Gabe's covering at the farm this morning instead of me. No sign of the car since last night. She said some things last night, Austin, that...that was disturbing." Emmett dropped the bead he almost had on the string. His hands started to shake as he looked around for the lost bead.

"Yeah, the chief called and relayed what she said. He wasn't too happy hearing about it and swore he'd find any sort of reason to have the bastard arrested. Peter's working on investigating what officers responded to the call she mentioned."

"How's he going to do that without more info from her?"

"He's got his top people on it. Looking up what calls, any sort of call, that came out of Dittmore's residence. He's going to question every officer about the call and what it entailed. He'll weed out the bad ones. Dittmore had to pay them to look the other way. How could any reasonable man think that beautiful woman in the kitchen could harm herself? He's trying to do it without involving Sophie. I asked him to. I don't want her reliving it if she doesn't want to. She never asked for any of this. Last night, when I told her I knew, she thought I actively sought out to find her secrets. I'd never do that. I just want her happy and fear free." Austin picked up a bead from the blanket. "Damn. These are tiny as shit."

"I know. Do you feel my pain?" Emmett said, holding out his hand for the bead. "Well, those cops need to be found. If they look the other way on Sophie, they'll likely do it again on another poor victim. Not that Sophie's a victim. She's a survivor. One of the strongest, bravest women I know. You have no idea how lucky you are, Austin. She truly is special," Emmett said, glancing at him.

"Trust me, I know. That's why I'm finally taking the plunge with love and a relationship. She is special. She's got you wrapped around her finger, too. Stringing beads," Austin said, laughing, picking up another bead.

Emmett held out his hand for the bead. "Watch it, she's gonna have you doing this in no time."

"Gladly. Anything for my Sophie." He sniffed again. "Man, I hope that pie's done soon. My mouth's watering just by the smell. You can go home now. I'm here."

Emmett glared at him. "I ain't leaving until I get a piece of pie, buddy. Don't try kicking me out. I'm not done with my strand of beads either."

"She made the pie for me, not you," Austin said firmly.

"What? You don't know how to share."

"Really? You boys are still arguing about the pie. Is that what you've been doing since I walked out of here?" Sophie said, a hand on her hip, looking cute and delectable in a shirt and sweats. Austin smiled. He sure liked her when she acted stern. She tried to get that fierce stern look down, but it only made him smile.

"Pie is serious business, Sophie. I don't have to share, do I?" Austin asked with his goofy grin he liked to give her. He stood up and walked over to her. "You made it for me."

"I did...but you have to share," Sophie said.

"Ha! Who's her favorite now?" Emmett said in a singsong voice.

"It's really just because I don't want to hear him pout. He's a big pouter. You understand, right, Austin," Sophie said, letting him pull her into his embrace.

"Oh, I understand. He is a big pouter." Austin kissed her on the lips.

"I don't pout," Emmett shouted.

She moved in his arms, positioning herself in just the right spot. If Emmett wasn't in the house, he would've made good use of that bed on the floor. Suddenly, he wanted Emmett gone. Sophie moaned delightfully, knowing then, he needed to slow it down. He pulled his tongue away, getting an angry moan from her sweet lips, and whispered against her mouth, "I can't wait for bedtime."

"Bedtime?"

"Mmm...bedtime. I've missed holding you, Sophie. I'm never going on a trip without you again. Bedtime is my favorite time. I need to explore this beautiful body. I need to kiss you everywhere," he whispered, still holding his mouth close to hers, peppering small kisses around her mouth as he spoke.

"Oh, yes, bedtime. I like bedtime, too," she whispered back.

"Oh, Sophie, my beautiful pixie. Is that pie done yet? I

need Emmett to eat his piece and then get the hell out of this house. It's bedtime."

Sophie chuckled. "Not quite. Another fifteen minutes or so. It's almost lunchtime, not bedtime."

"No, it's definitely bedtime," Austin said, grabbing another kiss before she could argue with him.

"So, when Sophie makes a pie I need to eat my share quickly before you get a whiff of it, huh?" Deja asked, walking into the living room where Austin sat on the couch watching TV.

"Yep. Sorry, Deja, it was good pie, too," Austin said with a grin.

"I believe you, since there wasn't a slice left for me. I knew Sophie was making a pie before I left and I didn't expect not to get a slice."

"I'll try to share better next time. I had to share with Emmett and that was hard."

"I was dying to try this mysterious grape nut pie. Well, it was a long day at the diner and I'm wiped. Here's another fifty bucks." She slid her hand out of her pocket and held the money out to him.

Austin eyed the money in surprise and grabbed it. With the new developments going on, he had completely forgotten about it. "Thanks, Deja. That's a hundred already. You must be making decent tips."

"Yeah, I do. Not my first rodeo at waitressing. I'm giving you most of it so we have that settled right away, and then I'll start saving for my own place. 'Night, Austin." Deja turned around quickly to walk out of the living room.

"Do you have your tire iron?" She made it to the foot of the steps when he said it.

She turned around slowly. "You still don't trust me?"

"I don't know this Kevin guy very well. I haven't really talked to Sophie about him because I know she probably doesn't want to. He doesn't know the lay of the house. At least, I'm assuming he doesn't. It's somewhat odd Sophie didn't take the master bedroom. If he would break in, I imagine the first place he would think to look for her is there. I just want to make sure you have your weapon handy in case...you know in case anything happens," Austin said, the concern evident in his eyes so she wouldn't be mistaken. He stood up, his hands fidgety by his sides. "I think you've earned my trust."

"Umm...wow. Yeah, I do. It's in my bedroom."

"Good. Keep it close by. Holler out if you need me tonight." Austin gave her a small smile, still fidgeting with his hands. "Thanks for last night. Making Sophie feel happy, you know, forgetting about him. You're a good friend."

"And you're a good man. I guess Sophie's the luckiest out of both of us."

"I guess so. Good night, Deja."

Deja nodded and turned around. She made it halfway up the stairs when Austin said, "By the way, Emmett sucks at cards. You're gonna get a run for your money when you play with me."

Deja glanced behind her shoulder and grinned wide. "You're on, big talker. I hate to take more of your money, but at least I wouldn't be stealing it this time." She kept climbing the stairs, her laughter floating down the staircase.

Austin couldn't help but laugh with her as he walked into the kitchen. Sophie stood at the sink, swaying her hips to, well, he assumed a song in her head since he heard no music himself. He would never get enough of her cuteness or how she made him feel, what she did to his heart with one sweet smile. She turned her head when he wrapped his arms around her.

"Are you almost done with the dishes? Can't they wait until tomorrow? I'm ready for bed," he whispered against her neck, kissing her just beneath her ear.

"You've been ready for bed since this morning. I hate dirty dishes sitting in the sink. I should have done them right away instead of lounging on the couch."

"What? You didn't like lounging with me," he said, giving her another kiss just below the first one he delivered.

"I did. But if I would've done them right away, we could be cuddling in bed right now." Sophie grabbed the last plate and shivered in his arms when he kissed her again, just below the last kiss. "You should really stop doing that."

"Why? Don't you like it?" he whispered in her ear, pressing another soft kiss just below her ear. "I guess I didn't do it right. Let me start from the beginning."

She dropped the plate and turned around in his arms. She grabbed his head with her soapy hands and kissed him soundly on the mouth. He tried to deepen it with his tongue, demanding entrance, but she refused to let him in. She pulled her mouth away and wiped her hands down his chest.

"You're all wet now. Go change and I'll meet you in bed."

"Fine. You win." He sighed, wiping the water from his face even as he smiled at her. "I'll let Axel out and I'll meet you upstairs. Don't be too long or I'm gonna put my foot down on not finishing the dishes."

"I have one plate left, that's it," Sophie said, turning back around to finish it. A soft kiss hit her neck and then nothing but air.

SHE HEARD him walk out and call for Axel. She quickly finished the last plate and placed it next to all the other dishes drying in the drip-dry. Normally, she liked to dry them all and put them away, but tonight she would let it go. His light kisses had ignited her body and she wanted more. She wanted all of him.

She was completely ready.

Maybe he thought it would be like all the other nights where they just kissed and went to bed. How did she tell him she wanted more? Did she just come out and say it? Did she show him? She didn't know how to show him.

As she placed a towel over the dishes, her hands trembling, she wondered how she could dispel the nerves. What happened if he didn't want her like that?

Silliness.

She turned the light off in the kitchen.

Of course, he wanted her like that. Only the nerves talking.

She checked the front door, even knowing that Austin locked it, and walked to the stairs. As she took each step, the urge to turn around came over her every time.

What if she did it wrong? She didn't look like all those other women he'd had. She could never live up to them and what they offered him. He was going to hate her. He would be disgusted with her.

She could never satisfy Kevin, he always—

Stop!

She took a deep breath, standing outside of the bedroom door, and tried to push all those nasty thoughts out.

Austin was not Kevin. He liked kissing her, touching her. He said so all the time. He whispered such wonderful words to her every time he touched her. That's what she needed to think about. She took another deep breath and stepped inside the bedroom. He sat on the edge of the bed taking his clothes off.

"That was quick. Thank goodness. I'm glad that last plate wasn't too dirty," he said with a grin. "Lock the door."

Sophie glanced at the door and slowly locked it. "You still don't trust Deja?"

Austin hopped into bed, clothes off except for his boxers. He gently patted her side of the bed, a tender look in his eyes. "Come to bed, Sophie. We'll talk."

Sophie changed earlier into her PJs—a simple shirt and thin sweats—and climbed into bed. He didn't wait for her to tentatively scoot closer to him. He grabbed her by the waist and pulled her close to his body. "I trust Deja. I think she's earned it."

She savored his soft touch, his warm heat. "Why are we locking the bedroom door?"

"Not the conversation I want to have right now, but we haven't talked about it since I got home. If Kevin breaks in, at least he has to go through a locked door first," Austin said softly, pressing her closer as a shiver rushed through her. "I won't let him hurt you again."

"I know. I don't think he would break in. That sort of thing is beneath him."

"But you don't know that. He always had you within his reach, and now he doesn't. You didn't hear him on the phone like I did. He might knock on the door first and try talking to you face to face, but when that doesn't work, don't think he'll be beneath breaking and entering. I heard the anger...the deep anger in his voice. I don't need to know anything that he did to you because I can guess just from what I heard. You have no idea the restraint I had to control not to walk over there and show him some pain."

Sophie put a hand to his cheek. "Please don't do that, Austin. I don't want to see you get hurt. He's a dangerous man."

"I can be dangerous, too," Austin said with a grin, turning his face a little to press a kiss onto her palm that held his cheek.

Sophie smiled. "I do believe that. I don't mean he's dangerous just physically, but—"

He put a finger to her lips. "Peter told me all about him. He's got money, he's got status, he's got a damn stick up his ass, and I'm about to shove it higher right through his damn throat. I don't care who he is. He will not touch you again. He will not touch the woman I love."

Austin rubbed his finger across her lips. "I know what I told you when we first met. But I was wrong. I said I didn't want love, but I do now. I love you, Sophie. I love every part about you, even the hard parts. I finally figured out that's what love is. Working through the hard parts of life with that one special person. I'm sure there's a slew of things I don't know. That's okay. That's okay if you never want to tell me. I will still love you. I will still love you if you share it with me and it's the most horrible thing in the world. Nothing in this world will change how I feel about you. Nothing."

His eyes glittered with his love.

"Buying the house next to you was the best damn thing I ever did. Finding Axel on your doorstep and knocking late at night was another good thing I did. Just meeting you was the best thing to ever happen in my life. That man can't hurt us. I won't let him. And I'm not talking physical harm. I'm talking about this," Austin said, tapping her head lightly.

"He has no control over you anymore. Don't let him think he does. If you start to hear his voice in your head, think of mine instead. Just think of me. Remember, I will make you forget him. I promise. He can't hurt us."

"He does randomly pop up every so often. But I can make it go away much faster now. I do think of you. I...I trust you," Sophie said as she scooted closer to him, even though she was already nestled as close as she could. "I have forgotten him."

"I don't think so," Austin said tenderly, brushing a hand over her hair and lightly down her back. "You just said he randomly pops up."

"Okay, maybe not completely. When you were gone, when I laid in bed at night, I thought of you, not him. I'm not good at this stuff, Austin. I don't know how to say it or...or what to do," Sophie whispered.

"What are you talking about? Good at what stuff? I think we're pretty good at communicating. Quite good, actually. I've never been so open with a woman before."

"That's not what I'm talking about. I wasn't talking about talking. I was talking about...this." Sophie took her hand that rested on his chest and slid it right to the edge of his boxers.

He inhaled sharply as she broke the barrier between cotton and skin, sliding her hand down to his cock, cupping him in a way she never had before. He always touched, explored, made her tingle in delight. She never had the bravery to try—until now.

She moved her hand down the length of him and back up, hearing another sharp intake of his breath.

"Yeah, I'm pretty sure you're good at it, Sophie. If you don't stop touching me, I might not last long," he said in a ragged breath.

She bit her bottom lip with a smile mingled in and slowly moved her hands again. He moved with her, igniting her to slowly rub her hand against his length again.

"Oh, Sophie, please stop," he moaned, closing his eyes.

"Really?" she asked with a smile. He moved his hips as she stroked her hands up and down. "You really want me to stop? You don't like it?"

He started to answer her when she increased the pace, grabbing harder and a little faster. Another ragged moan escaped from his lips instead.

"You always want to know what I like, Austin. I want to know what you like. Tell me," she whispered, leaning closer to him. She kissed his neck as she continued the steady pace.

She started to slow down when he didn't answer. Her hand stopped on his tip, then rubbed back down in a tender caress.

"I like it all. Don't stop," he said, barely getting the words out.

She smiled as she continued her torture on him. His boxers made it difficult sometimes to get a good grip, so she quickly divulged him of those. She threw them to the floor, picking up where she left off, increasing the pace, slowing the pace, and matching each movement he gave her. She loved it all.

She slowly trailed kisses from his neck to nibble on his ear, and whispered, "And to think I worried about doing it wrong. You're putty in my hands."

So close to exploding.

When she uttered those words, she had been absolutely

right. Complete putty in her hands. He would do anything for her. Let her do anything to him.

But he didn't want it to end like this. Now he knew what she meant when she said *I have forgotten him.* He couldn't be happier that she'd finally forgotten it all. He was forgetting himself as he met her stroke for stroke.

Her small kisses on his neck and the slower movement of her hand made him remember what he really wanted to do. He grabbed her hand to stop her and brought it above her head as he rolled her over and rested against her body in the most delicious spot. "My turn."

"I wasn't done. I enjoyed doing that. Wasn't I doing it right?" she asked, suddenly nervous.

He let her hand go, slowly caressing her body as he brought his hands to the hem of her shirt. "Oh, Sophie, you did it just right. So right that I would have made a huge mess on your hand." He chuckled as her face bloomed a deep red. "I want to be with you, inside you. I want to feel the pleasure together. Is that okay?"

She nodded as he grabbed her shirt, bringing it up and over her head. He tossed it on the floor, taking a good look at her gorgeous body. He bent down and took her nipple into his mouth, sucking, nipping, and kissing it just the way he knew she liked. She shivered beneath him as he continued to caress and kiss her breasts. He suckled hard on her nipple, making a path to her other one where he started all over showing her just how much she made him feel.

He took his time kissing and nibbling, barely moving his mouth from her breasts, enjoying the tiny movements she made as he hit a spot she really liked. As he devoured her, her hands ran down his back to rest on his ass. She grabbed hard, digging her fingers in, and pressed up into him as she moaned in delight. It was the first time she ever touched him back, taking from him, almost begging him for more. It made him harder than he could've ever imagined. Almost to the point of pain.

"Sophie, do you feel what you're doing to me?" he asked as he moved his hips when her hands pushed again.

"Yes," she whispered breathlessly. "Are you sure I'm doing it right?"

He shook his head in disbelief, cutting off any more crazy talk from her with a deep kiss. His tongue explored, ventured, soothed all in one as he kissed her with fervor. Her hands trailed up his back, latching onto his head as she ran her fingers through his hair. Her fingers, wherever they landed, did things to his body that set him on fire. He liked when she touched him. Couldn't get enough of it, in fact. He never wanted her to stop moving her hands. Oh, the delightful things they made him feel.

His lips never left her mouth. His body didn't stop moving with her as his hands made their way to her pants, pulling them down in one smooth move. He had grabbed her panties at the same time, nestling his cock right back down on her aching center.

Skin against skin.

He finally broke the kiss and became completely still. "We're naked."

"Yes, we are," she said with a giggle.

"Is that okay?"

"Yes. A little late to ask me, don't you think?"

"Maybe, but better late than never. I don't want to take advantage of you or make it seem like I am. You keep asking if you're doing everything okay and you have no idea just how much you're doing it all right. You're not the only one nervous here. I just want to make sure you're completely ready for me. For this," he said, still not moving an inch.

"I want this. I want you. I—" Sophie paused, biting her lip.

"You know what that lip biting does to me," Austin murmured, almost taking a bite himself, but knowing she still had more to say.

"I worry I can't live up to all those other women—"

"Stop." He placed a finger over her mouth to stop any more foolish words. "You can't live up to those other women. Because you surpass them. The thing is...they can't live up to you. Nobody makes me feel the way you do. One simple touch and I come undone. You, my pixie angel, you're the only woman to light my body on fire. I don't want to hear any more crazy talk. If you're not sure I'll like it, try it out. I'm here for your learning pleasure. I guarantee I'll love it. Simple reason, I love you. Now I will remove my finger from your mouth if you have something non-crazy to say," he said, moving his finger when she shook her head yes.

"That really wasn't what I wanted to say. That blurted out, but I do feel better. You always know the right thing to say," she said softly.

"Really? Because I feel like I never know what the right thing to say is. I'm glad I'm not saying the wrong thing. What is it you really wanted to say?"

She bit her lip again, the words tumbling out in a barely audible whisper.

His body became tense from what he thought he heard, making him jump a little, the movement placing him in just the right spot. He had been resting nicely on top of her and now his tip nestled perfectly in her opening. One little push was all he needed to make their joining complete.

"What was that, Sophie? I didn't quite hear you," he asked in a trembling voice.

She shifted, making him enter a bit more. "Umm..."

"Umm is right. You keep moving and I won't be able to get any closer than I am." It took all his restraint not to plunge deep inside her. "What did you say?"

"I...I love you, too."

At those beautiful words, Austin entered her completely. Her soft moan was enough for him to know it felt just as glorious to her as it did to him. He started moving slowly, taking in each pleasure, each tiny movement she made and the soft sounds that left her mouth. He kissed her, feeling her hands run down his back as he pushed into her at a slow pace.

He kissed the side of her mouth, down her chin, peppering a trail of kisses along her neck. "Sophie, I can't tell you what hearing those words mean to me. I can only show you," he whispered as he kissed under her ear, still thrusting slowly. She matched him every time he moved, almost knowing how he would move, so perfectly in tuned to him.

He kissed his way back to her mouth, groaning as she grabbed his ass, pushing hard into him. She slid her hands back up, dragging her fingers in a tender caress. His kiss deepened as he started picking up the pace. She never slowed down, matching each thrust as he took her to the height of ecstasy. The harder the kiss got, the faster they moved together.

The heat swirled around them, the love clinging to their bodies, the rightness in each delicious move they made together. He could have moved his hands around her body as he kissed her, loved her. Instead he kept them centered on her face, holding her. His pleasure rose each time she moved her hands to a new spot on his body. On his back, down his ass for a tight squeeze, back up his body, to his head, through his hair. Every spot she could reach, she touched. Each touch made him harder, made him crazy with need, deepening the kiss, and increasing their pace. She never faltered, she kissed him back with the same crazed need, met each thrust with the same frenzied desire.

He felt the moment she went over the edge, pushing into her one more time, and fell over the edge with her. They shivered together in satisfaction, ending the kiss in a quick fashion. He made no effort to move, resting his head in the crook of her neck, as she slid her hands up and down his back. He softly kissed her neck. "If that doesn't say I love you, I don't know how else to say it."

She pinched his ass.

"Hey! What's that for?" He lifted up on one arm to look at her.

"I just wanted to. You said if I wasn't sure that I should try it out. Yes or no, did you like it?" she asked with a twinkle in her eye.

"Did I just unleash a monster?"

"I have no idea what you're talking about."

"Yes...but only if you rub afterwards to soothe the pain," he said with a sly grin.

She pinched his ass again. He jumped a little, and then she rubbed the spot with sweet, tender circles. "If that doesn't say I love you, I don't know how else to say it either," she whispered with a devious smile as she brought her fingers to his sides and tickled. "Yes or no?"

He grinned real wide. "I see I did create a monster. I already said I would love everything you do to me. The answer will never change. Just be prepared for me to dish it back," he said, swiftly moving his hands to her sides and tickled.

She laughed as the pleasure started to rise again, his hardness taking permanent residence deep inside her.

"Thank you, Austin. For everything. For your sweet patience, your understanding, your love. For making me forget."

"No, no, my sweet pixie angel, thank you. For letting me," he replied as he continued to show her one more time how much he loved her.

21

"How's Sophie doing?" Zane asked, walking up to the pigpen Austin was mucking out.

"Great. Sophie couldn't be better," he said with a grin.

"You know, I've never seen you muck out a stall with a damn grin on your face. She must be really great." Zane looped an arm over the side of the fence.

"She is. Life couldn't be better. Well, no, that's not true. It could be a little better. It's been two weeks since I came home from New York and learned about Kevin. It does slightly unnerve her that he hasn't tried to make a move because she's positive he will. I make her relaxed enough to forget about him, for the most part. If he's gonna make a move, he'll do it when he's ready. And I'll be ready for him."

"Relaxed, huh? How relaxed?" Zane asked with a curious smile.

"You know, I remember the disgusting feeling of manure slithering down my back in a slow, oozing manner. I'd be more than happy to share that feeling with you." Austin held up a shovel of manure. "Not gonna talk about my sex life with you, Zane. Sophie and I are doing great. I found the one, so just be happy for me."

"I am happy for you. Just curious. When are you going to ask her to marry you?"

"What?"

"You are going to ask her, aren't you?" Zane asked, confused.

"I hadn't really thought about it. I love her. I know she loves me, but—I'm not going to think about that until Kevin's out of the picture." Austin grabbed another shovel of manure.

"What happens if he never is? What happens if he decides she isn't worth the effort? Chief Tanner managed to run off his spy since we haven't seen anyone watching her since that night. Kevin's still in New York that we know of, since Peter has had people watching him. Hell, Peter even managed to find the officers involved when Sophie tried calling for help. He has to know that Sophie is protected by people who care about her."

"Yeah, he does, you're right. Those officers haven't admitted anything to Peter about the incident. They haven't given one clue on why they did what they did, or if that bastard paid them off. They're staying silent on the whole matter, even with the threat of losing their jobs. I don't know how Peter's going to get them without Sophie's cooperation, and I don't think she's going to. She told him her side of the story, and that's all she was willing to do. She won't travel back to New York. She even kindly asked Peter to let it go. She downright refused to make a statement on any abuse Kevin afflicted on her. Peter can't even arrest him for that. He can't do anything about Kevin, and he almost can't do anything against those damn cops. He should just let it go, for her sake."

"Which we know he won't. Ava doesn't get her bullhead-edness from no one. They let an innocent woman back into the hands of an abuser, made her feel threatened, made her think she would get arrested. Nope, sorry, I want them to pay as well. Maybe this is Kevin's way of making her suffer. Make her wonder when he'll attack and never actually attack."

"Suffer? What makes you think she's suffering? I just said she's good."

"We've all changed our schedules around to accommodate Sophie, to make sure she's never alone. How long are we going to do that? Did she agree to install a security system yet?"

"No, damn it, she didn't. She doesn't have the money and refuses to accept any from me. She can be very stubborn when she wants to be. Look, if you have such a problem—"

"Whoa, whoa. I never said I had a problem. I'm just as worried about her as you are. I'm all for her being with somebody in case he comes around. He's a dangerous man, and I know this. I was just thinking."

"Thinking what exactly?"

"Well, what's mine is Ava's, what's Ava's is mine. That's kinda how it goes when you get married," Zane said tentatively.

"You want me to ask Sophie to get married because..." Austin waved a hand, trying to prompt Zane to continue.

"You just admitted she's stubborn. She won't get a damn security system because she has no money. You have the money. Put it together, Austin. You love her anyway. The next logical step is marriage. Unless you don't love her that much." Zane watched as the slight fear entered his eyes.

"Yeah, yeah, of course, I love her. She's everything to me. I guess marriage never crossed my mind. I mean, give me a break, Zane. I'm going from never having a relationship to loving a woman with my whole heart. It's a lot to take in. Even if I did ask her, what happens if she says no? That's a high probability."

"A high probability? You make it sound like she doesn't love you. I doubt there's even a small, minuscule chance she'll say no. She'll say yes. You're such an idiot. Nice to know it runs in the family," Zane said with a chuckle.

"It's not like we'd get married tomorrow and then a security system installed the next day," Austin said, exasperated.

"You never know. You seem to have better communication with her than I did with Ava when we first started out. I never told Ava how I felt. You've done more than I ever did. She needs to know she can feel safe without anyone there. There's gonna come a time when someone can't be with her. A security system isn't much, but it's something. Hell, we just installed one at the farm. Convince her to stay here for a while," Zane offered.

"We both know you had that installed because of Sophie. She won't like to hear that. She's very independent and...I don't know...she hate's help. She's never liked it from me. Ever. Still doesn't. I hold her at night, tell her I love her, I hear the words back, and the things we do...well, you get the picture. I still come home with something for her crafts and she insists on asking me if it was just lying around the farm. She'd be pissed if she knew half the stuff I brought her was not just lying around the farm."

Austin slammed his shovel against the fence. "It's a fanuzeling miracle she even lets me stay in her house still. She knows I trust Deja, but she worries about my mortgage payments on my house. I barely go to my own home anymore. I've kinda talked about moving in, but I stop when I see that hesitation in her eyes. She says she loves me, she shows me she loves me, but she hasn't completely given her full self to me. That's why I can't ask her to marry me yet. We've made progress, but I still have a ways to go with her."

"Fanuzeling...please use correct swear words in my presence," Zane said, trying to lighten his brother's mood. It didn't work when Austin's hard glare never wavered. "I'm sorry for touching a sore subject, Austin. I care about both of you, that's all. Think about this, though. Maybe she hasn't completely given herself to you because she's afraid you won't completely give yourself to her. You told her yourself you weren't a marrying man. You tell her you love her—do you love her enough for that step? If not, walk away. I imagine you'll do more damage than Kevin ever did."

"Thanks for those touching words, Zane," Austin muttered as he twisted the shovel.

"Truth hurt sometimes, bro. Just know, if you walk away, this family will still protect her."

"I'll never walk away from her. I said I love her and I meant it," Austin said firmly, as he gripped the shovel harder.

"Then what the hell are you waiting for? Go buy a ring and all that flowery shit. And are you using protection?" Zane shouted.

For a moment, the world went black for Zane. He stood still.

He cringed, wiping his face until he could see through the manure. It dripped slowly down his chest. Austin stood inside the pen, his shovel loaded with more manure, and an angry glare plastered on his face.

"I said my sex life wasn't up for discussion. I meant it. I would never, and I mean never, hurt Sophie. You aren't my dad and never have been. Quit giving me the sex talk. Better yet, how about you quit talking to me about Sophie. I'll ask her when I'm ready...and so is she. Go find something else to do before I decide to let loose with this other shovel of manure."

Zane held his hands up in surrender and backed away. For once in his life, he chose not to fight back with his brother. He deserved the manure thrown at him, maybe not in the face, but at him, nonetheless. He let his anger get the better of him.

He worried about Austin just as much as he worried about Sophie. Didn't it ever occur to Austin that this Kevin fellow might try to harm him, too? He needed to bring that worry up. Next time, though. Austin probably couldn't handle anymore talk today.

Zane tried wiping as much manure off his face, hair, and chest as best as he could, walking and stopping frequently on his way to the house. He'd find a good chunk, wipe it off with disgust, and continue walking just to feel more slide down.

So that's what Austin meant by it slithering in a slow, oozing manner. He learned his lesson. Don't throw manure at someone if you don't want it thrown back. Definitely don't talk to someone about an important issue when they are near manure.

He was about to step up onto the porch when a stern voice said, "Don't even think about it, Zane. You march yourself back to the barn and wash off with the hose first. I don't want a speck of manure in that house. Do you hear me? I just cleaned today. Why you boys can't argue without involving that disgusting stuff is beyond me."

Zane glanced over at the porch swing with a sheepish grin. "I have no idea, Eleanor. Austin started it."

"I highly doubt that. He was minding his own business in the white barn until you joined him. I know you're just trying to help, but you have to handle him gently. He's never been in love before, or with a woman who needs help as she does. Give it time, Zane. Give him time. He'll come around."

"Why do I feel like a kid being berated for trying to do something good?" Zane asked, as he turned around to walk away.

"Your heart's in the right place. Just going about it the wrong way, if the manure running down your head is any indication, which I think it is," Eleanor said with a chuckle.

Zane turned around. "I think you're right. I'll do better next time...or at least wait until he's not near any manure."

Zane made his way to the barn, chuckling to himself at Eleanor's scolding look.

"AUSTIN BOUGHT tickets to the baseball game in a few weeks and he said he got you a ticket, too," Ava said as Sophie worked on her crafts. She offered to help, but Sophie refused. She told Ava it was her job and she could do it.

"Yeah, I've been getting into baseball a little more these days. Deja was a wealth of information when you guys— well, when you guys were on vacation. Austin was surprised and quite excited when I sat down with him the first time and watched a game. It was nice to surprise him like that," Sophie said wistfully.

"A New York fan, then?" Ava asked hopefully.

Sophie stopped what she was doing to raise an eyebrow at Ava, gave her a funny look to go along with it, and then went back to her project.

"I'll take that as a no. It was worth a try. Ever been to a ballpark?"

"No. I'm sort of looking forward to it. Behind home plate, too. Emmett made it seem like a huge deal."

"Oh, it is. Best seats in the house. I've been to a multitude of stadiums in different seats, so I should know. It's going to be a blast. I'm glad you're coming with."

"Me, too, Ava. I can't sit around waiting for Kevin to make a move. He wasn't just good at hurting me physically, you know. He played mental games as well. Making me wonder is right up his alley. I refuse to allow him to do that to me anymore. I plan to enjoy life and live it normally," Sophie said firmly. She looked at Ava. "Perhaps I should now. You don't have to come over every day. It's been two weeks. How long are you going to come over when Austin leaves for the farm? You're pregnant. What happens if he really does come here and try to hurt me and hurts you and the baby instead? I would just hate myself, and I imagine Zane would hate me, too."

"If Zane was worried about that he wouldn't let me come." Ava sighed heavily at Sophie's disbelieving look. "Okay, maybe I have to console him a bit sometimes to come over, but I do remind him of the firearm I carry with me. I would have no qualms to shoot the man if he tried to hurt you. Why don't you let Austin pay for the security system he talked to you about? That could solve the problem."

"He gives me enough already. I just need to finish a few more orders and I should have enough money to install one on my own. It's important I do things on my own. I never have, Ava. Please understand. I think Austin does...and then sometimes I think he doesn't."

"I know better than to push you. That New Yorker in you scares me. You know us New Yorkers," Ava said with a grin.

Sophie grinned back, appreciative of her understanding.

"Knock, knock. I'm home," Deja said, opening and closing the door with too much enthusiasm.

"Hey, what are you doing home already? I thought your shift didn't end until four. It's not even lunchtime yet," Ava asked, surprised.

"Oh, you know, boss man gave me the rest of the day off. Slow day. So is life." Deja smiled brightly.

She was about to climb the stairs when Sophie said, "What's the matter, Deja? What happened? You always ask for extra hours. You are way too chipper for being told to go home on a slow day. Am I right, Ava?"

"Oh, yeah, you're right. What's up, Deja? We're all friends here," Ava said.

Deja turned around slowly, giving Ava a wary eye. "Are we friends? I know you're friendly with me because of Sophie and...her recent situation. You've been forced to be around me a lot more than you probably like."

"That's all very true. You've since paid Austin off, only taking a little over three weeks, which is impressive. Although, we both know that's because you work hard and haven't started saving money until you paid him off. That says a lot, Deja. Plus, you've had Sophie's back from the get-go concerning Kevin. That's a true friend," Ava said with a smile. "So I repeat, what's up?"

Deja sighed heavily. "I got fired."

"What! How did that happen?" Sophie exclaimed, standing up from her chair.

"Deja?" Ava prompted gently.

"My boss can get a little touchy-feely sometimes. He's never tried it on me, but I've seen him grab some of the girls' asses. Little slap here, little grab there. He decided to test me today and grabbed my ass. I kindly slapped him in the face. He responded by firing me," Deja muttered.

Ava stood up, her face covered with anger. "That fat, rat bastard. I'll have him arrested right now." She walked to her purse that sat on the table near the wall in the living room.

"What?" Deja asked, surprised.

Ava made it to the table and started to rummage through her purse. "You didn't really think I would think you did something wrong, did you?" Ava stared at Deja for a moment. "You did. Geez, Deja. No. It's called self-defense. That man sexually assaulted you. He touched you in an unwanted manner. That is not okay."

"I broke into Austin's home," Deja said, shocked.

"Yeah, and proven you've owned up to your mistake. Did you ask this man to touch you on the ass and squeeze?" Ava asked.

"No." Deja shook her head vehemently.

"Then it's a crime. Not to mention he fired you for defending yourself." Ava dug in her purse some more and finally found her phone. She started scrolling through her contacts when a hand covered the phone.

"I'm over my shock of your support. I do appreciate it and can't tell you how much that means to me," Deja said as Ava looked at her. "But I'm kinda like Sophie and just want to let it go. It wasn't the greatest place to work at, and I can easily find another job somewhere else. As long as Sophie lets me stay here still."

"Of course, Deja. Don't even worry about that. But Ava's right, it's not okay. I'm a wimp for not going after Kevin. I can admit that. Plus, I just can't step back into the city. I found a safe place, and I have no desire to ever return to that city. If he comes here...and...and does something, then that's a different story," Sophie said, barely getting the last words out of her mouth.

"You're not a wimp, Sophie. Stop uttering such silly

words," Ava said firmly, giving her a look that gave no room for argument. She whipped her head back to Deja. "Sophie's not a wimp and neither are you. That hard glare I see in your eyes half the time tells me that. That woman who admits her wrongdoing and owns up to her mistakes tells me that. You said it yourself, you've seen him do it to the other women there. That is not okay. He'll just keep doing it. Don't worry about slapping him. He deserved it and so much more. One person comes forward and the trickle effect starts. I guarantee more will, too. Let me make the phone call."

Deja barely hesitated, her strength coming back. "Fine. Make the call. That fat, rat bastard has it coming."

Ava smiled wide. "Now we're talking."

Sophie chuckled as Ava put the phone to her ear.

It didn't take long for Ava to call the department to send an officer to Sophie's house for an official report from Deja. Soon after getting all the information, the officer made his way to the diner, arresting Deja's boss without issue. It didn't take too long, after a short visit at the diner from Ava, of course, for a few more waitresses to file charges alongside Deja. The owner immediately fired her boss, the day manager, after five women total came forward. The owner even called Deja personally to offer her job back, but she politely declined. She really wanted no reminder of that place anymore.

Five hours. That's all the amount of time Ava needed to take care of the problem.

As Deja lounged on the couch looking through the classifieds for another job, she couldn't believe how swiftly and efficiently Ava had taken care of it all.

She knew it wasn't a good thing, but seriously, she broke into the best house she could have. What a gold mine. Instead of living on the streets, scrounging for food, money, and shelter, she now had shelter, food, and new friendships she never thought possible. She couldn't be more grateful for Sophie's kindness. She kind of wished Kevin would waltz through the door so she could whack him a few times in the head with her tire iron and show Sophie how appreciative she really was.

"Long thoughts going on over there. You okay, Deja?" Emmett asked, walking into the living room.

Deja looked up and smiled gingerly. "You know...things. It's just been a long day. We're good, Emmett. You didn't have to come over. Unless you were sniffing for pie. She can't make a pie everyday for you guys. You know that, right? Unless you're gonna start supplying the ingredients, you might want to lay off."

"Can't hurt a guy for trying. I sort of have a weakness for Sophie." His eyes got wide after he realized how that may have sounded. "Not that kind. I would never try to take her away from Austin. That isn't what I meant."

Deja gave him a sly smirk. "Just what do you mean, E-man?"

"I just worry about this Kevin guy, all right. Sophie's a sweet woman and I worry. She deserves happiness—with Austin. I swear that's all I meant. Plus, I want pie," Emmett added for good measure.

Deja rolled her eyes and looked back at the classifieds. "Start supplying the damn ingredients. I've got my tire iron, no worries, E-man. She's safe with me."

"Right, I know." Emmett stood there for a moment, then

started to turn around and walk out when he whipped back around. "I need a secretary."

Deja dropped the papers and looked at him. "Huh?"

"You need a job. I need a secretary. My business is growing and I just don't have the time to do it all myself. My office—if you want to call it that—it's a mess. I can't file worth a crap and I'm horrible at expenses. Sometimes, it's rare, but it happens, I forget where I write down a new client. I need a secretary. I won't grab your ass without permission." A light hint of red emerged on his cheeks.

"Meaning you want to grab my ass with permission," Deja countered.

"Of course not. I mean, you're beautiful. Very beautiful, in fact. I just—I'm gonna stop talking. If you want a job, you got one," Emmett said, swallowing hard.

"Can I think on it? I've never had a secretarial job, E-man. I might screw it up."

"Yeah, sure. Can't do any worse than I am. You'll have your hands full. It'll be a mess and a headache organizing it all."

"How are you even surviving?"

"With my wits...and my lawn mower," Emmett said with a grin.

Deja laughed. "Good one, E-man. Let me sleep on it."

"You do that. I'm gonna head out. Austin should be home soon, and I promised my brother I would swing by his place tonight and check out a lawn issue, as he put it." Emmett rolled his eyes, making Deja think it was a brother thing. "Have a good night, Deja."

"'Night, E-man. And thanks."

Emmett smiled, nodded, and walked out.

WHY DID he act like such an idiot? Put him in front of a beautiful woman and he became just that—an idiot. She'd never accept his job offer after that.

"Hey, Soph. Gonna head out."

Sophie turned toward him as she stirred a pot on the stove. "Okay, Emmett. Thanks for stopping by."

"I noticed some wood lying on the porch when I got here. You need me to put that somewhere before I go?" Emmett asked.

"Oh, that. No, it's fine. Austin said he'd bring it to the basement for me, but I insisted I would do it and I will. I just got busy doing other things today and then the thing with Deja's boss, I just forgot. I don't know how there's so much wood lying around the farm like that. He has to be running out soon giving me so much," Sophie said with a small laugh.

"He bought that the other day. I was with him...when he grabbed it from the barn where it was lying around," Emmett said, trying to cover up his mistake.

Sophie stopped stirring the pot on the stove and turned toward Emmett. "Austin lied to me?"

"I would call it more of a light fabrication of the truth," Emmett said tentatively. "I'm pretty sure that's the wood from the farm. That other comment was about some other wood we bought for something else."

"You ever want to step foot in this house again and have any sort of pie you will not make any light fabrications of the truth to my face, Emmett McCord," Sophie said with firmness.

"He loves you, Sophie. He just wants to take care of you. He's just trying to help," Emmett said, trying to fix his mistake and failing miserably.

"Get out, Emmett. I can't speak to you right now. Leave, please." Her voice started to waver. "Leave."

"I'm sorry, Sophie. Don't be mad at him, be mad at me." Emmett smiled. When she made no move to speak, or show any signs of lessening her anger, he turned around and walked out.

He made it to the foyer where Deja stood by the couch. She had a hard glare in her eyes and her tire iron in her hand. "What did you do?"

Emmett shook his head. "I didn't do anything. I slipped up with my words. She's not really mad at me as she is at Austin. Please, help him when he gets home. Everything he does is because he loves her."

"It doesn't matter. I'll always be on Sophie's side. He made a mistake. He's going to fix it himself. That's the way it works. Sophie asked you to leave, Emmett. I'm not gonna ask since she already did."

"Damn it. I'm leaving," Emmett said, pulling the door open with agitation.

He stepped forward and almost tripped, colliding with someone. He cringed. "Austin, you're home, buddy."

"Yeah, thank goodness. Not a good day at the farm." Austin gave Emmett a funny look as he walked around him and stepped inside. Deja stood in the living room holding her tire iron and the anger still in her eyes. "Am I missing something here? Is Sophie okay?"

Austin started to walk away when Emmett grabbed his arm. "Yeah, let's have a quick chat first."

Austin shook Emmett's hand off. "Make it real damn quick. I'm seriously not having a good day. What the hell is going on?"

"I screwed up, Austin. I'm sorry."

"English, please, Emmett. What did you do?" Austin

asked, confused. Suddenly squinting, an angry frown formed. He clenched his fists as he advanced at Emmett. "You didn't make a play at Sophie, did you? Because I will kick your ass, cousin or not."

Emmett put his hands up and backed away. "Never, no, no, I would never touch Sophie like that. I sort of slipped up, though. She knows the wood on the porch wasn't just lying around the farm."

Austin's angry frown turned into panic. "Oh, shit, Emmett."

22
_____

"Sᴏᴘʜɪᴇ, please, let's talk about this," Austin pleaded, as Sophie continued to grab his clothes from the closet.

"Talk. Now you want to talk. Now you want to tell me the truth. I point blank asked you, like I always do, if that wood was lying around the farm. You lied. You said it was. But you bought it." Sophie grabbed his last shirt and threw it on the rest of the pile.

"Is it such a big deal I bought it?"

"The big deal is you lied, Austin. From the beginning, trust was important. A little lie like that speaks volumes."

"But a little lie, I would never do a big lie. Never. I'm just trying to help you. Please don't make me leave. Please."

"I don't want your help," she shouted.

Austin backed up, her anger surprising him more than anything. If Emmett wasn't family, he would make him feel the pain like he never felt before.

Just as quickly as the thought entered, it swiftly exited. Absolutely nobody's fault but his own. He should've told Sophie from the beginning what came from the farm and what didn't.

He knew she wouldn't take it if he did. He was only trying to help. Why couldn't she just accept his help?

"Please, Sophie. I'm sorry. I love you. Don't make me leave. What if—"

"What if what? Kevin comes. I have Deja. You haven't been to your own home in a long time anyway. I'll be fine. I think we need to take a breather. I need a breather. Tell me, how much have you been buying for me? Was it just the wood?"

Austin wanted to look away and lie, but he couldn't. "No. It was never anything expensive and...shit, Sophie. Please. Pretty please. I'm begging you. Don't make me leave. Let's talk about this rationally."

"I'm done talking, Austin. I need you to leave. Your pretty pleases aren't going to work this time. You can take Axel with you."

"You're punishing him, too. He's just a baby. He didn't do anything." Austin waved a hand at Axel, who he swore knew what was going on. His face looked like it became sadder just by hearing Sophie voice what she did.

"I don't want to see you. I can't have Axel here. He's ultimately your dog, not mine. I need space right now. You lied, Austin. Maybe in your mind, it's little, but in my mind, it's huge. I'm asking you as nicely as possible to take your clothes and go home."

Austin thought about saying more, but the look on her face said she wasn't about to budge. And the tears brimming in the corner of her eyes. He hated that it was him making her feel this way.

Maybe the best thing would be a little breather. As soon as she realized how much she loved him and missed him, she would forgive him.

She had to. He didn't know what he'd do without her. His heart was breaking into pieces and it was all his fault.

He bent down and picked up his clothes. He didn't say a word until he got to her bedroom door. "I'm sorry, Sophie. I've never done anything to intentionally hurt you. I would never intentionally hurt you. Never. Everything I do is because I love you. Please don't forget that."

Austin hung his head down in sorrow when she made no effort to look at him or say a word. "Come on, Axel. We gotta go home, buddy."

Axel jumped on Sophie's leg and licked her hand, but she made no move to pat him or give him a scratch behind the ear like he enjoyed. Axel gave a small whimper and followed Austin out of the room with sadness.

SOPHIE HEARD VOICES DOWNSTAIRS, knowing Deja was talking to Austin, but she didn't want to know what they were saying.

Crying. That's all she wanted to do.

Hurriedly walking to her door, she closed and locked it.

The tears came down heavily.

Turning around, she eyed the lone shirt lying on the floor. He probably left it on purpose. It's something he would do. She refused to pick it up.

Whipping off her clothes in a frenzy, angry at it all, she grabbed new pajamas from the top dresser drawer. The nightgown hung in her hand, then suddenly went flying across the room. She snatched his shirt from the floor. With shaky hands, she put it on and climbed into bed.

She curled onto his side of the bed. The only sounds

that echoed around the room were her tears. He just didn't understand why she was so upset.

Everyone in her life always let her down with trust. In the end, when she really thought about it, she couldn't even trust her own mother.

This little lie left a burning hole in her heart. She didn't know if she'd ever recover.

She hated him. She hated what he did. She hated that he left this shirt. She hated that she put it on and felt closer to him. She hated she missed him, that he should be lying next to her. She hated the fact she would always love him no matter what.

Sophie stood behind her mother, shoulders dipped, the tears sitting in the corner of her eyes. "Why'd you lie, Momma?"

Her mother locked the front door, turned around slowly, and put on the bravest smile Sophie had ever seen. "It wasn't a lie, Sophie. I fell. I just told the officers what happened. It was an accident."

"He hit you. You only fell because he hit you," Sophie insisted, her little fists balling up.

"He didn't mean to hit me. He loves us. It was an accident. Do you hear me, Sophie? It was just an accident." Her mother reached for her.

She backed up, her fists still balled up, and stomped her feet. "You're lying, Momma. Why? You said lying is bad."

"Lying is bad. I wouldn't lie. He did hit me, but he's sorry about it. I fell into the wall from it. He didn't mean to do it. That makes it an accident. It doesn't even hurt. It's nothing. Nothing can hurt me, Sophie. Let's get supper started, sweetheart. Let's

put it behind us for right now. Please, for Momma," she said, a sad smile in her eyes.

"Only for you, Momma," Sophie mumbled.

Her mother gave her a weak smile and touched her shoulder softly as she passed by. Sophie turned around to watch her mother walk into the kitchen, noticing the way she touched her cheek and the cringe that followed.

It didn't hurt, huh, Momma, Sophie thought dejectedly. Her momma was still lying. Lying was bad. Why would her momma still lie?

23

"I'll be right back. I should really put in this application. I need a good job. Why don't you just come with me?" Deja asked hopefully.

"I'll be fine. You'll be gone less than an hour, and really, do I need a babysitter? I'm a big girl. I survived my whole life by myself. I survived over a year with him. I can survive an hour without you, Deja," Sophie said.

"I know. It's just...you know, why don't I call E-man? I need to explain to him why I'm not taking the job from him anyway, and you haven't seen him since—"

"Stop, Deja. I know you're trying to help, but it's not. I don't want to see Emmett or Ava or any other person in the McCord family. I want peace for a while. It's only been three days since I kicked Austin out. I need just a bit more time to process it all. Just go." Sophie opened the door for her. "Get that application in. Good luck."

"Thanks, Soph. I'll be no more than an hour. Tire iron's in the living room," Deja said as she offered Sophie a weak smile.

Sophie nodded and closed the door behind her. She locked it and walked into the living room. She wasn't scared. She wouldn't let any man scare her, including Kevin. She would fight back if he decided to show his face. Grabbing the tire iron that sat on the couch, she placed it on her craft table within reaching distance.

She wasn't worried about Kevin, anyhow. She should have reasonable warning if he was on his way to Minnesota. Despite the fact she kicked Austin out of her life, his family was still helping her. Deja had talked to Ava last night, who informed her that her dad still had his people, whatever that meant, watching Kevin. If he even looked like he was heading to the airport, they would know and would call her.

She wouldn't be surprised if he got around their little spies. He was a devious, cunning man. She didn't think they fully understood that, but she was putting faith in this family. Ava hadn't called and she decided not to worry about it. She refused to worry about Kevin and what he would do.

If he came here, she had no qualms about what he'd do.

He'd kill her. He told her so many times that if she left, she'd never live to see another day again. He was still playing his mind games not making a move yet. That's what he did. Played his little games.

Sophie attempted to focus on her work, failing miserably.

The doorbell went off.

A quick glance at the clock told her only fifteen minutes had gone by since Deja left.

Oh, Deja. She probably called Emmett anyway. She didn't need anyone babysitting her.

She walked to the door, cursing inside that she still had no door with a peephole. She suddenly felt like cursing on the outside.

Why did Austin have to hurt her like that? He made her want to curse and she hated cursing.

Everything started to boil inside, hoping against hope it was Austin on the other side of the door and not Emmett. She wanted to unleash her anger at him for making her want to curse.

She whipped open the door. "What do you want?"

Her anger slowly dissipated into a frown.

"To take you home, dear. Let's go pack your bags, shall we. And maybe teach you a lesson or two for running off like you did," Kevin said with a vile sneer as he stepped inside, shoving Sophie out of the way, and closed the door.

"Wh..what are you doing here, Kevin?" Sophie backed up.

Stay calm. Show no fear. She would never bow down to him again.

"What do you think I'm doing here? You're mine, Sophie. Nobody can have you. I don't know what made you think otherwise. Your behavior is unacceptable. I've had the police at my door, and you made me look like a fool. I've since taken care of that nonsense, and now I'm here to take you home." Kevin glanced around, the disgust obvious on his face at the simple means she lived in.

"Why are you still standing there? Go pack your bags, Sophie," he yelled.

The sudden increase in volume made her jump. She tamped down her frightful nerves, steeled her spine, and said, "No."

Kevin gave her a borderline sneer, trying to play his handsome polite persona like he enjoyed doing right before he really dished it out. "I will not repeat myself. I will forgive this little incident and chalk it off to nerves. You're nervous about getting married. I see that now. We'll have a long engagement."

"I never agreed to marry you, Kevin. You've never asked me. You've always just assumed I would. I won't. I will never marry you."

"I don't have to ask. You're mine, Sophie. You will do as I say. Because I love you, I will say it one more time. Go. Pack. Your. Bags." Kevin pointed upstairs, the mean, sinister look forming in his eyes.

Sophie braced herself for what she knew was coming, but she also tried to focus her mind.

The tire iron. In the living room. How could she get it?

"No."

Kevin didn't hesitate as his hand whipped across her face in one fluid movement. Sophie cried out in pain, losing her balance from the force of the slap, and stumbled onto the stairs. Before she could make a run for the living room, he grabbed her by the arm, gripping tightly, and started dragging her up the stairs.

"I see we still haven't learned our lesson, have we, Sophie dear? I guess we have to do things the hard way. I'm so disappointed in you."

She wasn't going to let him treat her this way. Not anymore.

Not when she knew how great life could be to live in peace, with happiness, with love—with Austin. She started struggling, almost making Kevin lose his balance on the stairs. He pulled her arm up and shoved her back down, slamming her hard into the stairs.

"You want to fight back, huh? You have no idea what's in store for you when we get home," Kevin said, making it to the top of the stairs. He dropped her arm and waved his hands around. "Which room, dear? Let's get packing."

Sophie lay on the floor, the tears threatening to flow, the pain in her arm and back swelling to the point of wanting to scream, but she clamped it all down. "No."

"Oh, we're going to do this the really hard way," Kevin said with a vicious smile and kicked her hard in the stomach.

AUSTIN GRABBED a bottle of water from the fridge, trying his best to ignore his annoying brother and wife, who stood in the kitchen staring at his back. He could feel their concern all the way from his head to his toes. He shut the fridge and started to walk back out of the kitchen when he heard, "Can we please talk, Austin?"

Inhaling a deep breath, he slowly turned around and gave Ava a weary look. "I'm not really in the mood."

"Austin, you haven't been in the mood since it happened. Come on, talk to us," Zane said.

"What do you want me to say? I screwed up. I screwed up the best thing in my life and I have no idea how to fix it. I've tried knocking on her door, calling her, and I'm always deflected by Deja. She won't talk to me. I lied. That's all that matters to her. It doesn't matter it was a little lie, or because I was just trying to help. All she cares about is that I lied," Austin said with defeat.

"Just give it time. She'll come around. I've talked to Deja, too. Deja's on her side, but she's let it slip how bad Sophie's doing. She's miserable without you. Just give her time," Ava said with a tender smile.

"How much time, Ava? She won't let you, Emmett, nobody but Deja over to the house. I worry about Kevin coming. Deja can't be there 24/7. She's gotta get a job soon."

Austin twisted the bottle in his hands, staring at it intently. "I worry about her, but mostly I just miss her. This is why I never wanted to fall in love. It hurts."

"Yeah, it does. It's unavoidable sometimes. Real relationships have their ups and downs. You think Ava and I don't argue sometimes. Most of the time it's because I'm in the wrong. Because, really, it's just easier to tell your woman they're right," Zane said, grinning at Ava.

She nudged him in the stomach, muttering, "You're gonna get it for saying that."

He leaned down and whispered in her ear, "Promise?" He kissed her on the neck and glanced back at Austin. "Austin, Ava and I were talking. We want to invite Sophie over for supper and try talking to her. At least about her safety. We want to help in any way we can."

Austin looked up, wanting to smile at the way his brother held Ava into his side, but couldn't manage it. "I don't know. You just said to give her time."

"I did say that, but I also want to try. She needs time from you, but not necessarily from us. Someone other than Deja needs to try because Deja isn't really trying on your behalf. Just let me make a quick call to her," Ava said, encouragingly.

"Why are you even asking?" Austin asked with a shrug.

"Because I don't want you mad at us. You have enough to deal with. I hated it when you ignored me last time. I'm not looking forward to that again," Ava replied.

Austin sighed. "Fine. Whatever. Probably won't work. She's stubborn as hell."

"That she is," Ava said, smiling as she grabbed her phone and dialed Sophie.

Ava tapped her fingers on the counter while she waited

for Sophie to answer. The light in her eyes shined when Sophie answered. "Hey, Sophie. How's it going?"

Ava shook her head. "Okay. Are you all right? I just have a quick question."

The light in her eyes dimmed as each second passed. Austin started to fidget on his feet, knowing the conversation wasn't going well. It killed him not to hear Sophie's voice and what she was saying.

"But Sophie, please, can we just talk about this? Don't say things like that. If you will just come over—"

Ava dropped the phone onto the counter and glanced at Austin. "She hung up on me."

"I told you it wouldn't work. She's stubborn." He didn't want to talk any more, or even know what she said. He didn't.

He turned around to leave, then whipped back around. "What did she say? You told her not to say things like that. What did she say?"

Ava stared at him with a frown, hesitating.

"Please, Ava. Just what did she say?" Austin pleaded.

"It was weird, actually. She seemed occupied and...I don't know."

"Ava, what did she say?" Austin yelled.

"Calm down, Austin." Zane stepped away from the counter to stand next to Ava. "Just spit it out to him, Ava. You can see he's already in pain. If she never wants to talk to him, just put him out of his misery."

"Wow, thanks, Zane," Austin muttered.

Zane shrugged, probably knowing no amount of words would make him feel better anyway.

"She said she never wanted to see you again, Austin. She was very quick to say that," Ava said softly. "I'm sorry."

"What's so damn weird about that? I knew I lost her when she kicked me out." He turned around to leave.

"That's not what was weird. She said to tell you, you were never a sexy beast. I've never heard her talk like that before. It was just weird." Ava grabbed Zane's hand.

Austin stopped moving. "What did she say?"

"Geez, Austin, how many times do you want Ava to say it?" Zane exclaimed. "She—"

"Sexy beast. She said those exact words," Austin demanded, as he turned back toward her.

"Yes, why? What is it?" Ava asked, recognizing his fear right away.

"Call nine-one-one, Ava. Get every available officer over there. Sophie's in trouble," Austin shouted as he ran out of the house.

He hopped in the truck, cranked the engine, and moved to shift it into drive when the passenger door opened and Zane and Ava piled in.

"Drive. Talk," Ava said, dialing her phone as she said it.

"That's our safe word. We made it when I went to New York. She was supposed to say those words if she had a problem with Deja. She has a problem now. She would never say that to you if she didn't. He has to be there. He has to," Austin said, as he took a right a little too sharply.

Zane's shoulder rammed into the door. "Slow down, Austin." He saw Austin's pointed look and grimaced. "Well, at least drive a little better. You don't want to kill us before we can reach her, do you?"

"Shh, both of you. Yes, I need all available units to Sophie Greene's residence. Possible hostage situation, subject is most likely Kevin Dittmore out of New York. Unknown if he is armed," Ava said.

She kept talking to the person on the line as Austin

drowned her voice out and everything she said. His focus centered on getting to Sophie. She needed to be okay. He refused to lose her to that lunatic.

He pressed his foot harder on the pedal, picking up speed, barely hearing his brother yell as he ran a red light. He didn't care. He only cared about getting to Sophie. That's all that mattered as he slowed on the brakes to take another hard right.

Five minutes later, he pulled in front of her house.

"Damn, I'm driving next time," Zane mumbled as he opened the door. He barely set a foot on the ground as Austin had already rounded the truck.

"Ava, where the hell are the police? He's gonna get hurt, or worse, kill that man inside. Stay in the damn car." He slammed the door before she could exit or even answer his question. As Zane ran behind Austin, the sirens could be heard in the distance. "Don't be stupid, Austin."

Austin whipped open the front door, stumbling inside from the force of opening it. "Sophie!"

He heard a soft yelp come from upstairs and took the stairs two at a time. He ran to their room, because no matter what she said it was *their* room, and stepped inside.

Immediately jerking in his tracks, he saw Kevin by the window. Sophie lay on the floor, a foot pressed to her throat and blood dripping from her mouth. Austin already saw a few faint bruises forming on her face, and his rage instantly bubbled to the surface at the sight.

Her clothes were scattered all over the room, her dresser drawers wide open. Her jewelry and the few things she found precious and dear to her that normally sat on top of her dresser were also scattered around the floor.

And her angel, her beloved angel with the broken wing,

in pieces, broken beyond repair. He refused to lose his angel. She was everything to him.

"Get off of her," Austin demanded. "You wanna fight? You wanna hurt someone? Why don't you try it with someone who can fight back, you bastard."

"I suppose you're Austin, the not so sexy beast she muttered about on the phone. I should have never let her answer it, but she was quicker than me. Very bad of you, Sophie. Very bad." Kevin pressed his foot down a little, eliciting another small whimper from her.

"You're nothing but a coward. A disgusting, poor excuse for a man. You have to beat a woman to feel good, is that what your problem is?" Austin took a step closer.

"What? You're telling me you showed her what a real man is? I highly doubt it," Kevin said.

"He is a real man. The only man in this room. Go ahead and beat me. He'll just make me forget because he's really good at it. He's good at it all," Sophie whispered, half laughing as she did.

A vein bulged in Kevin's neck, his eyes glazing over in anger.

"Sophie, let me do the talking, huh, my pixie angel," Austin said softly, never taking his eyes off Kevin.

"How in the world do you think you're going to get out of this mess? You hear those sirens. The police are here. Your ass is going to jail." Austin took another step closer.

"I highly doubt that. You'd be amazed with the power I have," Kevin snickered.

"Wow, you're more full of yourself than I realized. You're truly delusional. I guess you have no idea the power I have either," Austin said, one more foot going forward.

"I know about all you pathetic people helping Sophie. Farmers, nothing but little pathetic farmers. You are nothing. I didn't hurt Sophie, did I, dear? She hurt herself. She's sick. I need to take her home," Kevin said.

"That's right. I am a farmer. You definitely don't want to mess with this farmer. I will shovel the shit out of you before you even know what hit you. I can tell you with complete certainty, you're wrong. You messed up, Kevin. I will destroy you for touching the woman I love. I love you, Sophie." Austin smiled at her.

She smiled back, even though a foot lay pressed on her throat. "I love you, too, Austin. Go ahead, Kevin. Kick me again. Hit me again. It doesn't hurt. None of it hurts. You can't hurt me anymore."

Kevin lifted his foot to oblige her wishes when Austin jumped on him, slamming him into the wall. Austin grabbed him by the collar, hitting him squarely in the face, and knocked him to the ground. Austin tried not to step on Sophie, but thankfully, she managed to scramble out of the way as he advanced on Kevin.

Kevin tried to sit up, but Austin was quicker, the anger flowing through his veins for every hurt Sophie ever endured by the man, and started to pound him in the face.

Each time his fist hit Kevin's face, he thought of Sophie and her beauty, her smile, her sweet kindness. He thought of the memories they made and how her face lit up in delight at the littlest thing. He thought of her wrapped in his arms, safe, loved, sated from his warm, caressing hands. He would never let this man hurt her again. Never.

He didn't know how many punches he delivered before a pair of hands tried to pry him away.

He tried to fight them off until he heard his brother in his ear. "Stop, Austin. Stop. It's okay. Sophie's okay. She needs you. Let the police handle the rest. Let them arrest him, not you. Any more punches and they might."

His senses finally came to him as he focused his eyes on Kevin lying on the floor, blood pouring from his face. He was mumbling, groaning, and demanding the police get off him. Except his demands came out more as a murmur, his face too bloodied and bruised to speak very well. They paid him no attention as they cuffed him behind his back and carried him out of the room.

Austin turned around expecting to see Sophie, but the room stood empty except for him and Zane.

"Sophie? Where is she? You said she was okay." Austin whipped his head around the room as his panic started to well up inside.

Zane let Austin go. "She's in the hallway. The chief pulled her out when we couldn't get you off him right away. Be calm. She's okay now. She's fine. He can't hurt her."

"The chief's here?" Austin asked, surprised.

"When Ava calls something in, the whole damn department drops what they are doing and responds. Come on now, Austin. Haven't you figured that out yet?" Zane said with a laugh as he put a calming hand on Austin's shoulder. "Come on. Sophie needs you. She's pretty banged up."

Austin nodded and walked into the hallway where Sophie sat on the floor, the chief sitting right next to her. Sophie looked up when she noticed him. "Austin."

He dropped to his knees and gently pulled her into his arms. "Oh, God, Sophie. Please tell me you're okay. He didn't hurt you too bad, I hope."

"I'm okay. I'm okay," she said, hugging him back, even as the pain radiated throughout her body.

"I'll go see when that ambulance is going to get here.

Help me do that, Zane." Chief Tanner stood up and winked at Sophie when she glanced at him.

Austin gently let her go and rested against the wall next to her. He grabbed her hand, pulling it onto his lap. "I'm sorry, Sophie."

"For what?"

"For everything. For lying, even if they were little lies. For breaking your trust. For letting you get hurt. For not being here when that bastard came. For not...no, I can't be sorry for that. I'm not sorry for beating him. I just wish I got a few more punches in. I'm sorry for everything else, though," Austin said, pulling her hand to his mouth, lightly kissing it. He turned his head toward her to see a small smile light up her face.

"You're smiling. I love your smile. Don't ever stop," Austin whispered, kissing her hand again.

"My sexy beast."

"Yes, I am." He chuckled.

"Maybe I overreacted about what you did. You've never done anything to hurt me. I should have known that."

"Sophie, I was wrong and—"

"No, let me finish." Sophie inhaled softly, pulled his hand closer to her lap and traced his knuckles that were bleeding. "You know when I first saw this house and its horrible curbside appeal, I thought of bloody knuckles. Who thinks of something like that? Most people would see red peeling paint, but no, I saw bloody knuckles. My life has been one bloody knuckle after another. That's as plain as I can put it. My mother always taught me lying was bad. Yet, she lied all the time. To my teachers...the police...me. I could never figure out why. Why did she cry when my real father walked out? Why did she put up with the abuse from my stepfather? Why would she lie that it didn't hurt? I love my mother. She was the only bright spot in my life. She tried her hardest to make my life good and happy, despite all the beatings, the rage, the sadness, the loneliness."

Sophie paused, trying to find the right words as she continued to trace his knuckles, his blood smearing with hers.

"I saw the terror in your eyes when you walked into the room and I knew I had to be brave. Not for me, but for you. I get it now. I know why my mom lied, to me at least. She told me so many times it didn't hurt. That she felt no pain. Oh, she felt it. How can you not feel a fist pounding into your face or a foot jamming into your stomach? She lied to make me feel better. I guess that's what you do sometimes when you love someone. I said it didn't hurt in the room, but it kinda does." Sophie glanced at him, his eyes boring into her with a tenderness she never saw before.

"I knew you were lying when you said that. I could feel every ounce of pain you endured. That's how much I love you. I will never ever lie again. Please let me back in. I need to make you forget. You said I could. You told Kevin I would," Austin said, a slight pleading look in his eyes as if she would still deny him.

"The minute you walked into the room, I forgot. I can't sleep in that room again. I need to move to the other empty room...with you," Sophie replied.

"Best dam—nuzeling thing I heard all day," Austin said with his natural goofy grin.

"Still trying not to swear for me. That's why I love you. I truly do, Austin." Sophie laid her head on his shoulder and sighed in contentment.

"I love you, too, my beautiful pixie angel." Austin kissed the top of her head.

"He broke my angel. He saw it when he pulled me in the

room and immediately picked it up, slamming it against the wall," she whispered.

Austin linked his fingers through hers to stop her from tracing his knuckles and lightly squeezed. "I saw it lying there. It may be broken, but my angel sitting right by my side, holding my hand, resting her beautiful head on me, is not broken. You may have looked upon that angel for guidance and courage, but it's always been inside of you, Sophie. You are your own angel. You're my angel. He bruised you, but he didn't break you. He never did. Do you hear me?"

She squeezed his hand back. "I do. Thank you, Austin. What would I do without you?"

"That's a very good question. What would you do without this irresistible, charming, handsome fellow holding your hand, counting his blessings for ever getting the chance to meet you, to love you? The real question is...what would I do without you?"

"Hmm, I guess that means you can't leave me," Sophie said softly.

"I never plan to, Sophie. Never," Austin whispered, placing another soft kiss on her head, then glanced at the stairs.

"Oh, shit, Sophie. I knew I should've never left. I just knew it." Deja grimaced in pain when she saw Sophie's face, the bruises, and the blood splattered everywhere. "Oh, damn. Look at you."

"I'm okay, Deja. Really, it's nothing. Nothing that a little forgetting from Austin won't cure," Sophie whispered, not lifting her head from Austin's shoulder, suddenly the effort too much.

"Is that ambulance here, do you know, Deja?" Austin asked as Sophie's breathing became a little more ragged.

"Just pulled up, I think. Did you beat the shit out of him,

Austin? Tell me you did. Otherwise, I'm not above breaking and entering a jail to do it myself," Deja said, no joking tone entering her voice.

"For my piece of mind, probably not. For the police, must've been enough to be considered self-defense since they didn't arrest me. To be honest, I don't really know. They had to pull me off. I'd still be beating him if I could." Austin kissed the top of Sophie's head again. "I'd do anything for my Sophie."

24

"LOOK, I do remember saying that. I remember telling you that I'd do anything for you, Sophie. Because I love you." Austin grabbed a kiss before she could argue with him.

"But I'm not yelling at a two-hundred pound, mean looking, official toting ump...to take the big long stick stuck up his rump, as you so elegantly put it..." Austin raised an eyebrow at her previous words. "And how did you finish that? Oh yeah. And to shove that stick farther up his rump for making the idiotic calls he's making on the balls that should be strikes. It ain't happening, my beautiful pixie angel."

Austin grabbed another kiss before she could respond. "Now, stop hollering at the ump yourself and just enjoy the game. Please?"

"It isn't right. We're down two runs because of him. You won't let me yell at him anymore, the least you can do is yell at him for me," Sophie said, smiling a bright smile. The ones he really loved.

"Stop smiling at me like that."

"Why? Is it working?"

"No. I love your smiles, but I will not be blackmailed with one. I don't want to get kicked out of the stadium. I'd rather watch our team come back and win inside the stadium, not stuck outside of it," Austin said firmly.

"They are not going to win. And the ump seems fine to me," Ava added into their conversation.

"That's because your team is up by two runs," Sophie said, pointing at the scoreboard.

"You can always venture to my team. I am outnumbered here," Ava offered.

"No!" yelled all three men.

Sophie glanced at Austin, Zane, and Emmett, chuckling. "I have to agree with the very outspoken objection to that. I will remain a Minnesota fan."

"Worth a try. You're all gonna walk out of here losers," Ava said, cheering as her team got a base hit.

"Can you both just calm down, please? I don't want any of us to get kicked out. That ump has made several quick glances back at us and it makes me nervous every time. Sophie's been louder than I expected and you haven't exactly been quiet yourself, sweetheart." Zane gave Ava a pointed look at her frequent outbursts to the field for one annoyance or another.

"Sophie has a good point. He does have a very bad strike zone. What was that fielding incident in the fourth? Easy double play, but nooooo, he had to take his sweet time throwing to first. You wouldn't have your one measly run if the second baseman would've done his job correctly," Ava said with a critical look.

"Whose crazy idea was it to bring you to a baseball game?" Zane asked.

"Emmett's," Austin and Sophie said in unison.

Emmett picked his beer up, took a long swig, and

shrugged. "I'm having fun. I'm pretending I'm not with any of you. You all get kicked out, I won't be tagging along."

"You will be when I grab your hand, dragging you up the damn stairs," Zane said.

Sophie cleared her throat. Zane glanced at her and rolled his eyes. "I refuse to say that word."

"Then don't swear at all. It's not good for you," Sophie said. She suddenly sat straighter in her seat, her eyes bulging at the insane call the pitch just thrown was a ball and started to open her mouth. Austin reached her first and mingled his tongue with hers, taking the opportunity of her open mouth to plunge in and devour her. He felt her hands on his shirt as she pulled him closer, moaning a bit.

Goal accomplished. He pulled away from her tangoing tongue, bit her bottom lip, and smiled at her satisfied look.

"When you get the crazy urge to yell at the ump, kiss me instead. You'll feel much better, I promise. I know I feel better." Austin removed her hands from his shirt, kissing each one lightly before letting her go.

"It's only the sixth inning. I might be kissing you a lot because he doesn't know a strike from a ball," Sophie replied.

"I like your kisses. I can handle that punishment for every bad pitch my beautiful pixie angel thinks is being thrown," Austin said, grinning.

Sophie sat back, crossing her arms over her chest. "I'm not thinking anything, I know. We're sitting directly behind home plate. We see what he sees. He should be calling half those pitches strikes." She yelled the last bit a little louder just for the ump's ears.

Austin kissed the corner of her mouth. "Quit hollering at him. Remember, kiss me instead."

"We should've brought Deja with. She would tamper both of you down in no time," Zane muttered.

"Well, since Emmett's the worst boss in history, can't keep a clean office, and runs her rampant with work 24/7, she couldn't." Ava glanced at Emmett.

"Hey, don't make me the bad guy. She was still on probationary status with whether we trusted her or not when Austin bought these tickets. We tried looking to see if there was a seat available next to us and there wasn't. I don't over work her. She just started working for me two days ago. Two. Days. Ago. Why she didn't agree right away when I offered, I have no idea." He muttered the last part to himself.

"Don't try to understand women, Emmett. You'll hurt your brain," Zane said, grabbing his arm when Ava pinched him. "It doesn't mean I don't love you, sweetheart."

"Yeah, well, I told her she didn't have to work today because it is the weekend, but she refused. I know my office is a little messy and unorganized. I think she over-exaggerated a little on the extent of it," Emmett said dryly.

"She did not. I stopped by yesterday and she did not over-exaggerate. It's horrible. You have no filing sense whatsoever," Sophie said.

"And I hired the right lady to organize it. I have no doubt she'll have that office whipped into shape in no time," Emmett said with a smile.

"Not the only thing she'll have whipped," Austin muttered under his breath.

"What was that?" Emmett asked.

Austin shook his head in confusion. "I didn't say anything."

"I thought you did." Emmett gave him a funny look and then shrugged. He leaned back in his chair, clapping his hands as Minnesota got the third out. "Let's get some runs in the bottom of the sixth. We can do this."

"Don't tease him. He's sensitive," Sophie whispered to Austin.

"I didn't say anything." Austin looked at Sophie and saw her penetrating eyes bore into him, knowing he did say something. "You baby him too much. She will, you know, whip him good."

Sophie shook her head, smiling as she did. "Whip him into a good filer or...something more naughty like?"

Austin grinned and leaned in close to her mouth. "I have no idea. Maybe both. He likes her. He's just too scared to admit it. I can't figure her out. Quit babying him. Baby me."

Sophie kissed him. "You pout just like him."

Austin leaned back in his chair and felt inside his pocket when he heard Ava say, "Oh, the kiss cam. I love this part. Pick me, pick me."

"Please don't, please don't," Zane muttered.

Emmett chuckled with Sophie while Austin sat still, the nerves suddenly rampant through his body. He blew out a small breath when he heard Ava say excitedly, "Oooo, Sophie, they picked you. Look! Look!"

Sophie looked at the big screen, her eyes wide with surprise as her mouth dropped in disbelief.

"Sophie, my beautiful pixie angel, will you marry me? It's kinda fast, it's been kinda hectic, but I can't imagine my life without you." Kneeling on one knee, his hand held hers tightly, and the other lightly shaking, holding a beautiful diamond ring.

When she didn't respond, but continued to look at him with glazed, shocked eyes, he grabbed her hand tighter. "Sophie, will you marry me?" repeating the same words plastered on the billboard.

"Austin...really?"

"Umm, yeah. Why are you so surprised?" Austin asked as his hand holding the diamond ring started to shake a little more.

"I don't know. We're in public," she said, leaning closer to whisper the last part.

"I know," he whispered back. "The whole stadium is watching for you to put me out of my misery."

He watched her slyly glance at the field. When he knew he had her full attention again, he said, "I love you, Sophie. Nothing is ever going to change that. I would do anything for you, including yelling at the ump when we're done here. If you're gonna get kicked out, then I'm getting kicked out with you. I never thought of myself falling in love or getting married until I met you. Now everyone else knows it, too. Will you, pretty please, marry me?" he asked again with his usual goofy grin.

Sophie smiled wide and glanced at the ump. "Start calling the game right, ump! An engaged woman is going to be far worse than I was before."

"Yes, Austin," she said quickly right before she grabbed his shaky hand and kissed his sweet mouth.

Austin squeezed her hand tightly as he kissed her back, their tongues meeting each other in a desired frenzy. Austin heard the ump holler, "play ball," the crowd cheering, and congratulations from his family that surrounded him.

The only sound that truly mattered to him was his Sophie's sweet, beautiful moans as he kissed her senseless in front of everyone.

DON'T MISS THE NEXT BOOK IN THIS ANGSTY, YET
HEARTWARMING SERIES!
DESERVING YOU

FOR ZANE & AVA'S STORY
PROTECTING YOU
A McCORD FAMILY NOVEL, #1

He wanted to hate her.
She needed his forgiveness.
Love has a way of healing even the deepest wounds.

Zane McCord has always been there for his brothers, no matter what. But when his brother Jimmy dies, leaving unresolved tension hanging between them, he turns all his hatred and blame onto Ava Rainer— the woman he holds responsible for Jimmy's death. He doesn't want anything to do with her, but when she unexpectedly shows up on his farm, needing his help, Zane finds himself drawn to her, despite every effort to push her away.

Ava can't escape the guilt weighing heavy on her shoulders, and she's desperate to make amends. Working together gives her the perfect opportunity to break down the walls he's built around his heart and set them both on a journey of forgiveness, healing, and unexpected love. But with the painful memories of the past looming, can they ever truly move forward and find happiness in each other's arms, or will the guilt prove too much and destroy everything?

*Grab your copy of **Protecting You** today and witness the power of forgiveness and love.*

FOR EMMETT & DEJA'S STORY
DESERVING YOU
A McCORD FAMILY NOVEL, #3

She doesn't think she's worthy of his love.
He knows she's the only one for him.
But the ghosts of her past could shatter any chance they have at happiness.

Emmett McCord has been captivated by Deja from the start, despite the circumstances that brought her into his family's world. Her strength, determination, and unwavering loyalty make it easy to forgive, but Deja's fear and self-doubt threaten to push Emmett away.

He can't risk losing their friendship, but when Deja's brother, the only person she's ever trusted and known love from, is released from prison, Emmett can no longer stay silent. Her brother doesn't want to stick around and Deja's determined to follow him. Can he find a way to break through Deja's walls and prove to her the depth of his love before she runs again?

*Don't miss this emotional journey of love and redemption. Grab your copy of **Deserving You** today and discover if Emmett and Deja can overcome the past to build a future together!*

For Ethan & Penelope's Story
Always Kind of Love
A McCord Family Novel, #4

He wanted to forget her.
She longed for a second chance.
The flames of their love never died.

Ethan McCord has spent the last ten years trying to forget his high school sweetheart, Penelope. When she left town for college, she took his heart with her, leaving him to pick up the pieces. Now, while battling burning blazes and an arsonist bent on destruction, Ethan finds himself face-to-face with the woman he's never forgotten.

With danger lurking around every corner and the temptation of rekindling past desires growing stronger every day, can Ethan and Penelope overcome heartbreak and reignite the spark they once shared, or will the pain and danger of the present consume them both?

*Get your copy of **Always Kind of Love** and experience the heat of second-chance romance mixed with heart-pounding suspense as Ethan and Penelope struggle with the flames of the past and present to find their way back to one another.*

Note: This story was previously a part of the **Risking Everything Charity Anthology**.

FOR GABE & OLIVIA'S STORY
FINDING YOU
A MCCORD FAMILY NOVEL, #5

What happens in Vegas doesn't always stay in Vegas. One wild mishap could be the best thing that ever happened to him.

Being shy makes it hard for Gabe McCord to talk to women, but throw in a fun, wild night of drinking and it's not so hard. Until he learns he didn't just wake up next to a gorgeous woman—he married her. Nine months later and he's still trying to find her...when she accidentally finds him.

Olivia Brenson is the new arson investigator in town trying to find the person responsible for multiple fires, the latest one which almost took a life. When she learns they're married—because neither remembered their nuptials—Gabe finds himself on another fun adventure. She wants to stay married for a short time to keep her overprotective, demanding father off her back. He doesn't protest as it gives him a chance to prove he isn't always the shy guy. But if he's not careful, he might lose more than just his reserved tendencies. He'll lose his heart along the way. Because he's finding Olivia is the woman he never knew he needed in his life.

With nail-biting suspense and smoldering romance, dive into the danger and desire with Gabe & Olivia's story!

FOR DARE & JULIE'S STORY
DARE YOU TO LOVE
A McCORD FAMILY NOVEL, #6

He's looking for a fresh start.
She only wants to unwind and relax.
But when opposites attract, anything can happen.

He's done his time, but once a felon, always a felon. Nobody lets him forget that. Dare needs to leave town, get a new start somewhere else where no one knows him and what he's done. If only it were that simple. Not only is it impossible to find the right time to tell his sister he's hitting the road, he meets a woman who gets under his skin without even trying. There's something about her that he can't resist. And she knows it. So when he's asked to do something that could send him spiraling back into his old life, he wants to say no. He wants to run in the opposite direction and never stop. If only she'd let him.

Vacation time is meant to relax, not bring the stress and tension bearing down on her. Of course, meeting a man who challenges her in so many ways, well, Julie can't ignore that. Nor can she combat the desire that attacks her body every time he looks her way. Fighting comes easy to them, and so does the pleasure. It should be just sex, yet it's turning into more than she bargained for. It would never work between them. She works for the law, and he...is only trying to find a new path, and she respects that. If only it were that easy.

ABOUT THE AUTHOR

I'm a *USA Today* Bestselling Author that loves to write contemporary romance and romantic suspense novels, although I am partial to romantic suspense. I even dabble in paranormal. Honestly, I love anything that has to do with romance. As long as there's a happy ending, I'm a happy camper. And insta-love...yes, please! I love baseball (Go Twins!) and creating awesome crafts. I graduated with a Bachelor's Degree in Criminal Justice, working in that field for several years before I became a stay-at-home mom. I have a few more amazing stories in the works. If you would like to learn more about me and my books, head to my website by scanning the QR code. Thanks for reading!

Scan me

www.ingramcontent.com/pod-product-compliance
Lightning Source LLC
Chambersburg PA
CBHW021958010726
47494CB00003B/798